T0125600

LIGHTNING CHASERS

Visit us at www.boldstrokesbooks.com

By the Author

Lightning Strikes

Lightning Chasers

LIGHTNING CHASERS

by

Cass Sellars

2017

LIGHTNING CHASERS

© 2017 By Cass Sellars. All Rights Reserved.

ISBN 13: 978-1-62639-965-5

This Trade Paperback Original Is Published By
Bold Strokes Books, Inc.
P.O. Box 249
Valley Falls, NY 12185

First Edition: September 2017

THIS IS A WORK OF FICTION. NAMES, CHARACTERS, PLACES, AND INCIDENTS ARE THE PRODUCT OF THE AUTHOR'S IMAGINATION OR ARE USED FICTITIOUSLY. ANY RESEMBLANCE TO ACTUAL PERSONS, LIVING OR DEAD, BUSINESS ESTABLISHMENTS, EVENTS, OR LOCALES IS ENTIRELY COINCIDENTAL.

THIS BOOK, OR PARTS THEREOF, MAY NOT BE REPRODUCED IN ANY FORM WITHOUT PERMISSION.

Credits

Editor: Ruth Sternglantz
Production Design: Susan Ramundo
Cover Design By Melody Pond

Acknowledgments

Thank you always to Ruth and everyone at BSB for allowing me to be here and for constructing a space to create and find so many stories about us. A special thanks to Cara who manages to read and proof right along with me despite her crazy life. To Ashley, Michelle, and Tracy who were Sydney and Parker's first friends.

Dedication

Love and gratitude to Dee for your unwavering support
and indelible belief that I am capable of anything.

CHAPTER ONE

Sydney Hyatt worked diligently from her home office that was tucked into the loft of her nineteenth-century repurposed warehouse. A large window formed the longest wall and offered her a sweeping view of her living space below. The old red brick contrasted perfectly against the modern white columns, visually separating the rooms from each other. She mused at how different the space felt now she often shared it with someone else.

A black convertible swept into the space next to hers and she leaned over to watch the driver walk toward the building. Parker was wrestling to balance her workbag on her shoulder and she clicked the car's remote key before managing a graceful march toward their building on three-inch heels. Syd forced herself to return to her current project, despite the fact that she would rather be across the hall with Parker, her neighbor who long ago stopped being just someone who lived in her building.

Parker undressed and laid her suit over the slipper chair in her small bedroom and relished the feel of shedding her dress clothes after what had turned into a twelve-hour workday. Cotton shorts and a fitted T-shirt bearing a unicorn straddling a rainbow was as dressed up as she planned to be before she began it all again in the morning. She dragged her long brown hair into a loose ponytail and took a moment to appraise the space she spent little time in anymore. The journey had been paved by obstacles of wild emotions, a failed relationship, and fresh discoveries. The final destination brought a welcome independence and the person who had managed to round out her universe in a myriad of unconventional ways.

She snatched her keys from the table and locked the barn style, rolling door despite the fact that the other tenants, who ran businesses out of the space, rarely graced the halls after five p.m. She padded across the dark foyer carpet to Unit *A*.

She smelled the coffee that regularly accompanied Syd throughout her workday and a faint reminder of the cologne that her girlfriend wore. She glanced up to see Sydney hunched over her desk and proceeded to the bar which spanned the old brick of the outside wall. She deftly assembled a double scotch on the rocks and filled a stemless Riedel glass with a cabernet franc, taking a grateful sip of the earthy red before heading to the loft.

She could still hear Syd clicking away at the computer as she climbed the black iron stairs. She awkwardly balanced the drinks and pressed her thumb to the bio pad, releasing the door lock.

Syd turned her chair and smiled as Parker offered her the heavy rocks glass filled with the amber alcohol.

"Not what I want," Syd said seductively and she curved a finger meant to encourage Parker to come closer.

Parker smiled and placed both glasses on the counter. "Fine. I'll just let you get back to work then." She shrugged playfully and turned toward the door when she felt strong arms around her waist. She was pulled onto the chair and into the crushing embrace that never failed to spur her heart into a drumming rhythm in her ears.

Syd skimmed her hands under Parker's long hair, pulling the tie away, and bringing their lips together. Parker sank into the kiss that always felt like home base for her. The place she reset and regrouped. Syd's arms were firm around her as Parker curled against her.

"How does being here always make me feel better?" She emphasized *here* with a tap on Syd's chest. "You make all the daily crap seem insignificant." Parker breathed into her neck and skimmed the skin below Syd's ear with her lips.

Syd shivered at the contact that invariably caused her breathing to deepen and goose bumps to skim down her arms.

"I'm glad." Her voice was husky from the sensory assault that Parker had delivered. "It means you still love me."

"Maybe a little," Parker teased and closed her eyes for a moment. "What are you working on so late?"

"This case from Bob's office." Syd knew she sounded frustrated as she turned the screen so Parker could see the DA's latest pretrial case video she was constructing.

"You usually love these."

"Well they're usually much easier. Facts are all there and I just have to put them all together and make it look like a movie."

"And?"

"And according to the investigator, the wife says the husband came home early from a business trip and walked in on an intruder. He died in a bullet exchange with the neighbor, who was allegedly breaking into their house. She says she only heard the commotion, but I have to replicate the wife's movements from the bedroom. She says she was sleeping and hadn't woken up until she heard the shots."

Parked leaned into the animation that Syd had created on the screen, still pretty fascinated that she could make it look so real. "Okay."

"Bob is fairly certain she's lying about something significant and he sort of hopes we can prove it here"—she pointed at the now frozen image on the monitor—"since neither man is around to talk."

Parker turned away from the video and bent over the police pictures of a tall woman with auburn hair tipped with platinum. The woman stood, looking distraught, in satin sleep shorts and matching top. The hooks of a lacy bustier peaked from the blood-stained camisole.

"She says she bent over her husband, which is fairly consistent with the staining on her pajamas since he was bleeding across his torso." Syd pointed to the photo of the prone man's body contorted between the walls of a narrow hallway. "They couldn't find any GSR on her hands or any indication that she had changed clothes."

Parker briefly considered the fact that she could now look at crime scene photos with Syd without wanting to throw up. She declined to consider it progress. "No gunshot residue just means she didn't fire the gun—it doesn't mean she wasn't involved somehow," Parker reasoned.

"True, and that's what Bob says too but his new investigator is struggling with how."

"Did he ask her about any affairs?" Parker glanced back at Syd.

"I have to imagine he did. Why?"

"Because she wasn't asleep." Parker was certain of this. "And I doubt she planned to be alone that night."

"Oh, really. Do tell, Inspector Duncan, why do you say that?" Syd reclined in the chair as Parker dragged the woman's photo toward them both, and pointed at her pajamas.

"She's supposedly by herself because her husband is out of town? Please," Parker scoffed. "I wear your faded Forensics Academy T-shirt and boxers when you're out of town."

"Still sexy as hell," Syd said as she glided a palm along Parker's thigh before Parker slapped it away playfully.

"Even if you are home, I would save satin bustiers and matching lingerie for special occasions. No woman sleeps in that crap. It's ridiculously uncomfortable and a waste of a *come get me* outfit."

"Do you have any such outfit you can wear for me right now? It might help me visualize," Syd said teasingly, pulling Parker against her.

"You're not listening to me." Parker laughed at the playful bites Syd was doling out across her shoulder.

Syd straightened and released her hold on Parker so she could resume her explanation. "Sorry. I'm listening. I promise." She snuck in a last peck against Parker's cheek and angled the chair back toward the photos.

"Her hair is perfect and looks newly colored. Her manicure is fresh and she's wearing earrings. I bet Bob's investigator fell for the damsel in distress story, assisted greatly by her long legs and big boobs."

"And you think she was meeting someone for a rendezvous of the sexual kind. Makes more sense than being sound asleep looking like a Victoria's Secret model, I suppose. I guess I should have done the math myself." Syd shook her head and began clicking the screens.

"You were probably admiring her big boobs and long legs too. I seem to remember that you had a type."

Syd colored slightly and shook her head at the reference to her dubious past. "We both know my type consisted of willing and not too bright. I lucked out when you reformed me."

"Damn right, you did," Parker lobbed back jokingly and watched Syd work. Being reminded of Syd's regular prowl of the Pride Lounge and less than significant encounters no longer made Parker feel wary or the least bit jealous.

"Did they see if there was any connection with the neighbor? Maybe while the mouse was away…"

"Great minds think alike." Syd felt the new avenue of investigation taking shape and she scribbled thoughts onto a notepad for her conference call with the District Attorney in the morning. She pushed her new list of questions at Parker. The last one said, *Affair with neighbor?* "Maybe she and the lover wanted her husband out of the picture or hubby discovered that she was cheating and came home to confront them." Syd marveled at the fact that the investigator seemed to have left those stones unturned. "Doesn't mean she had a hand in it, but it certainly means she's possibly being less than honest."

"Right. Now how about you stop working for the night and order us Chinese and a bad movie?" Parker sipped her wine and slipped off Syd's lap to stand beside her chair.

Syd skimmed a hand over her military short hair and leaned in to save her file. "Way ahead of you. Food should be here any second."

"You think you know me, huh?" Parker levered her from the chair with comically exaggerated effort.

"Indeed." Syd followed her down the stairs and fought the urge to steer her toward the bedroom instead of waiting for dinner. "I still think I need to study your *come get me* outfit, though."

"Maybe I'll give you a show later." Syd was enchanted by the way Parker still flirted with her. The buzzer sounded from the lobby door and Parker jerked a thumb in the direction of the entrance. "But you'll have to feed me first."

CHAPTER TWO

Sergeant Mack Foster tapped her thumb on the steering wheel of her SUV and watched for signs that her wife would make it to the car before the event was over entirely. The life she shared with Jenny now was many shades different than the carefree existence they had known before a baby and careers complicated it. She wouldn't trade the life with her daughter for anything but it felt nice to be headed to an event with their friends for what Jenny had coined *adult time*.

"Sorry," Jenny breathed as she heaved her tiny frame into the passenger seat and slammed the door. "Olivia was playing with the dog and I wanted pictures." She held up her phone promising a later slide show.

"It's okay. I called Sandy and they were running a bit behind as well." She wound her fingers through Jenny's thick blond mane absently as she backed down the driveway.

"Sorry."

"Stop apologizing, it feels weird leaving her for me as well," Mack said reassuringly. "Anyway, they understood. Sandy's been a cop as long as I have—schedules are nice, but never guaranteed, as you can attest."

Jenny nodded with a wry grin. "Tell me about it." She smoothed a hand over her midnight blue silk column dress and Mack planted a chaste kiss on her wife's pale shoulder when a stoplight afforded her the opportunity.

Jen turned, smiling. "You look very handsome, Mack. I kind of miss doing these grown-up things together. I mean, I would do anything to be with Olivia Grace," she rushed out guiltily, obviously thinking of their daughter now probably sleeping soundly at the neighbors', "but it means a lot to be able to have this, just you and me." She caught Mack in a soft kiss and sighed.

"You don't have to qualify that with me. I miss my hot, carefree wife sometimes. We just need to remember to have date night more often, okay?" She considered her light gray pantsuit and midnight-blue shirt, and the small square silver cuff links at her wrists. "I kind of feel like we're going to the prom since my shirt matches your dress." She laughed and looked self-consciously at Jenny.

"I planned it like that. This way someone can return you to me if you wander off," Jenny joked, gently kissing Mack's cheek as she drove.

"We both know that is something you'll never have to worry about." Mack covered Jenny's hand with her own.

"Are you happy, Mack?" Jenny's tone was suddenly serious.

Mack looked carefully at her wife. "What would make you ask me that? I tell you how much I love you constantly."

"I know, but there have been so many changes for us since last year and I just feel like I need to check in sometimes."

Mack smiled as she pulled Jenny's hand into her lap. She stroked a thumb over her fingers and glanced over at her. "I walked into a party many years ago expecting boring people telling half-truths about their accomplishments and overselling their dim children." She brought Jenny's hand to her lips. "But I walked away knowing that the only thing that would ever make me truly happy was a tiny blonde in a bad peasant blouse and the highest heels I'd ever seen someone stand upright in."

Despite her attempt to insert humor in her answer, Mack was totally serious and her emotions rode close to the surface. "Do you know that I look at you every morning before you wake up and wish we could have known each other longer? That way I could have more years with you." She couldn't imagine sharing her life, her home, her daughter with anyone else.

"You know, I bought that blouse just for the party. It was very expensive." Jenny looked mock-wounded.

"And it was very ugly, sweetheart." Mack smiled and turned onto a residential street lined with dark brick bungalows.

"You're lucky you're cute, Foster. I don't let just anyone insult my wardrobe." Jenny leaned against Mack's shoulder. "But thank you for saying those things, Mack. I love you in a way I never thought would be possible." She suddenly sounded wistful. "You know, when I realized I was attracted to women, I never thought I would grow up and get married, not to mention have a baby. You gave me all that. You make me feel very loved."

Mack glided a strong hand over her wife's back and took a deep breath. "If I ever forget to make you feel those things, hit me with something, okay?"

"Deal." She held on for several more seconds, as if silently absorbing the woman who loved her so completely.

Mack stopped in front of an unassuming Craftsman bungalow just as the front door opened.

Sergeant Sandy Curran's five foot nine frame was thick but she kept in decent shape, evidenced by a tailored black tuxedo sans the bow tie. She'd opted instead for a nontraditional shirt with the top button unfastened. Her partner Mia wore a long green dress adding to the dramatic portrait sketched by her curly red hair and emerald-colored eyes. She stood just an inch or two shorter than Sandy and Mack thought they looked good together. She was happy for her oldest friend and watched Sandy hold Mia's hand tightly as they walked to the car.

"Smurf!" Sandy slid across the back seat and leaned over to peck Jenny on the cheek. She clapped Mack on the shoulder. Mack laughed at the nickname Sandy had devised for *Sergeant M. R. Foster* shortly after their promotions ceremony six years earlier. Once she decided her initials spelled *SMRF*, she'd never let it die.

"Sandy Feet! Long time, no see," Mack lobbed back. "Mia, you look stunning as always."

Jenny turned to offer a half hug to Mia as Mack drove toward the venue.

"Thank you, Mack. How does it feel to have grown-up date night?"

"We're somewhere between ridiculously excited adults and woefully neglectful parents," Jenny responded, glancing over at Mack who nodded in agreement. "But considering she barely looked my way when I left her with Maggie and her sheepdog, I guess I should quit thinking about it."

"Good idea," Mack scolded lightheartedly. "I'm not even on call tonight, so I plan on enjoying twenty-four hours of freedom."

"I'm with you. I don't go back until nineteen hundred tomorrow night. I could use a little R & R." Sandy sounded relieved to have a few hours away from the bustle of the patrol division. "Even though this is sort of a command performance for you, Detective."

"It seems you're actually the official rep for the Lesbian Cop Guild, San," Mack joked, referring to a recent newspaper interview profiling female police officers in Silver Lake. They had not been circumspect about Sandy's orientation.

"Funny, we both know all that means is I get more sideways glances and a few less propositions."

"Really? I just get eyes-down bypasses in the hallway and people who stop talking when I enter a room." Mack glanced in the mirror at Sandy.

"Maybe they're just devising how to put us on the next recruiting poster for a more diverse police department."

"Very funny. That would mean that the chief and her lackeys would have to acknowledge that there are already a dozen of us in our little department. And we all know that isn't on the agenda." Mack fingered her index card notes for the evening's speech.

"A dozen and one, Smurf. I'm pretty sure Lora Hayman in Records might break out of the closet anytime now."

"She does always look like she might burst into flames when we're around, so you might be right. I'll leave the welcome kit to you."

❖

The vision of Sydney standing in her signature black suit and white collared shirt made Parker stare appreciatively. The Prada jacket clung to her broad shoulders and the bright white of the shirt made her coal black hair look even darker.

Syd leaned against the tall painted column near the kitchen and Parker could see her watching. She attached an earring as she walked down the hall toward her. She wore a short black cocktail sheath and strappy heels, raising her five foot four inch height closer to that of her six foot tall lover.

"You know I can't focus when you dress like that." Sydney smiled and looked approvingly at Parker preparing for their Saturday night event.

"You'll be concentrating on drumming up new business, love." The way Sydney looked at her made her feel like a runway model every time. And the sight of Sydney in the formal ensemble never failed to make Parker's stomach find all the butterflies that she thought should have been gone by the relationship's anniversary mark.

"How about we stay home and I'll have my way with you, instead?" Sydney suggested.

Parker watched Sydney's gray eyes flash and she leaned against her. She had never imagined feeling so connected to anyone before. "How about you let me just enjoy being on your arm? I get to be the luckiest woman in any room when I walk in with you, you know." Parker rolled to her toes and pressed her lips against Sydney's. "Afterward you can have me any way you want me." Her voice was seductive as she closed her eyes briefly and breathed in the scent of Sydney's skin and expensive cologne.

Sydney's arms encircled Parker's waist and trapped her there. "Deal." She winked as she leaned in to take her mouth possessively, skimming her fingers underneath Parker's hair. "Plan on being up very late."

"I love you, you know," Parker said locking into Sydney's gaze.

"I know that. Almost as much as I love you."

❖

Three soaring white tents graced the lush green lawns of City Park for the Silver Lake event of the year. Limos deposited flashy social climbers at the steps while well-dressed valets waited for the guests who opted to drive personal vehicles up a long path from the street.

Although Silver Lake was a relatively small city, its proximity to the nation's capital drew an abundance of wealthy residents looking for their peace and quiet outside the rumble of the Beltway. Similarly, medium to large sized companies hung their shingles in Silver Lake, allowing them to save on real estate but enjoy the closeness to DC for both their clients and their employees. The city worked hard to foster goodwill with those citizens and their companies, not to mention to preserve their contribution to the city's tax base, so they wined and dined them every summer when Silver Lake held the Silver Stars Ball.

Syd had laughed when she'd opened the gold trimmed parchment inviting her as a guest of the DA's office, one of her largest clients. Syd imagined her mother, a member of a city council committee, fainting at the prospect of attending such an event with her only daughter. Sydney would admit that had been at least half the reason she had accepted the invitation. Of course fostering new potential client relationships was also useful. Attorneys were always looking for her video reconstruction expertise, which helped them win favor with many a jury.

Syd glided the black Porsche 911 to the curb and strode confidently to the passenger side, nodding at the attending valet who held Parker's door as she collected her from the passenger seat.

"Chivalry is certainly not dead," Parker remarked as she slipped a hand through Sydney's elbow. Syd considered it a small thing, but she relished Parker's appreciation. As they ascended the steps toward the tents, the cadence of their silent walk together was an effortless dance, one Syd believed they had been practicing for their whole lives. Tiki torches lined the narrow approach, creating a well-lit path as they made the long climb to the graceful landing under a painted arbor.

Syd stopped just as they reached the top, turning to face Parker. She guided both hands down her back, coursing the tips of her fingers along the zipper. "In case I ever forget to tell you, you are the best thing that has ever happened in my life." Sydney stroked her fingers under Parker's hair and delivered a slow kiss against her forehead reinforcing the message that Parker had become, and would always be, Sydney Hyatt's world.

Syd, once addicted to casual affairs with less-than-substantial women, took every opportunity to remind Parker that those days were far behind her.

Parker breathed raggedly, "I don't know what I did to deserve you, but I'll take it…forever."

"Remember that when I act like a jerk, okay?" Syd smoothed a hand across Parker's bare shoulder.

"Deal." Parker snaked her arms around Sydney's neck and held her tightly before they steered through the gauzy curtains.

Sydney held the draping away from the entrance as they both ducked through. The huge white tent boasted giant crystal chandeliers that hung from billowing linen draped low over the created space, easily the length of a football field. A sea of white-cloaked chairs and tables were set off by gauzy fuchsia sashes and coordinated centerpieces of stargazer lilies and baby's breath. White-painted panels created table platforms and walkways, and a dance floor at the opposite end of the long expanse. A few couples sat chatting at the tables while others mingled in the growing crowd, issuing obligatory air-kisses and enthusiastic handshakes. The night air carried the fragrance of lilies and fresh cut grass.

"Wow, it's really beautiful." Parker looked at Sydney and stood tightly against her. "It's kind of like a fairy tale, huh?"

Sydney stroked her hand and admired the genuine way Parker embraced their moments together. She turned as a tall female figure made her way through the tables in their direction. "More like a fairy tale than you thought—here comes the evil witch."

Parker followed Syd's gaze until she saw her. Pamela Hyatt wore a long bronze column skirt and matching jacket in slightly iridescent taffeta. An abundance of gold jewelry dripped from her skin making her look rather like an overdecorated Oscar statue. Her dark hair streaked with pewter strands was cut into a shoulder-length bob, framing a creased face and her trademark dour expression. It was amusing to watch it transform when some political player got within ten feet of her. Her countenance became instantly open and friendly, smiling broadly at whoever bestowed attention upon her.

Syd's mother looked them over just as they entered the bar area and she scowled in their direction.

"Apparently she was expecting her other daughter this evening," Syd jested. She was an only child.

Parker knew that seeing her mother hurt Syd. She always fought to ignore her mother's obvious disapproval of her life. She would never admit that it was more than an inconsequential irritation, but Parker felt the brief crack in Sydney's resolve every time she was forced to face her.

Syd turned toward Parker. "Watch out," she said quietly, her gaze fixed on something far away, over Parker's head. "The jackal is descending."

Parker slid her arm more firmly into Sydney's as they stepped away from the bar with their drinks. They sipped casually as the dour widow marched toward them on dyed-to-match bronze satin heels.

"I wasn't aware you would be attending, Victoria." The air seemed to thicken at her arrival and her clipped delivery, aimed at Sydney's back.

Syd turned reluctantly. "And good evening to you, too. Would you like to verify my invitation, Pamela?" Sydney had long since stopped referring to the bitter woman as *Mother*.

"I just came over to ask you something. Could you please... could you show some"—she seemed to struggle with her word choice—"decorum this evening, simply out of respect for the distinguished attendees who will be here tonight, of course."

Sydney took a long draw of her scotch, unmistakably choosing her response carefully. "Do you think you could be more specific, Pamela?" Sydney sounded weary as she regarded the woman who took every opportunity to attempt to belittle her daughter.

"Perhaps you could refrain from flaunting your...whatever this is." She swept a scathing finger between Sydney and Parker, who accepted her lover's strong arm around her shoulders. "Not during this evening. It's uncomfortable for our guests to see you demonstrating that type of behavior." The words seemed to create a foul taste in her mouth and produced an even more sour expression on her face.

Parker squeezed against Sydney when her muscles tensed at the exchange. Sydney's jaw flexed as she squared her shoulders. The elder Hyatt was tall but Sydney was taller and much more imposing as she prepared to address her mother's latest inappropriate commentary on her life.

"So, Pamela, does that mean I shouldn't hold her hand, or would you rather I didn't French kiss her over the sorbet at Table One?" Sydney delighted in delivering such a blunt hammer blow to her sad excuse for a parent.

A look of utter revulsion crossed Pamela Hyatt's face.

Sydney leaned against Parker and said, "I think I need a refill, you?" She locked eyes with Parker and forced the interaction with Pamela to fade into the periphery.

"That would be fabulous, love."

Syd could see Pamela watching them walk away. She didn't spare another glance in her direction but she grazed her hand across Parker's back and down, just briefly, over her bottom, for effect. She smiled as she heard her mother cluck her derision before her fake voice swiped over some unfortunate new target.

"Do you know how much I hate that woman?" Syd rotated her shoulders attempting to release the tension that had built there.

"I have some idea." Parker lifted onto her toes to kiss her cheek. "She's just trying to impress everyone. Her opinions mean nothing, love."

As Pamela stalked away, Jen and Mack breezed through the drapes. Mack greeted Syd with a firm handshake. "Too late for the floor show?"

"Unfortunately. But not much variation on the regular theme. You know, mother embarrassed by deviant and hopes I will agree to pretend we aren't related." Sydney's tone was wry and tired.

Mack shook her head and Sydney attempted to dispel the residing bad temper that had taken hold of her.

"You know she's on the Concerned Citizens' Coalition for the city council now?" Mack looked toward Sydney's mother who was accepting polite embraces from members of the city council. "I don't understand what exactly they are concerned about—their mission statement seems a bit thin. It buys her a seat at the table, I suppose."

"Speaking of, are we sitting together?" Jen asked hopefully of Mack, reaching for her hand and skillfully changing the subject.

"I listed all our names when I RSVP'd." Mack nodded at a table near the stage. "Sandy and Mia are sitting with us, too." Mack indicated Mia and Sandy still wading through the crowd.

"Wow, six lesbians at the same table—my mother might just call in the CDC." Sydney drained her drink and slid it onto a passing tray.

The rooms slowly filled with local dignitaries and the who's who of city government. Syd watched Sandy stop to speak briefly with a member of the command staff before walking with Mia to the bar.

When they reached the table, Sandy exchanged a hearty embrace with Sydney. "How's business, President Hyatt?"

"Couldn't be better," Sydney replied happily. "How is fighting crime street side?"

"Maybe Sandy will tell you why we never see her outside of newspapers and banquets, Syd," Mack lobbed at Sandy as Mia maneuvered around to introduce herself to Parker.

"Um," Sandy returned, "because you can make one case last a month or better and I have a hundred blue shirts busy harassing the public to deal with." They laughed as they regaled the table with the tale of their first traffic stop together. A well-known citizen had screamed to a late night crowd a warning that they should watch carefully since the Silver Lake Police were intent on harassing the public for no reason. He had blown a .25 into the Breathalyzer just before passing out on the blacktop.

"So what was your tête-à-tête about when you came in?" Syd asked and Mia rolled her eyes, groaning playfully at the question.

Sandy caught her girlfriend's hand and kissed it briefly. "I promised no shop talk tonight but let's just say I'm still a detective at heart." The former detective in the white collar crimes division was vocal about the fact that she missed the challenge of investigations. "Patrol sergeants get to hand off cases and maybe never see them again. It's not in my nature to let someone else play. I'm working on trusting that someone will listen to me one day."

"You mean to tell me that people don't feel compelled to work on a case that doesn't spell a promotion? I can't imagine." Sarcasm dripped from Sydney's lips as she shook the ice in her glass.

"Ah, so you've met some of our esteemed commanders?" Sandy looked at her with amusement.

"One of them and my mother scheme to save the world from anyone not worthy of oxygen in their opinion." Her jaw clenched as she scanned the room and located her mother speaking animatedly with Major Williams.

Sandy's eyes grew huge. "I never put it together before. Pamela Hyatt is your *mother*?" She gawked briefly.

Syd smiled drolly and ran an absent finger around the rim of the glass. "Well, we've never actually had confirmation from her home planet, but it is a fairly persistent rumor." A sneer overtook her attempt at a grin.

Despite the moratorium on department-related chatter, Mack and Sandy continued to recount tales of their rookie days over dinner. Syd appraised the duo; their genuine admiration for each other was evident. Their enduring friendship was solid.

CHAPTER THREE

As the meal drew to an end with the arrival of a decadent chocolate dessert garnished with fresh raspberries and whipped cream, staff in white coats and black slacks rapidly buzzed around the room filling coffee cups and clearing plates before the spirited sounds of the crowd fell into a retreating hush. Pamela Hyatt climbed the short stairs to assume her post behind the podium. Sydney was continually mystified how her mother contributed practically nothing valuable to the running of the city but still managed to ingratiate herself with the movers and shakers of the community.

Her normally pinched expression spilled into a broad smile at her audience. Sydney thought a good audience might be something she loved more than anything.

"Good evening, ladies and gentlemen."

Parker turned in her chair toward the stage and leaned slightly against Sydney's chest. She closed her eyes and savored the jolt of electricity that still found her body every time they touched. Sydney turned Parker's face gently, softly grazing a kiss over her cheek.

"Love you," Sydney whispered as Parker smiled and drew Syd's arm tighter around her shoulders.

Pamela continued, "What a pleasure to see all of you, our esteemed citizens and city leaders. The other cities in Fairfax County are certainly poorer for this gathering tonight, am I right?"

A smattering of applause greeted her painfully awkward attempt at a joke, Parker observed, entertained by the fact that Pamela actually clapped for herself.

"We have some truly inspirational guests here to address everyone this evening. Tonight we begin with our most esteemed and accomplished law enforcement leader, Chief Jayne Provost, who came to our fair city a scant five years ago from our nation's capital. She brought with her thorough knowledge and a dedication to ridding our lovely city of violent crime and the unwelcome behavior of delinquents and deviants." Pamela seemed thoroughly impressed with herself.

Syd leaned into Parker's ear. "I love it when I get mentioned in my mother's speeches." Parker giggled and rubbed Sydney's hand, remembering briefly how the elder Hyatt had referred to both her and Sydney as deviants during a thoroughly unpleasant exchange last Christmas.

"Please give a warm welcome to Chief Jayne Provost!"

Everyone clapped politely as she climbed the stairs of the dais revealing the red soles of her Louboutins. Parker had heard that it consistently bewildered the officers sworn to protect and serve Silver Lake that their top cop behaved more like a fashion-addicted celebrity than a law-enforcement professional.

The slender, auburn-haired woman smiled and waved as the reception quieted. "Thank you so much for that warm welcome and for coming out tonight to this beautiful event." Her manicured hands swept grandly over the venue. "It is my distinct pleasure to welcome my officers here tonight as well as our community's business and government leaders. Our esteemed district attorney Robert Fillmore is also with us—please stand, Bob." He waved awkwardly garnering a quick round of applause. "Now please give a hand for Marco Hamlin, our city manager." A short round of applause followed again as the small man in a dark suit did a half stand from his place at table two.

"Let me now offer a special welcome to our local celebrities from the world of business who were most generous in their sponsorship of this event. First, please offer a special welcome to our Platinum sponsor, representing CacheTech Incorporated, one of our largest corporate partners in Silver Lake as well as the city's largest employer—Lawrence and Bryce Downing."

Pamela worked her way through the corporate sponsors, recognizing each one. "And finally, representing the PRC Advertising Group—"

Parker tensed as she heard the company's name and glanced around uneasily, wondering how she hadn't seen anyone from PRC during the cocktail hour.

"—senior account manager and vice president Dayne Grant, and account manager Tom Simmons." Applause rang out as Parker's ex-wife was the first to stand followed by her shorter, pudgier colleague.

Parker watched as Dayne waved to the crowd as if she had just been crowned Miss America. Anyone who knew the brash Dayne Grant would expect nothing less.

Jenny leaned over the table and whispered to Parker, "Did you know she was coming?" Jenny looked at her best friend and boss, as if to read her unspoken thoughts. After more than seven years together at Davidson Properties they worked together like sisters. Parker knew she likely looked unsettled to her best friend. After all, Jenny had watched the daily struggle Parker endured to get to the other side of her horrific separation from the unfaithful Dayne.

Parker took a long steadying sip of her wine before answering. "I had no idea. Richard told me months ago that he had declined this invitation because they would be on their cruise. I suppose I should have assumed that they would send her in his place." She shrugged and watched Dayne lean over to other tables to shake hands with acquaintances as the speech continued.

"Are you okay?" Mack asked.

Syd hugged Parker more firmly against her adding her other arm around her lover's shoulders. "Parker has nothing to worry about from Dayne. I don't think Ms. Grant would attempt a repeat of our New Year's gathering, do you?"

Parker looked warily at Dayne who had made a pointed play for Parker before knowing that she and Sydney were together. Syd lifted Parker's hair and dropped a kiss on the nape of her neck.

Parker turned to look at Syd. "Are we okay?"

Sydney looked incredulous for a moment and pressed the side of her face against Parker's as she spoke. "Of course we are. I'm not, nor will I ever be, threatened by Dayne Grant. Surely even she has better sense than to behave inappropriately at a citywide event like this. New Year's Eve was bad enough."

Parker laughed and nodded. "Yes, I think even she has more common sense than that."

Sydney looked at her steadily, her sharp gray eyes locking into Parker's. "She missed an opportunity to spend the rest of her life with you, so you'll forgive me if I give her common sense a failing grade."

Parker smiled and turned farther in her chair to kiss Sydney's mouth slowly. "I fell in love with a hopeless charmer."

"As long as you stay in love with me, you can call me anything you like." Sydney watched Dayne as she resumed her seat, flicking a glance over to her ex's new girlfriend before focusing elsewhere. Syd made sure that her silent warning was clear. Dayne would steer clear of Parker because Sydney wouldn't permit an attempt to lure Parker from her. It should have been out of consideration for Dayne's new girlfriend; however, Syd wondered if Dayne ever considered anyone other than herself.

The evening ambled by slowly as Major Williams gave his State of the City address, regarding the reduction of crime in Silver Lake. Major Cash had happily escaped the obligation, normally his responsibility, since he and his wife were celebrating their twenty-fifth wedding anniversary in Belize.

Syd people-watched as Major Williams spent the majority of his speech verbally kissing Chief Provost's designer-clad behind. It was no secret that Major Williams coveted the chief spot. He had been summarily overlooked five years ago by the city council but no one had expected them to select an even more mediocre cop, which Jayne Provost had proven to be. Pamela hovered nearby, seemingly entranced by the speech. Typical.

As Major Williams finished, he angled toward their table. He introduced a reluctant Mack and invited her to the podium. "Our Detective Sergeant Mackenzie Foster, over the west side homicide division, has helped bring our little city into the new millennium, overseeing a number of new and progressive projects. Please help me welcome this rising trailblazer in the Silver Lake Police Department."

Mack politely thanked the major. Sydney wondered if her disdain for the incompetent leader was as apparent to the rest of the room as it was to her. She spoke quickly and knowledgeably about the progress her division had made and the sound solution rates they had achieved. She noted that crimes like homicide affected predominantly the homeless and drug-involved populations in the city. She reviewed recent programs and initiatives to help the underprivileged populations in their city as well as announcing the CIT certification of thirty-five officers, dedicated to helping the mentally challenged residents of Silver Lake. Mack finished as her fellow officers gave her a louder than necessary round of applause which made her blush, but gave her the opportunity to return to her seat quickly, swallowed by the celebratory din.

Finally, District Attorney Robert Fillmore took the stage and spoke about the successful prosecution rates of some of the city's more publicized criminal trials. He took a moment to address his staff and the administrator of the courts, then made special mention of Sydney Hyatt and DRIFT, asking her to stand as he cited her invaluable contribution to a recent successful prosecution.

Syd sat down as soon as it was appropriate and took a swallow of her now-watery scotch. The group at the table clapped loudly for Sydney who gestured away the uncomfortable kudos.

The speeches ended and Syd knew the remainder of the evening would be dedicated to rubbing elbows with people who thought networking might garner them future business advantage. She could manage the task easily but it wasn't her favorite pastime. Several attorneys pulled her aside and asked to set up meetings for cases that were pending. While she did many personal injury cases when she believed the claims were bona fide, she had no patience for ambulance chasers and staged reconstructions of minor accidents. She happily stepped aside as her competition snatched those cases aimed at big settlements from large corporations who were often just victims of a litigious wave. Syd's true love was pro bono work, reconstructing violent incidents where the defendants were long forgotten and resources were slim by the time new evidence came to light.

Parker watched Dayne make the rounds with the local elite, no doubt touting the work she could do publicizing their businesses. Dayne had glanced over once, catching Parker's eye and raising her scotch in salute. Dayne had then darted her eyes over the crowd as if to locate Sydney before her girlfriend grabbed her arm and her attention possessively. Parker felt nothing for her ex-wife and was glad she was no longer part of the ad exec's sales pitches and endless diatribes of self-aggrandizement.

Parker accepted a fresh glass of wine from a passing tray as she watched Sydney speak with the DA about the latest project she was finishing for him. She was dark and serious and cripplingly sexy as she talked business and inadvertently charmed her audience. She scanned the room and noticed Mia and Sandy walking with Mack and Jen to the coffee station, when a stocky, light-haired man in a gray suit approached her.

"Nice gathering, don't you think? I'm Bryce Downing." He thrust a clammy hand toward her and she shook it reluctantly but graciously.

Parker smiled at him politely. "Yes, it's lovely. The tent and the lighting make it feel really special." He finally released her hand and she reflexively rushed hers back as if it had touched something unpleasant.

"My company is the major sponsor of this event every year. I was assured this time it would be better—more upscale—or I wasn't interested in having the company name up there." He smiled smugly as he turned her toward the sponsor board behind the coffee bar. Parker caught Jen's bemused expression as she observed Parker tensely and awkwardly engaging the self-important little man. He attempted to appear assured and laid back but instead she thought he came off as uneasy and arrogant. Parker remembered a man once telling her that confidence could easily be mistaken for arrogance. She was quite sure that he had made the comment because everyone thought he was arrogant. By contrast, she thought, Sydney was coolly confident in any situation; this guy was just a pretentious ass.

Parker moved away slightly, causing his unwanted hand to slide off her upper arm. She took in an unexpectedly shaky breath and struggled to corral her reaction. "Well, it was nice to meet you." She tried to smile but she was positive the attempt could have been called a grimace at best.

Clueless or completely unconcerned about his acquaintance's attempt to extricate herself from the conversation, he continued speaking too closely to Parker.

"So what do you do—or are you married? I don't see a ring." He sang the last word as if he had dug for gold and come up a millionaire. He sounded slightly drunk. He smelled like whiskey and had begun to slur his words. His breath fell hotly over Parker who still tried in vain to subtly increase the distance between them.

"Well, I've been married and I also had a job at the same time." Parker felt the affront for any of his potential girlfriends and hoped the new sheen of indignation would coat her unsettled mood. "I guess I'm just multitalented like that. And no I'm not—"

"Well, I just mean, when *I* decide to get married, I expect *my* wife to stay at home and tend to the duties there. A lot of women would appreciate a traditional guy like me."

Some women marry imprisoned serial killers, too, she thought. She also thought the number of his potential girlfriends could be statistically similar.

Out loud she managed, "I'm sure they would. I guess I'm one of those pesky, self-sufficient types." Parker tried a grin again but she was finding the exchange with the boorish man increasingly unsettling. She skimmed a hand over her neck where a glaze of perspiration was forming despite the relative cool of the room.

Parker noticed Sydney deep in negotiations with an attorney who had spent weeks practically begging for help on a case he hoped to fast-track for his corporate client. As if feeling her gaze, Syd glanced over to wink at Parker before she turned back to face the attorney. Parker stared at her, willing her to turn around again.

As if the footlights on his personal stage had just snapped on, Bryce Downing leaned in. "People are finally dancing, looks like our chance." His watery eyes and stale breath contributed to the churning in her stomach. Without any warning or indication of ca-pitulation from Parker, he grabbed her upper arm, more tightly this time, and endeavored to move her toward the dance floor.

"Thank you, but no." She attempted to pull out of his grasp but he held her too firmly. She scanned the space for a place to relinquish her glass, suddenly wanting both hands free. "Please let go," she said a little louder as a cold sweat broke over her face. She suddenly felt short of breath and, despite the room full of people, desperately isolated. Alarm flushed over her body and her knees felt weak. She mentally evaluated her visceral reaction to the situation. She bordered on panic which she knew was irrational so close to the safety of hundreds of people, but she couldn't seem to break its spell.

"Come on, honey, I'm a great dancer." He leaned into her and attempted a wink that wound up looking like some sort of nervous tic. Parker supposed his alcohol consumption made touted prowess of any kind easy for him to believe. She was sure she wouldn't be finding out firsthand.

Parker endeavored once again to twist out of his grip but felt weaker from each attempt. She hardly managed words now as she struggled for a breath. Edges of her vision narrowed and she felt locked on his face which seemed only inches from hers. She closed her eyes and fought for oxygen which seemed to catch in her throat. Her internal admonishments told her that she was being ridiculous and that she was overreacting. They did nothing to calm the pounding of her heart.

"She said no." Sydney stood too close, towering over Bryce, her hands inches from his. "Let go."

"Not sure this involves you," Bryce responded. Parker thought something akin to beer muscles just overtook his logical brain. His sarcastic delivery sounded feeble in the face of her physically imposing girlfriend. But the sudden tension caused him to squeeze Parker's skin even harder.

Sydney sneered as she peeled his hand from Parker's arm and twisted his fingers roughly, holding them in hers for a few unnecessary seconds. Once free, Parker tried urgently to rub away the legacy of him from her flesh. Sydney moved between her and Bryce Downing, creating a shield with her body. Parker knew that Sydney's move to protect her was more instinct than calculation. Parker placed her hands against Sydney's back using the moment to ground herself, feeling suddenly silly at her reaction.

"I beg to differ," Sydney stared at him treacherously, not moving a muscle. "Don't ever do that again." Parker moved around and accepted Syd's arm around her back.

Bryce Downing smirked at Sydney and sidestepped to look more directly at Parker, who still felt strangely off balance by the peculiar encounter.

"You're queer?" He sounded incredulous as he dragged his eyes lecherously over Parker's body, increasing her discomfort. Sydney remained partially in front of her, her other hand half clenched at her side.

Parker laced her fingers into Syd's and attempted to sound flip. "Yup, I got a toaster oven *and* the T-shirt."

"Good luck with that." He threw the words over his shoulder as he began to walk unsteadily away. "You don't know what you're missing." Parker was grateful for that at least.

Parker hoped he might be embarrassed, but then doubted if he even understood how inappropriate his behavior had been. She sighed loudly as Sydney turned to fold her arms around her, causing a shudder to wash over her.

"I'm sorry I didn't see him earlier." Sydney was visibly steaming. "Let me see your arm."

Parker forced a smile. "I'm okay, really. It was just so weird. I'm thinking that guy is used to getting what he wants and alcohol is not his friend." She presented the angry red ring on her arm quickly before shrugging it away.

"I'm going to go talk to Bob about him, okay?" Parker knew Sydney's reassuring tone was no match for the blind rage she could see simmering behind her eyes.

"No, please, love, it's okay. He just doesn't seem to have much experience wooing women, I guess. He seems harmless enough." She chuckled as she now felt Sydney's heart beating loudly in her ear instead of her own. Syd brushed long soothing strokes over her back.

"You don't know how close I was to choking the little cretin." Her words sounded much less lethal than her voice.

"Thank you for not making a scene. It's okay, really. I'm just going to run to the restroom, all right?" As she turned, Parker still felt her face burn from the encounter—whether a blush, or the heat created by the crush of the crowd, she couldn't arrive at a satisfactory description.

Parker walked quickly through the door of the deserted bathroom and leaned against the wall in front of the sink. She felt grateful for the cool tiles at her back. Pressing a damp paper towel to her cheeks, she dabbed carefully under her mascaraed lashes. She marveled at how easy it had been for him to unnerve her and how instantaneously she recognized the feeling. It had been nearly a year since one of Sydney's acquaintances began stalking her and ended up taking her hostage. Becky Weaver had held her at knifepoint until Sydney talked her way in and eventually overpowered the unstable woman. Since then, feeling defenseless against some unwanted touch, some stranger's grasp, was more of a frightening trigger than it should have been.

The Becky incident had left a now-tiny scar beneath her right eye and some other faint legacies from the deranged woman's knife, but otherwise she had escaped significant injury. Parker breathed slowly and pushed the memories back. This was the first time she could remember the recall coming so vividly or affecting her so dramatically. She pushed the damp towel under her eyes again and over her forehead before wetting it again in the sink.

Sydney tried to carry on casual conversations while repeatedly turning toward the restrooms, expecting to see Parker making her return. Finally catching Mack's ear, she whispered to her, "I need to go check on Park—make my excuses, okay?" Mack nodded as Sydney nearly jogged through the crowd and through the door marked by a skirted silhouette.

She only had to see Parker for a second before she knew instinctively that she was still fighting unwanted feelings from the Becky episode. Sydney moved her up and away from the vanity, gathering Parker protectively against her without a word.

"I'll be okay." Parker attempted a laugh but Syd could feel her body tremble in her embrace. "I don't know what got into me."

"I'm so sorry. What he did wasn't okay." Her voice was ragged and she knew it revealed her poorly restrained fury.

Parker took a deep breath again and relaxed in Sydney's still unyielding grip. "I'm okay now." After a moment, Parker arched away from Sydney, just enough for her to see her face properly. "Any makeup runs?"

"Stunning as always." Sydney held a tiny distance between her lips and Parker's allowing the heat to build before she pressed her mouth into a gentle kiss, reassuring herself, and hopefully Parker, of the impenetrable bond that cemented them.

Parker responded gratefully and then hungrily. Syd relished the building heat and endeavored to replace Parker's feelings of unsteadiness. She felt the deepening kiss to her soul, always amazed at the spell Parker could place over her.

The contemptuous gasp from behind them caught Syd by surprise, lost as she'd been in the moment.

"Victoria, when will you stop humiliating our family? When will it be enough?"

Sydney unhurriedly finished the kiss, looking only at Parker, still shielding her. "Let's go home." Her eyes locked into Parker's intense blue ones as if no one had invaded the solitary space in their very personal universe.

Neither of them looked at Pamela; she wasn't allowed to spoil their moment. Sydney felt triumphant.

Chapter Four

Sergeant Sandy Curran watched a white box truck back up to the dock door of the vacant building on Forty-Sixth and Lincoln. She had spent numerous late shifts eating her dinner in the car, casually watching trucks unload crates into the unadorned space.

Tonight, sitting in her unmarked black Taurus sedan, she reclaimed her covert spot between the train tracks and an adjacent structure. She had anticipated finishing her coffee and her growing stack of reports before heading home at end of her final shift in less than an hour.

Part of her had hoped this truck would be back and she wasn't disappointed. Investigations might not be in her job description anymore as a patrol sergeant, but once a detective, always a detective.

She aimed her phone and snapped a picture of the truck and the short sandy-haired man driving. Not risking the flash, the only light on the subject filtered from the street lamp and the overhead door. She attached them to a text with the time. After three years with Mia, all she could think about was waking up with her in the home they shared. Instead she was sending her random texts of nondescript night scenes from the sketchy side of Silver Lake.

Another sexy text, sweetheart. You sure are lucky, lol.

Sandy then deleted the text to leave no obvious trace in her department-issued cell phone. She had no intention of leaving evidence that she was sharing an investigation with someone outside the department even though she knew it could be found if someone really wanted to look.

Silver Lake had started seeing more vacant properties taken over by partying teens with unobservant or absent parents. Because the city was growing in popularity as the site of the second homes of wealthy DC movers and shakers, empty houses in which to party were becoming more plentiful. Sandy knew, however, that what she was observing wasn't overindulged children hoping for a rave and some Ecstasy. She had been watching too long and seen them too often. Six months of evidence gathering would prove that soundly enough.

She waited another forty-five minutes, when the nondescript truck drove away. Disappointing for her unofficial investigation, but she was happy to report in that she was 10-7 and headed home.

Mia met her at the door instead of waiting in bed for her to come in, which had long been their routine on her second shift weekends. Sandy was grateful for the reminder of normal life outside of department politics and criminal diversions. Sandy would gladly admit that she truly loved Mia Wright and looked forward to planning their long life with each other.

"I missed you." The lanky redhead slid her arms around Sandy even before she had time to shut the heavy wooden door behind her. Mia wore the blue and white striped button-down shirt she had swiped long ago from Sandy's closet. She claimed she wore it as a nightshirt because it was comfortable but admitted she had taken it at first because it smelled like Sandy. And Sandy found that extremely sexy. She admired the milky white skin that smoothed down over Mia's long legs to her perpetually painted toes. Mia made the old house come alive for Sandy who still mourned the grandmother who'd left it to her family. Once the estate was settled, she and Mia planned to buy it and make it their permanent home.

"Wow! Send a woman a couple of pictures of random trucks and you might get lucky," she joked, kissing her gratefully when Mia offered her lips to Sandy. The kiss was deep and needy and a harbinger of the sexy evening Sandy had not been expecting.

"Actually, *in spite* of the unsexy texts." Mia raised her eyebrows comically. "When are you going to turn all that over, anyway?" Mia dropped her hands and walked at Sandy's side through the living room.

"As soon as someone in Investigations calls me. I'm trying not to step on toes—you know how the brass is around here. I go over someone's head and mine is likely to roll." She was only partially kidding, thinking about the political nature of any police department let alone the one now run by Chief Provost. "Besides, I'm not sure who the players are. Something tells me that there's more to this than one truck and one guy. And I can't be the only one who has noticed the activity there every Sunday night." Sandy wondered if someone was discounting her reports because she was no longer part of the detective squad. She had long ago discovered that just because things looked to be insignificant, it didn't mean they were.

Sandy had never questioned her loyalty to her employer in her twelve years at Silver Lake or in her twenty in law enforcement. She never wanted to be in the position to question the work ethic of others. However, she was becoming increasingly frustrated by the inaction of her department.

"You would just think it would be easy enough to prove. They are obviously using the warehouse for something covert—read, illegal." Mia tickled her fingernails over Sandy's neck as she loosened her tie and unpinned Sandy's badge from her uniform shirt. She laid it carefully on the table.

"That *is* easy to prove, but I would sure like to know what they're moving and where it's going first. I only have that one picture of cargo and I couldn't even get close enough to see what it was. All I know is by the time Monday night comes, it's all locked up and desolate again. They only have to get careless one time and I'll have them tied up in a bow—we can get a warrant. Even the lazy butts in Investigations can't complain about that kind of easy closure. I was thinking I might try an overnight in my own car, and then I might see what happens after the drop."

She unknotted her tie and pulled it away from her neck, then draped it playfully around Mia's shoulders. She hung her duty belt on the spindled dining room chair that had belonged to her grandmother. Sandy couldn't wait until the estate was settled and her family had picked through what was left in the house so she and Mia could start putting their own touches on the 1920s Craftsman bungalow they had moved into nine months earlier. If it wasn't for Mia's bedroom set, there would be nothing but their clothes to distinguish it from the home her grandparents had lived in since it was built nearly a century ago.

She walked to the bedroom, unbuttoned her uniform shirt, and hung it in the narrow closet. Velcro straps ripped loudly away from the shoulders of her Kevlar vest before she draped it over a hanger, ready for her shift on Wednesday. She felt much freer in her long white T-shirt and briefs as she padded into the bathroom. She rolled her shoulders and bent over the sink to wash the night from her hands and face.

"You're not usually up so late on a Sunday night, Mi," she called into the bedroom as she turned off the tap. "Did you have something in mind for this evening?" She patted her face dry on a fluffy white towel that Mia must have bought since Sandy's collection had consisted of four rough and dingy yellow ones.

She found Mia leaning seductively against the bedroom door frame.

"How about a White Russian and a redheaded Canadian?" Mia smiled as she passed her the drink she had made and posed dramatically with her red hair scooped haphazardly on top of her head. She batted her eyes exaggeratedly at Sandy and cocked a hip.

"Fascinating." Sandy looked serious. "I don't know how you do it. Those are my two favorite things." Sandy laughed and took a grateful sip of the milky concoction before drawing her lover in for a zealous, Kahlua-tinted kiss. "Let's go to bed my little Canadian."

Sandy had been in numerous relationships before Mia but they had all been plagued with typical drama and petty jealousies. Sandy hadn't been perfect either, often being the cause of the jealousy. Cops were notorious for being unfaithful and she hadn't done much to combat the stereotype. After finding a love note from a fellow officer, her last girlfriend changed the locks on their apartment while Sandy was at work. She remembered loading garbage bags stuffed with her belongings into her SUV in uniform at eleven o'clock one night. She had hoped the neighbors weren't watching the activity as she'd called Mack for a temporary spot on her couch.

A more mature Sandy made sure that Mia had all the relevant information about her past before they started dating. Mia was understandably cautious at first, but made it obvious that she loved Sandy with everything she had. Sandy was grateful when Mia decided to take the leap three years earlier. Sandy swore to herself she would never make Mia regret a moment of their relationship or doubt Sandy's commitment to her.

Sandy shed her clothes and slid into bed next to Mia. She felt a chill as she ran her fingernails through her wavy hair. Sandy shifted Mia on top of her and kissed her powerfully. A glowing Mia moved with her, arched against her, and Sandy felt the flush of heat draw over her skin.

"I missed you," Mia said.

Sandy knew Mia needed to feel her this way, just to cement their life together, to bring her back to the place they were before Sandy left to do the job she knew was dangerous. Sandy didn't know if Mia ever would get used to life as a cop's girlfriend.

Sandy spoke softly, "I will always love you."

❖

Parker had spent the lazy Sunday after the ball running errands and crafting a cream of vegetable soup while Sydney worked to finish the project for the DA. Now dressed in cotton gym shorts and a knit camisole, Parker climbed the loft stairs. She pressed her thumb to the biometric pad and listened as the lock clicked open. Syd had added her to the access control system just after the New Year when they were spending more and more time at Syd's two-bedroom loft. Parker had no reason to be in Sydney's studio except in emergencies. The incident with Becky had left Syd overprotective and overly cautious about their safety.

Parker watched her lover pore over eight-by-tens of a crime scene as she scanned them into her encrypted PC on the long counter that occupied two of the walls. Syd clicked through pictures as the images were deposited onto the huge monitor.

At Parker's arrival, she minimized the program and worked to gather the photos back into their file. Syd often tried to spare her the unpleasant images she worked with in her forensics reconstruction company. DRIFT paid her bills and then some, but the images could often be disturbing.

Holding a drink, Parker skimmed her hand over Sydney's shoulder and down over her chest glancing over the stiff points under her shirt, causing Sydney's breath to stutter. Parker presented the heavy Waterford glass to her over the other shoulder and skated her lips seductively across Sydney's neck. Syd turned her chair slightly, inhaling the scent of lilies mixed with the faint aroma of cooking spices on Parker's skin.

Sydney's husky voice found Parker's ear. "To what do I owe this honor?" Sydney leaned against her high-backed captain's chair, offering her neck to Parker. She sifted her fingers through Parker's hair, firmly clasping a handful when Parker found the spot behind her ear.

"Well"—Parker continued her ministrations as Sydney took a shaky sip of her scotch—"as your undertipped serving wench, I try to make myself useful whenever I can."

"In that case"—Sydney set her glass on the counter and drew Parker onto her lap—"I have a very good tip for you." Parker's touch made Sydney instantly weak and immediately flushed.

Depositing a slow, deep kiss onto her full lips, Parker bowed into her lean body and moaned at the effective assault. Syd greedily scraped her fingers over her lover's narrow hips as the kiss became hungrier.

"I am so in love with you," Parker breathed. Sydney's skin responded as she heard the words she never thought she would want to hear and now couldn't listen to enough.

"I love you." Sydney could say those words willingly without hesitation, unlike the many years of her life when simply the thought had terrified her.

"Don't you...uh...need a break?" Parker's words were suggestive, as she hooked a finger in the collar of Syd's T-shirt. The look in her eyes left no doubt what she was proposing.

"Like you wouldn't believe." Sydney took a long pull from her glass and set it back on the counter, still cradling her lover against her.

Parker extricated herself from Sydney's lap and dashed to the door as an amused Sydney took another leisurely swallow from her drink and started to stand. Her words were slow and assertive. "I'll give you a head start, but after I catch you, all bets are off."

Parker laughed as she danced down the metal stairs. "Thanks for the warning but I'm way ahead of you."

Parker squealed when Sydney caught her waist in a powerful forearm and threw her playfully onto their king-sized bed. Syd pushed her long body onto Parker's, suddenly hot with the desire the proximity to Parker always brought. Syd watched her lover's mood transform as the feel of Parker's body and the intensity of the moment consumed her.

Sydney framed her face gently with long fingers and grazed her tongue across Parker's. Parker pressed against her in answer.

"I need you, Syd." Parker seemed captivated by the fire on her skin, and lost at the sensations where her lover's body touched hers.

Sydney removed the only remaining item of clothing from Parker's narrow hips and grazed her lips down Parker's neck before discovering her hard nipples with her teeth. She lazily tortured her willing body as she felt Parker grind against her.

Sydney Hyatt could draw an intricate diagram of Parker's body from memory by now, having explored, so many times, the hills and valleys and intimate ridges as Parker begged to be consumed by her. Syd's fingers slowly found the burning center that would propel Parker and commanded her lover's response, browsing her thumb gently past the hard, insistent core. Parker dipped her forehead under Sydney's chin as she pushed her toward her release.

"Not yet," Sydney teased as she glided into her more slowly, searing heat fusing them together. Before Parker, Sydney had never conceived of the mesmerizing sensual power that one person could have with another. Her navigation, her control over Parker's surrender consumed Sydney every time she was granted the privilege of drawing Parker to the edge. Parker's thigh connected solidly against Syd whose own punishing release was only seconds behind her lover's.

Moments later, Sydney found Parker's ear, knowing instinctively the words and the sensations that would cause the maddening rush she could elicit from Parker. She drew her tongue hotly along her collarbone and up around the rim of her ear. She savored her influence over Parker's desires, the power to siphon her lover's resolve as she thrust deeper into her. Finally the insistent, quenching demands found purchase on them both.

"Now, baby," Sydney's deep voice instructed. "I need you to come for me. Please, for me."

She was rewarded with an insistent *Now* from Parker as Sydney met her in a simultaneous yielding, once again fascinated by the dominion Parker had over her body and over her mind.

Sydney studied Parker as the grip of her contractions faded quietly, pulling her tenderly against her, strangling against her own ebbing sensations.

"You are so amazing. I can't believe we're here sometimes." Sydney tried to steady her breath as the traveling swells along her skin subsided.

"Please don't let go," Parker managed.

Syd waited for those words each time they were together. "Never." Syd held Parker, slowly stroking over her hair, always just a little terrified that something would tear Parker from her someday. She was sure she could never desire another woman the way she did Parker. She attempted not to focus on the small finger-sized bruises she could see on her girlfriend's arm.

After a few languid moments, Parker murmured, "I made that soup you like and I got some yummy French bread and I was thinking that we could have dinner in bed. What do you think?" Parker stretched lazily against the woman she had become addicted to, basking in the feeling of Syd tightly holding her, inhaling the intoxicating fragrance of her fading cologne mixed with the scent of her skin, a combination she was sure she could identify blindfolded in a room of thousands.

"Well, I think that sounds very indulgent and really good. Of course anything you ask me that ends with my being in bed with you sounds really good." Sydney settled her body onto Parker's and bit her neck playfully.

"You have a very dirty mind, Sydney Hyatt." She watched as Syd bounded off the bed and headed naked toward the kitchen in search of the rumored meal.

"I thought that's why you loved me," she called back down the hall while Parker padded across to the spare bedroom for TV trays. The room held a Murphy bed latched snuggly to the wall but predominately served as Sydney's home gym since she rarely had guests. Parker peered into the large double closet along the back wall and dodged a punching bag suspended from the ceiling. She found the trays behind customary odds and ends routinely dumped in a closet, that no one ever used but everyone failed to get rid of. She stepped past the inversion bench and back to find Sydney.

Parker knew the week would be busy with Sydney spending long days with her client going over her presentations and testimony. Parker had two new projects to prepare before breaking ground on office expansion in the fall, which would cost her the mundane moments she relished with Syd. She padded toward the kitchen where she found Sydney ladling soup into stoneware crocks, pouring slowly so as not to scald her naked flesh with the boiling liquid. She watched appreciatively from the hall as her faithful warrior smiled back at her.

CHAPTER FIVE

Independence Day found Sandy Curran piloting her black sedan into her familiar hiding spot. Because the industrial area saw very little night traffic, the lot was still and the railroad tracks would host no freight for hours.

After ten o'clock, she wondered if the routine had been broken. Normally the nondescript truck had arrived by now and would have been unloaded and preparing to leave again, but so far nothing. Perhaps the holiday had affected their schedule. She listened idly as fireworks exploded in the distance. The fairgrounds hosted the legal fireworks display, but closer, erratic explosions told her the illegal festivities were in full swing as well.

She returned her stack of reports to the passenger seat and draped her thin nylon raid jacket over her mobile computer terminal to dim its glow. She heard a helicopter above her just before her attention was drawn through the windshield. Twin streams of light completed a wide sweep onto the road and then the lot. A different truck than usual, this one with a logo, backed into the dock. She aimed her phone camera at the faded image through the dark. She jotted the license plate number onto her notepad and snapped a picture of the truck. The flash was bright and pierced the night's calm. She cursed at herself for not remembering to switch it off. She send the image to Mia and a reply text came immediately.

Stay safe, sweetheart

Mia never told her to be careful—she was always careful.

Sandy expected no further deviance from the routine but watched the action nonetheless. A jolt of excitement sparked in her mind, and she wondered if she might finally see the merchandise which she had never been able to identify before now. A dim light seeped around the edge of the box truck as the roll-up door was raised. The same sandy-haired man she'd seen before backed the truck a few more inches and sealed it against the rubber frame of the dock door.

As he exited, she could now estimate that he was closer to his thirties instead of the twentysomething she had originally thought. He disappeared inside the windowless building.

She rested her right hand reflexively on the butt of her holstered weapon, flicking the snap loose with her thumb before fastening it again. Something felt off, more charged than usual. She snapped a last picture of the warehouse and slipped the phone back into its home on her belt.

The report of the gunshot found her ear a microsecond before the crush of gravel under shoes communicated the approaching danger.

❖

Lab manager Darcy Dean glanced at her watch. It was just after midnight and the crime scene analysts in white Tyvek suits were scanning the empty lot for anything to collect. As they approached, Jamie Amana, a slightly built African American man, raised his camera and began taking careful pictures of the scene and the body. The lead technician's attractive almond eyes were intense as he swept the area and squinted into the viewfinder.

Darcy, sound asleep just an hour ago, was now laser focused on the body that lay in front of her. Neither she nor Jamie spoke as they processed the scene that held the lifeless body of their colleague which sat just inside her official vehicle. Her weapon sat securely in its fastened holster, her uniform pristine but for the fine red blood spray which had flowered across her starched blue shirt and pants.

"Looks like an ambush to me." Darcy broke the silence, speaking quietly to Jamie as she struggled to recreate the scene in her mind. She tilted the cap off her hair briefly and rubbed her forehead against her sleeve. She positioned herself outside the driver's door in an effort to approximate where the shooter might have been standing. She unspooled a measuring tape and stood away when Jamie took several photos from outside the door.

"Jamie, I'd like you to take some photos in the building if that's okay." She glanced at the hulking warehouse structure behind her.

"I already asked, but they told me it was locked up tight. The major told me they had determined some drug runner got spooked during a deal. He said this one will be open and shut," Jamie informed his newly minted supervisor, never disengaging from the viewfinder of his camera.

"How about just from outside then?" She glanced back at the browning strip of weeds serving as landscaping along the perimeter of the warehouse.

"Got those." Jamie bent to photograph the door, capturing the fingerprint dust along its edge.

"You do good work."

"Not exactly my first scene, Darcy."

"I know, but this is different." She tried not to let the sadness in her voice belie the stern professional look she wore. "Have you ever...?"

He closed his eyes and shook his head before obscuring his face with the camera again.

Major Damon Williams approached them and Darcy regarded the sweaty man carefully. Supervisors like Williams typically dealt with the medical examiner, leaving her to the science of evidence and research she analyzed quite on her own. Since the ME, Dr.

Alison Gray, was enjoying two weeks in Hawaii with her new husband, Darcy was the ranking member of the Silver Lake field office for now.

"Dean, I hate to have you pull two in one night but I need you on the double homicide we got in earlier." Williams spoke loudly and leaned in to be heard over the noise of an approaching helicopter. Darcy could smell his stale breath.

"Really, sir?" She tried not to let her face betray the fact that she was loathe to leave the scene before she had exhausted every angle of investigation. She had only been in Silver Lake and on this job a few weeks so her approach was cautious.

"Don't you want us to wait for Homicide and Major Crimes?"

"As much as I'd like to find the bastard and hang them for taking one of ours, we have to play fair tonight. Hear that helicopter? That's your next major crime, Dean. Some dirtbag committed a home invasion robbery and killed two grandparents while they slept in their bed. You need to get your team to Parkside Village." She had heard the call come in before they arrived, but this one was, in her mind, a priority. A dead on-duty cop always took precedence. "We'll finish up as soon as we can."

Silver Lake might have been new to her, different from her larger lab in DC, but she knew an officer-involved shooting would be handled as a priority anywhere. A homicide where a cop was the victim always did. She had watched those scenes stay hot for days, and Darcy didn't want to leave Sergeant Curran just yet. She let Jamie continue taking photos while she lifted prints from the door handles. She was certain that the more documentation she had, the better her boss would like it. She watched Williams walk away, his shoulders slumped in defeat.

Darcy walked to the back passenger door, careful not to encroach on Jamie's shots. She lifted the handle with one gloved finger and slipped inside, her knee denting deeply into the dusty black vinyl seat. The sergeant's car was thankfully without a transport cage so Darcy could lean over between the seats. Curran's

MCT was covered by her black jacket and paperwork sat neatly stacked in the front seat. A steno pad also rested on the seat near the console, under a pen.

The veteran officer's corpse was leaning awkwardly against the steering wheel angled uncomfortably as her left shoulder pushed against the upholstered driver's side door. Darcy scanned the compartment slowly trying to avoid focusing on the exit wound that glared at her from Sandy Curran's head or the darkening red shade that bloomed along the exposed skin of her face. She made notes and sketches and tried to imagine what Sandy Curran was doing right before she was shot. She acquired temperatures and made notes of the state of the body to confirm time of death.

She searched in vain for a cell phone or notation anywhere on Curran's MCT detailing her reason for sitting vigil in the lonely lot. Jamie held a clear plastic container so Darcy could deposit the bullet she had plucked from the dash, the last piece of the puzzle she would reconstruct at her lab. When she believed she had collected as much relevant evidence as she could without appearing to dawdle, she turned to see the major swaying on locked knees.

"Well, I guess we'll head out then, Major." She nodded at him when he walked back toward the car.

"You get those?" The major pointed at some wadded and cloudy plastic close to the rear tire of the sergeant's patrol car.

Darcy crouched to study small sandwich bags on the gravel, grateful that they weren't missed completely.

"Sure." She plucked them from the ground and sealed them in an evidence bag. She then added them to the form on her clipboard.

"I just need your signature on the chain of custody please." She thrust the clipboard at Major Williams. He seemed to be preoccupied, likely by the tragic scene and the sparse inventory they were bringing back. He scribbled his initials quickly as Darcy tried to imagine him as a rookie on patrol instead of the world-weary man who stood before her.

"Oh, one question." Darcy waited a beat before continuing. "Did anyone go inside the car before we got here?"

"Nope. No one touched anything. Why do you ask?"

"Just routine questions for the report."

He nodded thoughtfully. "Please let me know when everything is processed."

Jamie changed lenses and continued taking shots while she packed up the scene kits. She was loading the last of the equipment into their truck when the coroner's van turned past her. "Major," Darcy said, "the body bus is here. You're sure you don't need us to wait?"

He smiled as she began removing her scene suit at the edge of the lot, revealing snug jeans and a form-fitting polo shirt displaying the SLPD logo.

"I can assure you, I've been doing this a long time," he said wearily. "But thanks for the offer."

"Yes, sir. I was just making sure." Darcy turned back to the van and she caught him watching her walk away. She shivered when she felt his eyes on her as she returned to the van. Although she didn't date men, she could appreciate the appeal when a handsome specimen crossed her path. Not, however, in Williams's case. His six foot one frame carried at least fifty extra pounds which spilled over the waistband of the uniform pants he had likely outgrown years ago. His hair was composed of sparse outcroppings of black and gray strands corralled across a sweaty forehead which she bet had been expanding for decades. Some guys never stopped the chase even when the situation made it wholly inappropriate.

"Check in with Foster and Hicks tomorrow, okay?" He continued to stare at her.

"Of course." She quickly backed the van out of the lot, secretly happy to be out of his field of vision.

❖

Mack quickly silenced her cell phone when it shattered the quiet of her home. After a long evening with a cranky baby, Jen and Mack had hoped for a peaceful night of sleep.

She swiped over the screen to accept the call but didn't speak until she had closed the bedroom door and made it into the hallway, away from her sleeping family.

"Sarge, we just got a call." Detective Hicks's voice sounded strained. "The watch commander is at a homicide at the old warehouses, Forty-Sixth and Lincoln."

"Okay. Nothing new out there. Homeless?" she asked knowing the unkempt pockets of trees were host to tents and shanties for the city's neglected citizens and transients. She rubbed the sleep from her eyes. "Why is the watch comm—"

"Mack, listen. They think it's Sandy Curran."

Mack stopped to lean heavily against the door frame, pressing her shoulder against the only support she could manage.

She swallowed burning tears that she couldn't afford when she heard her friend's name, "How do you know?" She wanted to vomit. She pressed the phone to her ear and walked to the bathroom. She felt along the tile and perched on the side of the tub as she forced herself to listen.

"Dispatch reported a 9-1-1 caller who said they heard a shot and saw someone slumped over the wheel. They apparently saw an SLPD uniform." He breathed audibly before he continued. "They gave dispatch the unit number from the car. It's hers, Mack. No one has been able to raise her on Channel 1 since the report." He waited quietly.

"I'll meet you there in twenty." She stared at her phone as tears stung her eyes. She dressed quickly and moved blindly through to the all but empty spare room where she kept her gear. She was glad she could avoid disturbing the rest of the house in situations like this. She paused. Not situations like *this*. No one ever wanted to imagine a situation like this, especially not in Silver Lake, not to her friend.

She pushed her holstered gun onto her belt and thought about Mia. She wondered if she had been told yet, if the devastating news had been dropped at her door. They would need to go to her soon. An agonizing storm had just blown through Mia's once peaceful life.

She knew waking Jen wasn't necessary—she had left in the middle of the night plenty of times in their years together—but she needed to feel her, if only for a second. "I love you, Jen." Mack gently stroked a finger over her arm.

"You okay?" Mack smiled. Jenny had been sleeping soundly but she could wake in an instant when duty called her spouse.

"Yeah, I just wanted to hold you for a second," Mack whispered as she stroked her fingertips through her wife's long blond hair.

Jenny curled against Mack who strained to stop her body from trembling. "I love you," she offered sleepily before Mack forced herself to pull away.

❖

Mack and Detective David Hicks parked quickly near the quiet lot as the crime scene van drove past them toward the main road. Hicks had barely managed to bring the car to a stop before the thick sole of Mack's shoe wedged into the gravel.

Mack's jaw tightened as she marched at the uniform guarding the side of the lot. "What the hell, Perry? Why is the scene team already leaving? Tell me you aren't moving my body already." She couldn't begin to process what was happening yet and her emotions were transformed into anger and frustration. Detective Hicks stood close to her as if poised to step between her and the uniform.

Perry spoke quickly and nodded to a point beyond her. "Major's running this one, Sarge—I'm just handling check-ins." He held up the clipboard where he was logging names, hers now appearing at the bottom of the long list. Mack turned slowly and saw Major Williams staring in her direction.

"What's happening, Major?" Mack drove her short fingernails into her palms as she walked toward him. The large man looked sweaty and tense as he fiddled with his cuffs and straightened the bars on his chest, perhaps a reflexive reminder to Mack of his authority.

"I hate you got called on this, Foster. I know you were close to her."

Mack toed the ground and reined in her emotions before she spoke. "Yeah, I was."

"Look, I got here right after and I tried to call in anyone else besides you. I was pretty sure you didn't want that image of her in your head." The major looked at her sympathetically. "I really tried but no one else was available."

"I'm Homicide, sir. It's my job." Mack forced her voice to steady with concentrated effort, mentally conceding that she indeed wanted nothing less than to see her friend's lifeless body.

"I didn't go inside the car but I would bet money Curran fell on some kind of a drug deal. Crime scene got some baggies near the car. There aren't any cameras around here, already checked. Guess maybe she thought she could do this without backup."

"Do what without backup, Major?" She didn't want to accept the obvious answer—in fact she was still intent on denying this was really happening at all.

Mack seethed at the taking of any life, let alone of a fellow officer she admired as much as Sandy. She bit her tongue to keep her true thoughts on the situation from becoming words. Something felt off. Collecting plastic bags from the ground of an abandoned area adjacent to train tracks was not unusual but she wasn't ready to rule a drug deal in or out.

"Foster, drugs out here aren't uncommon, in case you forgot. It's been a while since you rode a beat." He sounded stern.

"I didn't stop being a cop, Major." Her voice was noticeably strained this time.

"Look"—he seemed to police his own tone and softened for a moment—"I know you two were tight. None of us ever wants to be here but it's part of the job, Foster." His words were meant to soothe, she supposed, but nothing was helping.

"Well, we'll get started," she said on a sigh before turning toward the unintended tomb of her best friend. "I'll complete the field report here and add whatever notes you have when you send them to me, sir." She could barely contain her fury. She had written a thousand reports, but never one detailing the loss of another officer.

"I told crime scene to call you when they get results in the lab. They had to go clear a home invasion in Parkside. I'll get you a supplement later." He looked tired and unfocused. He nodded toward the car. "I told everyone that the scene is your call. You tell them when the cruiser needs to get back to the yard. Only when you feel like everything's wrapped up, okay?"

Mack nodded, at once appreciating the vote of confidence while wanting someone else to seize the responsibility from her. She began making notes for what she knew would be a lengthy and scrutinized report. After a heavy breath she bent inside the open back door and forced her eyes to focus. She stared at gray dust coating the back seat and thought Sandy wouldn't like her car being dirty. She began listing the items in Sandy's car on her report.

The pop of gravel meeting the tread of car tires drew her attention toward an older blue Crown Victoria parking at the perimeter. Ford had stopped making the police interceptor sedans but some departments still had them in their fleet. Virginia Bureau of Criminal Investigation Special Agent Dan Jonas stepped out looking tired in rumpled cargo pants and a faded VBCI polo.

Jonas was a former Silver Lake detective as well as a former Williams squad member who spent his life looking positively bored. Of medium build with strawberry-blond hair, his hooded blue-green eyes made him look perpetually sleepy. His narrow sloping shoulders made him appear frail and weak, an unfortunate characteristic for a state investigator. Dan Jonas had had a reputation for being fairly useless in the field during the ten years he spent on the SLPD and Mack knew he had been promoted far above his capability level at the VBCI and was simply biding his time until the end of the year when he could retire. He was the poster boy for the Peter principle, having risen to his level of incompetence. His presence only added to Mack's ire.

After speaking briefly with Major Williams, he wandered toward her and waited for her to turn and look at him.

"Sorry to hear about this, Mack." His delivery was casual and not remotely fitting the situation.

"We just got here so I don't have much to tell you yet." Mack assumed he would begin to take his own notes for his own report as the bureau always did.

"Williams filled me in already so I have the gist. I'll get out of your way soon." Jonas seemed no more interested in the paperwork that would come from processing what he had likely been told was a drug deal gone bad, than staying in law enforcement one more day than he had to.

Protocol dictated that the bureau would run their own concurrent investigation since the case involved a law enforcement officer. Their expertise and resources could often be helpful, though she doubted that would be the situation with Jonas on the case. After just a few minutes of observation, she watched Jonas walk back to his car where Williams still stood.

Returning her thoughts to the scene, Mack tried not to focus on who had died in the patrol car, or on who lay in front of her; otherwise, she would fall apart. She'd heard other cops report that one of the hardest things in working an officer-involved homicide case was that the officer looked just like them, was dressed like them, and could just as easily have *been* them.

There was no use looking for footprints since the area seemed to have seen every shoe of every authorized personnel member over the past two hours. She wished she had been here sooner. She wondered how many other detectives had been busy or just ignored the call from dispatch. She knew Williams had tried to find someone else so she wouldn't have to be here, but she wondered if the delay would prove detrimental. She resented being handled because Sandy was her friend. However, she wondered which would have felt worse, investigating Sandy's murder or having to let someone else do it instead.

The coroner's team was preparing their paperwork at the road, a reminder that Sandy would be taken from her soon. Mack finally forced herself to look at the body in front of her.

She wondered, not for the first time, what kind of human could disregard the life of another person. She knew dealers valued their supply more than the lives of the addicts that kept them in business but murdering a police officer was something else entirely.

Detective Hicks left to scan the wider perimeter. Mack unclipped her cell phone. She made a video she would go through later. She took a second to lay a gloved hand on Sandy's cold arm and whispered a private message she knew her friend would never hear.

After an hour of photos and documentation, Mack was drained. She searched in vain for more she could do, more she could find that would point to the person who took the life of her friend. The covered gurney was being loaded into the transport van and Mack focused on brushing stubborn white dust from the knees of her black pants instead of watching Sandy being driven away. Mack saw Williams bid Jonas farewell just minutes before he sauntered back in her direction.

"You'll get my supplement over the next few days, Foster."

"Jonas didn't stay long, Major. Doesn't the bureau always require a full report in officer-involved cases?" She knew the answer before she asked the question.

"He'll work from your report. I filled him in and we both know you're better than he ever will be."

Mack stared at him without reply. She changed the subject since commentary on the prior one could land her in serious trouble. "I'd really like to contact that warehouse and see what we can find."

"You can get the warrant but I don't think it's got anything to do with this. Make sure you don't do anything you'll regret, Foster." He drove away from the tragic scene leaving Mack with a list of questions and no answers.

A warrantless search would make anything she found inadmissible in court if they ever arrested the killer. She waited until the area was clear and walked to the warehouse anyway. Keeping busy was the only thing she could do. She saw fresh tire treads at a dock to a building that was seemingly empty and, according to warning signs, under construction by Peticor Commercial Building. The treads near the dock were wide and deep, nothing unusual for a construction scene she supposed, but she started to record the area anyway. She videoed behind her and toward Sandy's unmarked police car while walking toward the main door at the side of the building.

Unexpectedly, she found it wedged open. She rationalized that she could have just been checking a potential property break-in, or clearing places the killer might be hiding, as part of the ongoing homicide investigation. She continued to film across the expanse of the dark interior. Despite her own argument, she didn't feel comfortable being there without a warrant—or, more precisely, she didn't feel comfortable getting caught there without a warrant. Especially after the major's warning. If the open warehouse *was* related to what happened to Sandy, the last thing she needed were evidentiary challenges. She panned the video across the center of the cavernous space one last time and exited quietly, avoiding her colleagues still working perimeter control. Hicks stood at their car scribbling furiously in his notebook. If he had noticed her movements, he did her the courtesy of pretending otherwise.

She wished she was anywhere else at that moment. The hours of work behind her and the days of work ahead of her would not bring Sandy back, but she was determined to make them count. She brushed her shoes against the grass and smacked at the film of white construction dust which clung to the hem of her pants and painted the black rubber trim of her shoes. She briefly considered the danger to people who were forced to breathe it every day.

Chapter Six

Mack finally pushed through the door late Monday morning. Olivia was down for her morning nap, and Jen stopped working as Mack dropped heavily onto the sofa and held her wife against her without a word, tucking her face into Jenny's neck. Mack fought to steady her voice and spoke softly against her. "I need to tell you something."

Jen tensed and pulled back to look at Mack's weary expression. Mack imagined that the dark circles she saw in the rearview mirror were visible to Jenny now.

"Okay," Jen replied cautiously.

"The homicide I got called out on was—" Mack breathed quickly as if forcing the words to rush out. "It was Sandy."

Jenny's hands flew over her face as she wrenched out of her arms and stared. Very few times had Mack allowed her emotions to overtake her in front of Jenny, but at that moment, tears streaked freely down her cheeks. Jen hugged her tightly and they cried together.

Gradually, Mack gathered her emotions and made herself continue.

"She worked second shift yesterday." Mack managed the inane details as a way to steady her voice.

"But we just saw her, it doesn't seem possible." Jenny sounded bewildered. "How? Does Mia know?"

"She was shot in her patrol car near Forty-Sixth and Lincoln. There aren't any suspects. I don't know what happened. While I was writing up my initial report, David Hicks went to their house to tell Mia. He stayed with her until one of her neighbors came over." Her voice was quiet and exhausted as she stared blindly at a distant spot on the wall before she could continue. "We need to go see her. See if Syd and Parker will want to go with us this afternoon." She drew an absent pattern over Jenny's hand.

"I know they will. She'll need all the support she can get, Mack."

Mack just nodded wearily as she snatched her badge from her belt and chucked it on a pile of newspapers on the coffee table. She suddenly felt bitter disdain for the job she had, until now, always loved doing, the same job that had stolen the life of someone she loved.

❖

Night was still hours away but the late afternoon felt dark as the solemn contingent walked slowly and silently up the walk to the unassuming bungalow on the east side of Silver Lake. The neighborhood, once an exclusively older community, was being slowly taken over by young couples buying and remodeling the old brick homes after the owners had died or could no longer live alone.

Parker smiled as she watched an elderly couple link arms and guide each other up their driveway. She walked closer to Sydney, as if the move would ensure that they would have each other that long. Perhaps reading her thoughts, Sydney squeezed her hand and brought it to her lips.

Mia's pale, blotchy face appeared as she answered the door. She stepped into Mack's arms without saying anything and just sobbed loudly. Mack stroked her back and spoke comfortingly into her ear.

Syd closed the door behind them as Parker took in the dark room that hosted an old yellow sofa and a heavy coffee table mounded with wadded up tissues and frayed-edged notebook paper covered by haphazard words and telephone numbers. Mia straightened and issued an audible breath as Parker moved to hug her new friend.

"What can we do?" Parker was desperate to offer something useful but she knew the months of agony would progress without regard to their sentiments or actions.

"Bring my Sandy back?" Mia laughed painfully, sounding as if that was all she would want forever. Jen took Mia's hand, leading her back to the couch where she sat close to her. "She didn't want anyone to see this place until we had fixed it up." Mia drew a shaky finger over the faded brocade cushions. "She said people would think we were a hundred years old if they saw this house now." She stared bleary-eyed at the worn wooden floor. "Thank you all for coming. I don't think it has quite hit me yet, that she isn't coming home." The words sounded thick on her tongue as she struggled to maintain her composure. She looked over to the old mahogany entryway. "I can still see her coming through that door."

"We're going to find who did this, Mia. It's my case and I'll make sure we get justice for Sandy, okay?" Mack sounded hopeless as she offered the inadequate pledge to find her lover's killer.

"Thank you. She loved you, Smurf." She laughed as Mack looked embarrassed.

"We all thought the world of Sandy, Mia." Syd squatted in front of her and held her hands. "We're here if you need us. If you need to stay with us anytime, we're close."

"Thanks. I don't think I can leave her...I mean here, yet."

Syd knew she indeed had meant *her*. She watched the redhead pull a much too large shirt up to her face. Her eyes closed as she inhaled the scent; Syd briefly imagined the horror of having Parker ripped from her life in the abrupt way Mia had lost Sandy. No amount of mementos would salve the wound.

Mack pushed the pile of Kleenex into a small plastic trash can and arranged the papers into a pile. Syd knew Mack preferred keeping busy; it was better than feeling helpless.

"I mean it," Syd continued. "We have an extra room or we can come stay with you, okay?"

Mia nodded and twisted her fingers tensely, spinning the silver Tiffany band that matched the one Sandy had worn. Her phone rang from the end table and she reached to answer it quickly. She listened for several minutes and new tears rivered down her face.

"I understand. Can you give me a few weeks, please?" Her chest heaved as she listened again. "That will be fine, I'll let you know." She bit her bottom lip and hung up. She dropped the phone angrily onto the surface and balled her fists against her eyes.

"That was Sandy's mother," she said through clenched teeth when she managed to look up again. "She wanted me to know that they would be selling the house and wondered if I could move out as soon as possible." She folded over her knees and cried almost silently.

"What the hell?" Syd stopped herself from continuing the stream of curse words in line to leave her mouth. "What do you need right now?" She managed a verbal course correction.

"I need to know what happened to my life. I want the one I had yesterday." Jen rubbed her hand over Mia's.

Syd shook her head at Mack and seethed at the insensitivity. Sandy had told her that they had planned to get married next year. Their finances were in order and Mia didn't need the house, but being forced to move out by Sandy's so-called family, only hours after her death, would have made Sandy livid.

"Maybe it's for the best, too many memories"—she glanced over the tired décor—"too hard to be here without her, I think. It's for the best." No one believed her words but they were quiet as they helped her tidy the living room and then make up the spare bed.

"Thanks for this." Mia looked at Jenny stuffing a pillow into a clean case. "I don't think I can sleep in there right now." She gestured toward the master bedroom.

"No one could blame you, Mia," Jenny said pensively.

Ninety more minutes of crying and reminiscing left Mia looking shattered. Grief and exhaustion were etched in her features.

"Will you promise to call me if you need to talk?" Mack held Mia's hand as the group filed out the door.

"Promise. I'm going to lie down for a bit, that will probably help."

Mack doubted that anything would. She listened for Mia to engage the lock before falling behind Parker.

Jen clutched Mack's hand tightly. "I don't think I've ever hated being a cop's wife more than now. I can't imagine if I were Mia."

"It makes me sorry that I do this job when you say things like that."

As Parker hugged Mack good-bye, she whispered, "It will pass for Jenny. She just needs to let it all sink in."

"Maybe that's what I'm afraid of," Mack replied.

Parker watched the blurry black of the passing road as Sydney steered the Porsche through the slick streets. A steady rain tapped out a sad melody on the windshield as she pictured Sandy and Mia together at the ball. "They were really happy together—you could see it," Parker said softly and looked over to Syd.

"They were. That's why I'm still stuck on calling your daughter's partner hours after she was murdered and throwing her out of the house they shared together. Can you imagine?" Syd was visibly angry.

"No," Parker almost whispered as the reality of a death so close to home crashed over them both once more. Syd parked the car next to Parker's in the otherwise empty lot; after-hours parking was almost always exclusively theirs. Sydney opened the passenger door as Parker joined her in the building downpour.

"I can run in and get an umbrella," Syd offered as she felt the chilly sting of the large drops hit her bare neck.

Parker shook her head and looped her arm into Syd's. "Let's just walk for a minute." A different woman might have dashed for the house but Syd knew Parker was remembering another planned dance through the rain just a few months earlier. Another moment when Syd realized she never wanted to be without Parker.

Syd nodded and wrapped her arm around Parker's waist. They walked silently to the grassy hill overlooking the city lights in the distance. Water sheeted over them as they stood together, remembering their friend and thinking about the devastated Mia. Syd didn't want to imagine what it would feel like to not be able to have this moment with each other, ever again.

Sydney closed her mouth gently over Parker's, breathing in a kiss like it could save her life. She believed that it once had. Parker clung to Sydney. They stayed tangled together as the coalescing storms of rain and loss raged around them.

"I was thinking." Sydney looked down at her lover as she squinted into the deluge and watched drops cascade off Parker's cheeks. "What do you think about offering Mia your loft? We've never talked about you renting it out but it seems kind of a waste that it sits empty all the time."

"You want me to move in with you?" Parker stared up at Sydney and smiled.

"Well apart from some pretty sour milk and a few pieces of furniture, your stuff is mostly at my place. Making it *our* place is just a technicality—it kind of already is."

"I think you're amazing." Parker paused before finishing the thought. "Are you sure it won't make you feel crowded?"

"I'm sure." Syd welcomed the question. She hadn't realized how long she had wanted to answer it. "I want us to live together."

"I just have clothes and odds and ends I can send to storage."

"The spare closet is practically empty so I can move some of my stuff in there. And I'm sure we can probably rent one of those industrial storage things for your shoe collection," Sydney teased Parker who poked her in retaliation.

"And what do you propose we do with all the skeletons currently in that closet, Ms. Hyatt?" she teased back at the reformed womanizer.

Syd was grateful for the moment of lightness that fell over them. "I don't think there's anything wrong with souvenirs, Ms. Duncan." She smiled and led a laughing Parker back toward the door to plan the next phase of their lives together, while feeling guilty that theirs continued as Sandy's had so abruptly ended.

CHAPTER SEVEN

Darcy Dean badged into her lab still trying to right her brain from the twenty-four hours on duty thanks to the home invasion and the Curran case. The few hours of restless sleep she had managed afterward would have to suffice for tonight. She wanted to start on ballistics testing and try to locate any trace evidence that might exist on the lifeless body.

The elderly couple from the home invasion could wait, sadly, until she was done with Sergeant Curran. They had been brutally beaten by some thug who left with eighty bucks and a thirty-two inch tube television. She had listened to the officer make notification to the family when they had arrived outside the home. The gut-wrenching wails she heard from her place in the couple's bedroom would stay with her for a long time. All so some crack addict could get his next fix. The world treated some lives like they were nothing and revered others like they were sculpted from precious metals. The only thing any of them could cling to in this line of work was hope, and Darcy mused that she often had a hard time finding hers.

Entering Sergeant Curran's name at the top of a new document, she transferred her notes and questions to the empty page. She took the custody form from her folder just as she heard the passenger elevator arrive on her floor. Darcy glanced through the window above her desk and saw Sergeant Mack Foster striding purposefully toward her office. She had been told that Sergeant

Foster was a good cop, a tough woman but a talented law-enforcement professional nonetheless. That didn't mean Darcy wanted her in her lab. She didn't like cops trying for early answers or offering useless speculation.

"Mack Foster." The homicide cop stopped and offered Darcy a stern handshake while she waited for a response.

"Darcy Dean, Sergeant. I assume you're here about the Curran case." Darcy straightened and addressed her guardedly.

"I am. Do we know anything yet?" Her voice wasn't as hard now. Darcy had heard the two had been good friends and could see her struggle to remain composed.

"I'm sorry, no. I just got back in here. I pulled twenty-four hours in the field. I'm starting ballistics and trace now."

"Any thoughts from the scene?"

"Nothing yet, some questions maybe, but I need to lay it all out. I'll have some information for you then, Sergeant."

"Can I ask a favor?" Mack lowered her voice and scanned the lab. She looked wary and uncomfortable.

"Sure." Darcy couldn't imagine what she wanted of her.

"Will you call and let me know what you find before you make the official report? I know that isn't protocol—it's just that she was…" She paused and tapped the dented metal desk with the black portfolio in her right hand. "She was my friend." Mack's words faded to a whisper. She seemed to barely manage to finish the sentence.

Darcy knew that didn't explain the unofficial request but considering her own questions about the scene Sunday night, she didn't need the official explanation.

"I get it. No justification necessary." She waited for a moment to see if the brooding cop would ask her anything else.

"The assumption is a drug deal too near the police." Mack spoke quickly and quietly.

Darcy considered her response. "Yeah. We'll run all the tests we can, but like I said, we haven't got anything yet, I'm sorry," she said patiently. "I'll check back when I do, I promise."

"It's okay. I know you haven't had much time." Darcy watched the sergeant dance around protocol. Foster's rep was that she was strictly by the book, and her discomfort seemed to confirm that. "What about her phone?"

"The clip was empty, assumption is that the shooter took it." Darcy watched frustration mount in the officer's expression.

"Thanks for the help." She unzipped the portfolio cover and jotted a number on the back of her business card. "That's my cell. Whenever you can call."

"Will do." Darcy took the card and slid it into the pocket of her work pants.

She watched the officer head back to the elevator spinning her wedding ring absently. *Too bad she's taken,* Darcy thought and pushed aside the inappropriate musings. She began the task of identifying microscopic fibers before analyzing the tiny chunk of distorted lead that was responsible for altering so many lives.

She lifted the intake sheets from the clipboard and walked down the hall to the positive cold chamber in the medical examiner's locker. She slid her master key into the lock beyond which Sergeant Curran's body rested. She stared for a few seconds and forced herself not to feel profoundly sad at the mental picture she would carry for a long time. She collected a packet of fibers left by the autopsy technician and returned to the lab.

She tried reminding herself how much she liked her job, ordinarily. After years in DC, doing less of a job than she was qualified for, Silver Lake seemed like a perfect solution. Three relationships in ten years had left her worn-out and jaded. When Molly, her last girlfriend, had finally gotten sick of Darcy's inability to commit, Darcy found her belongings waiting alone in the apartment they had shared for nine months, a sparse reminder of yet another failed relationship. Molly had been right and Darcy didn't fight it. The pattern had started long ago when the woman she really loved left her after finding her in bed with an ex from college. She was ready for a clean slate at work and some anonymity within the lesbian circle, although she wondered how much there was of one in Silver Lake.

Darcy couldn't believe three hours had passed when Jamie Amana pushed through the lab doors. Darcy jerked out of her mental cocoon and turned to him before he dropped his backpack under his desk.

She pushed her fingers into her temples and rubbed in small circles. "I need you to process the plastic bags from the warehouse for residue as soon as you can."

"I'm on it. Any theories?" He glanced at her nervously as he spoke.

"You sound like Foster. I don't have anything yet." She tried to look like everything was routine but since one of their own was thirty feet away, she didn't believe it. "I'm just logging in the trace report and I typed the bullet. Standard ten millimeter. No foreign prints and nothing to match it to."

"Let's hope the PD works its magic and brings us a perfect specimen." Jamie spoke with the defeat of a man who had done the job just long enough to be thoroughly jaded but not completely without hope for the occasional miracle.

"Yeah, wouldn't that be nice." She started arranging the results in the order she would put them in her final findings document. "Can you start on the Parkside prints after that?"

She didn't hear him answer before her mind was entrenched in the task ahead of her.

❖

Long after the expected end of her shift, Darcy sat in front of her notes, discouraged. A list of questions without hint of explanation dominated the page she had hoped would be a useful, cogent investigative tool for detectives. Instead it was a catalog of things that didn't match up and a scene that provided inadequate information.

Seconds later, the phone rang and Darcy snatched the receiver from the cradle mounted to the wall. "Silver Lake lab, Dean." Her words were clipped and cold.

"Dean, Sergeant Foster, time to talk?" Her shorthand delivery was jarring to Darcy.

"Honestly? Not really." Darcy exhaled loudly at the impatient cop. "Things are still in progress and a little crazy around here right now." They weren't particularly crazy but Darcy thought that sounded better than *unsettling*.

"I understand. Perhaps we can talk over a cup of coffee. I'll buy. After shift, you pick."

Darcy was mildly cautious. It was common knowledge that Foster was a lesbian, and it was even more commonly known that she was married to the mother of their newborn, so this wasn't a date or even a social meeting. Not that Darcy would have accepted anything social at this point. She'd moved out of DC partly to gain some perspective and some distance on her love life.

"Yeah, how about I call you tomorrow, when I get a handle on things?" She expected Foster to continue to push.

"Fine, call my cell?"

"Sure, Sergeant." Everyone knew Foster's no-nonsense reputation. Darcy trusted her but wasn't sure how much.

"Call me Mack."

Chief Jayne Provost twisted her fingers around the cord of her telephone as she reclined at her desk. She thought about how she had finally made it five years in what she considered a pit of a city outside DC, all that was required of her before layering on another pension and retirement. As far as she was concerned, she deserved it. After all, she had slummed through every patrol unit in the District and never once saw rank above major thanks to obvious politics and untalented pricks who didn't recognize her skill as a law enforcement administrator. When she retired out of DC, the squads she was overseeing were considered the dregs of the department and she certainly didn't consider that any of her responsibility. She had spent barely a week packing her things before bidding the cutthroat District of Columbia good-bye and starting at the helm of the SLPD. After all she had done, no one even offered her a retirement party. She saw it as their jealousy rearing its ugly head.

Not for a moment did she plan on staying long in the role of Silver Lake's police chief. This was simply a means to a lucrative end. She admired her new heels, which complemented her designer ensemble. She had worn a uniform for twenty years and she wasn't about to parade around the city looking like every other beat cop in her department.

The only tolerable aspect of the job had come in the form of a referral to a profitable new private sector position. While it wasn't official yet, an executive position at a Fortune 500 corporation was all but hers. This was what she was meant to do her whole life; the money and the respect would set her up for another retirement in five years, but she could stay as long as she wanted. Who knew, maybe she could grow the job and make a bigger splash in the business world. They would be lucky to have her.

She'd practically drooled at the opportunity take over the CSO seat when the current security executive had tipped her to the opening. Although Major Turner from Raleigh was also in the running, Jayne had already made sure that she was indispensable to executive management. She was a shoo-in for the job that would keep her in designer shoes for the next five years.

She dialed a number she knew by heart.

"Chief," Major Damon Williams answered formally. Major Williams had been doing her bidding since she had arrived, practically killing himself to kiss every aspect of her well-toned ass in the event he could curry favor with her and the city council and, one day, warm his backside in the chief's chair.

She silently congratulated herself for cultivating him when she saw that he was focused solely on his own advancement, suiting her purposes perfectly. She treated him like an errant child who happily did her bidding. She wouldn't be there much longer and he was welcome to the job for which he was woefully underqualified. He was incompetent, but the post didn't require too many brains, making him perfect for the job.

"Damon, I've spent a lot of time cleaning up this pathetic little department and I don't want to see all my efforts go to waste." She slid the reports back into the pile on the floor.

"Nor do I. What's the issue, Chief?" She imagined him biting his lip as was his habit when he spoke to her.

"That's the problem—I shouldn't have to tell you what the issues are. If your ass is ever in this chair, you better know the answers before anyone else. When I'm running a real business, I can promise you I won't give a crap about stats in this town, but right now, my numbers need to send a positive message to the selection committee next week."

"Yes, ma'am."

"Why then am I showing a disturbing trend in commercial burglaries and at least three too many unsolved homicides? Why do we think that is, Damon?"

"They are wrapping up the burg cases as we speak."

"And why are the media hounds still standing outside the building speculating on the identity of a cop killer on the loose?"

"I'm doing what I can on the Curran situation. How would you suggest I get a dead cop case solved with no viable suspects?" His scowl was evident in his voice.

"You listen to me," she ordered in a scathing tone. "I will not lose this opportunity because my legacy is a department full of bull dykes who couldn't make it in a real department and couldn't solve some random murder. Got it? Maybe Foster needs to be looking for lost puppies and missing bicycles, not some long-gone killer on the Curran shooting if it's too big for her. The city wants a hero on this case and I've given you ample space to be one. Do you understand what I'm saying or should I perhaps be grooming Major Cash for this job?"

"I got it."

"The point is, get those detectives to clear the case or find someone who can. Am I clear?"

"Perfectly."

Williams longed for the days when you could slam a receiver into its cradle instead of delivering the impotent press of a digital *end* key. That woman couldn't be gone soon enough. She got this job because the city council believed her endless line of big-city bullshit. They thought they were getting some expert crime fighter in the role that had been vacant for a year after Chief O'Brien's untimely death.

He considered that instead they got some self-interested ladder climber just waiting for the private sector to come calling. He had deserved the chief's job then and would get it now, whatever it took. As far as he was concerned, it would only be a few months until he could run this pathetic department the way he wanted. He daydreamed about someone taking her down every time she leaned on someone in the department, especially him.

Contemplating his growing disdain and his next tactical move, he snatched up his phone and dialed. He warred between toeing the party line and serving ethically. He briefly wondered when that had become a choice instead of an imperative.

"Where are we on the Curran case, Lieutenant Charles?" Williams demanded.

"Foster has it, Major, you assigned her and Hicks, right? They are waiting for the lab report. They think we're missing something, Major. Captain Hale thinks so, too." He sounded puzzled.

Williams was circumventing the chain of command. It wasn't uncommon in an emergency or when advancing a political football; Williams hoped it wasn't obvious which one this was.

"Maybe if they were busier working cases and not looking for conspiracies, we wouldn't be sitting on an unsolved homicide of a dead cop. We both know some lowlife took her out when she stumbled on drug negotiations, don't we, Lieutenant? This isn't a hard case to solve, so solve it. Didn't Romano and Summers just transfer in to your unit? You could get some fresh eyes on it."

"Yes, sir. But they've never even worked a B and E case, Major. You really want them on the murder of a Silver Lake police officer?" Lieutenant Charles sounded incredulous. "She was one of us, Major."

"You know what? They gave me these cute little bars to wear on my shirt, Lieutenant. I guess somebody thought I might know what I'm doing. Would you like to call the chief personally and tell her different?"

"No, sir," Charles stammered in reply.

"Foster is needed in Central, Lieutenant. Summers and Romano worked drug interdiction, they know the players. Am I understood?"

"I…yes, sir," Charles managed.

Mack emailed her request for Sandy's cell records and watched her Lieutenant as he slammed down his phone and marched into the bullpen headed for her desk.

"Foster, I need you to hand over your files on the Curran case to Romano and Summers." He squeezed his eyes shut as soon as he said the words.

"What? Are you kidding me, Lieutenant?" Lieutenant Charles stepped back as the meltdown he appeared to be expecting began in earnest. "I haven't even gotten the labs back yet."

"You've been reassigned to Central District effective immediately, Foster."

"Why?" She could barely contain her rage without being insubordinate. She respected her longtime lieutenant, but she knew that he wasn't going to fight the system, especially this close to his retirement.

"I don't know, Foster. It's above my pay grade. Just fly under the radar on this one, okay?" Charles replied wearily.

"She was one of us, Tim. You know they can't do this job. Does Captain Hale know about this?" She wondered how high and how deep this bullshit went.

"He's off. I got the call from Williams. Just cut me a break, Mack. No one's going to buck Williams on this and you know it. Just go to Central, I'm begging you."

"This isn't over, Tim." Foster snatched her files off her desk and glanced back at him.

He held out his hand. "The files?"

Mack stared. "I think I left them in my car. I'll make sure they're in order and back here first thing." Mack was pretty sure he knew they were in the stack she was shoving into her backpack, but he didn't question her. She was seething as she threw herself behind the wheel of her patrol car. Her shift was over but she was sure that the fight had just begun.

She launched her phone camera and began scanning pages of the case file. She might not be officially assigned to Sandy Curran's murder but that didn't mean she was planning on letting go.

The file was ludicrously thin. Photos of the abandoned car holding her friend's lifeless body stared up at her from the pathetic stack of notes, initial requests, maps, and corporate filings. She didn't need the career profile document. Sandy and Mack had spent the duration of field training in the same district and were boosted to sergeant during the same promotions cycle. They worked cases together for years until she was transferred to the West patrol unit and Mack went to Homicide. Sandy had been a good cop and an even better friend. There was something Mack wasn't seeing.

She dialed the lab as she headed home to her family. Before she could park in the driveway, a department email chimed through her phone announcing that her request for the warehouse warrant had been denied.

Chapter Eight

Mack jogged quickly up the stairs into Syd's open studio and closed the door behind her leaving Jenny and Parker alone on the sofa.

Mack felt both concerned and conspiratorial as she handed over unofficial crime scene photos to the forensic reconstruction expert.

"I know this is wrong"—she pointed at the police files she was sharing with a civilian—"but I also know that there's something I'm not seeing, that people aren't saying." Mack watched Syd pull out the glossy photos of Sandy and begin to sift through them.

"You know what I'm asking you to do is potentially risking your career or at least your business with our agency, hell, any agency in Fairfax County if it got out and this turns out to be nothing." Mack met her friend's intense gaze. "I'm perfectly okay if you turn me down, Syd."

"I appreciate that, but I'm willing to help if you're telling me that this smells funny." Sydney's acute sense of right and wrong was anchored deeply in her soul.

"That's what I'm telling you. It stinks." Mack nearly spat the words. "Sandy was killed in the line of duty and practically no evidence exists."

"That's not completely unheard of, Mack," Syd offered reasonably.

"I know that but I get the feeling from the lab that things seemed off for them, too. No leads from the car or the scene. An easy warrant gets denied out of hand and the next thing I know they're yanking me off the whole damned case."

"Maybe they thought you were a little too close to this?"

"Then why dispatch me at all? Why am I reassigned before I can even get her phone records? I don't even need a subpoena for a department cell."

"I hear you, all good questions, but it could also be exactly what it looks like."

"What if it isn't?" Mack's glare was furious.

Syd acquiesced. "Okay. How are you wanting to play this?"

"I took video of the scene and the car. I also filmed the warehouse next door. Something makes me believe that there's something worth looking at there."

"That isn't a lot. The best thing I can do is load in what you do have"—she held up the photos—"and start to look for what's not obvious. It may take me a little time." Sydney half shrugged as she looked back at Mack.

"Clearly I have time. No one wants to hear what I have to say anyway." Mack paced the short distance behind Syd's desk.

Syd spun her chair to face Mack. "What's the party line when you ask them?"

"Well, *them* is an unknown quantity, but I saw Major Williams in the hall after my transfer and he almost rolled his eyes at me when I told him that I thought there should be a more thorough investigation than two rookies could handle. He told me that I was overreacting since we were friends. When I challenged him, he told me that I was very close to holding paper for insubordination. He has never said anything even remotely like that to me. In fact, he normally avoids me like the plague. I don't think he relates very well to women he can't hit on." Mack looked incredulous.

Sydney sighed loudly. "You should know, Williams is not my biggest fan, Mack. He's the reason I lost the contract on two big cases last year. He's still very close with my mother and he seems to hate me by proxy. If he so much as smells me near this case, you'll never hear the end of it."

"I'm already on the outside of this, Syd. Something's got to be there. I just want the opportunity to prove myself wrong. If someone with a gold badge and a white shirt is pushing me out, I just want to know why."

"Clearance rates are a big deal. Especially after the show they put on the other night about ridding Silver Lake of all crime. This case is pretty embarrassing," Syd noted.

"Yeah. How can we protect the city if we can't even protect ourselves, right? Still, I can't imagine putting clearance above this case."

"Agreed. But, again, if the chief is any barometer, appearance is everything."

"True."

"If you want me to go on this, I will." Sydney spoke carefully. "Use Jenny's phone to call Parker's when you want to talk. You can't leave any trail that the department owns now that you have been pushed off the case." Syd pointed to her SLPD cell phone. "I'll need whatever you have regarding the murder weapon and the scene team report if you can."

Mack nodded. "Most of that is in the hands of the lab." Mack filled her in on her plans to meet with the lab manager.

"Do you think you can trust this new person?" Syd didn't trust easily.

"I do. I have to. You don't know how much this means to me, Syd. I think if I can just get a handle on the scene—all of it—maybe we'll see something someone missed...or that someone couldn't hide."

"We'll find it if it's there, Mack."

"She was our friend. As a peer, I owe her more than the PD is putting into it. As her friend, I can't let this get pushed under some political departmental rug."

"I get it and we won't." Syd turned to look directly at Mack. "You told me once not to be stupid, and now it's my turn. Be safe. You have a wife and a daughter. No matter what, they need you to be safe and, of course, employed. They're your primary responsibility."

"I know." Mack stared at the photos.

"Get me what you can."

❖

Mack had just slammed the drawer on the scuffed wooden desk in the corner of the Central District bullpen. She tried not to look furious when the district admin dropped a desk calendar and some generic business cards onto the surface. She managed a thank you before her phone began to buzz from her belt.

"Mack, it's Dean." Darcy's words rushed out through the phone. "I haven't had a chance to call before now. Can we talk?"

"Sure, go ahead."

"Not on the phone." Darcy sounded distracted and Mack could hear papers rustling in the background.

"I can come down there later."

"Not sure it should be here...or anywhere near here for that matter."

The hair on the back of Mack's neck stood up as she realized someone might have found something she could use. "Just so you know, I'm not officially—"

"On the case anymore, I know. I met your replacements this afternoon. Interesting."

Mack smirked at the restrained assessment. "How about I pick you up at the Second Street Mall after your shift and we'll head to a good meeting spot?"

"Okay." Darcy sounded resigned and just a little nervous. "I'm trusting you with a lot."

"I have just as much to lose, believe me." Mack contemplated just how much that was.

"I guess we'll just call this a mutual leap of faith."

"I guess we will. Call me from the mall." Mack disconnected and went in search of a case assignment that might make her appear busy.

❖

Mack paced nervously in Syd's office when her phone began to ring. "That's the lab, you ready to do this now?"

Syd nodded and listened to Mack arrange to meet another city employee for some decidedly un-city business.

"You bringing her here?" Syd asked cautiously. Mack nodded.

Syd was direct. "Make sure she knows what she's getting into and you better be damn sure she won't compromise us."

"I'm sure." She glanced into the living room from the loft window. "I'll be back, and then we need to fill everyone in."

Mack walked heavily down the stairs, kissed her daughter briefly, then focused on Jen. "I'll be back in ten minutes and then we're all going to talk." She looked over her shoulder as a serious Sydney walked to stand near Parker, winding her fingers through Parker's hair.

"I'm not going to like this, am I?" Jenny looked up at her wife.

"Probably not, but we both think everyone should know what's happening," Mack responded gloomily.

"That doesn't sound normal." Jenny laced her fingers into Mack's.

"It isn't. That's what I want to talk about."

"Don't be long and please be careful."

Syd knew Jen had been a cop's wife long enough to recognize the feeling of dread when it crept up on her. Mack kissed Jen briefly and escaped to her SUV.

Ten minutes later, Mack returned, leading a curvy blonde through the door.

The room tensed slightly in anticipation. Syd emptied her glass and headed back to the bar to pour another scotch.

Parker studied the stunning blonde with large breasts and huge green eyes. Her tight jeans and scoop-necked T-shirt left little to the imagination. Jenny raised an eyebrow at Parker as Mack and the newcomer entered the loft.

Mack pointed toward Jenny first. "This is my wife, Jenny Foster, and this is Parker Duncan. Her girlfriend is the person I wanted you to meet." She bent her head toward the kitchen, as if expecting to find Sydney there.

Instead, Syd walked into the living room from the other side of the room, stopping abruptly. Parker watched her lover's olive complexion turn pale, her stare welded into cold steel.

Mack continued, "This is Sydney Hyatt. She owns DRIFT. Everyone, this is—"

"Darcy Dean," Sydney finished.

The blonde flashed Syd a smile. "Hey, SyFi. It's been a while. Wow, you look great." Her voice was smooth and sexy, maybe unintentionally, but for some reason Parker didn't think so.

She crossed the room to hug a stunned Syd who didn't move to return the embrace. Parker eyed them both as seemingly unwelcome arms snaked around Syd's neck.

"Well, perhaps you can fill us all in later." Mack was clearly focused on the task at hand. Parker felt no need to derail the meeting for the, albeit intriguing, story of how the two women were acquainted since Sydney was clearly unenthused.

"Yeah, can I get anyone anything?" Syd scanned the others while they stared at her, as she stood glued to the small square of rug she had occupied since she saw the visitor in her home.

Mack stepped into the kitchen and grabbed a beer, holding one out for Darcy.

"Thanks, Mack." The sexy voice sounded more professional now.

"Let's go up." Sydney nodded toward the stairs. She dragged Parker to her feet and whispered in her ear, "I'll explain later." She stopped to double lock the front door and looped a finger over the waistband of Parker's slacks as they walked up the stairs together.

When the small contingent, including one sleeping baby in a carrier, had assembled in the loft studio, all eyes fell on Mack and Syd as they sat in front of the large monitor.

"I guess I'll start." Mack sighed. Syd, as if given some unspoken cue, began launching programs that typically held her reconstruction videos.

"As everyone knows, Sandy Curran was murdered on July 4th near a warehouse in the West District." Mack looked, for the moment, like she was briefing her squad during roll call.

"As soon as I got to the lot with my partner, Major Williams was standing by as the scene was essentially dismantled. The lab was leaving and the coroner was ready to move her body. I was the lead for Homicide that night but it took a while for them to call us. Williams said he was trying to spare me."

She turned to Darcy, with a formal professional demeanor. "Darcy is running the Silver Lake lab and was standing in while Dr. Gray was on vacation. She had the first crime scene techs there—in fact, she was the first person inside the car. I've been speaking with her over the past few days and on the way here. She agrees that we have reason to be concerned and she can explain. After the lieutenant yanked me off the case and essentially buried me in the Central District, he told me to hand over the case file to two rookies just out of Northside Patrol, and needless to say, my access to information has dried up considerably since then.

"Syd has agreed to help me with some reconstruction and evidence analysis. Darcy has brought some new facts to light that I want Syd to hear. Parker and Jen, you have nothing to do with this but I'm afraid that if anyone finds out that we're investigating this case, axes could fall and things could get pretty ugly." Parker tensed at the mention of potential danger to her chosen family. "I don't expect either of you to be involved."

Syd leaned over to click on a couple of frames and Parker noticed the telltale bulge of the Sig Sauer P232 in the concealed holster she wore at her back. She bristled at the implications of the situation and the fact that her partner was, once again, armed in their home.

Bringing a dingy gravel lot onto the screen, Sydney addressed Darcy. "Perhaps you should walk us through this, Dean, so we can all see what you did that night. These are the images Mack shot, right?" Sydney's voice was tense but she was now focused on her keyboard, not the woman Parker had so many questions about.

Darcy walked to the screen and pointed to the black sedan. "My photos aren't approved yet so I can try to work from these." She pointed to a photo of Sandy Curran's body wedged behind the steering wheel.

"When I got there, there were about four uniforms and a couple of EMTs walking all over the scene. Major Williams was standing over here by the car. Pretty typical I suppose, just not what I'm used to, in DC anyway." She glanced quickly to Sydney. "Syd and I worked on a couple of officer involved shootings a long time ago and they were never like this—remember, Syd?"

Sydney didn't respond as she continued to adjust settings on the display. Darcy finally looked away and turned to address Mack directly. "We did the best we could when we realized what we had and who the victim was." She looked sympathetically at Mack. "I didn't know her but I understand that she was a great police officer and I'm really sorry this happened."

Mack nodded and looked back at the screen. Parker watched her seem to force the memory of her friend away.

"I processed the scene like I would any other priority homicide, even though there was a huge perimeter. Williams was just waiting for detectives to arrive, I guess. There wasn't much direction. It sort of felt like we walked onto a movie set. He told me that Curran must have stumbled onto a drug deal in progress. There were some plastic bags on the ground behind the car which had meth residue in them as it turned out." She pointed at the screen.

Syd was looking at her intently. "Not a long leap, by the tracks."

"True."

"Where was the wound?" Syd asked. "Do we have trajectory or theories where the shooter might have been standing?"

"That's sort of why I wanted to talk to Mack. Based on the entry wound, she was shot in the left temple from behind her left shoulder and just outside the driver's door." She reached over to point at the sergeant's head. "All my preliminary data and, quite frankly, common sense says that the impact would have caused her to fall onto her right side. However, she was lying in this position, more on her left and kind of over the steering wheel." She tapped the screen with a short manicured fingernail and drew an arc with her hand.

"When I first got on scene, keys were in the ignition, driver's window halfway down. No one had been in the car until us according to the major. I examined her body and livor mortis was present along her right side even though she was lying on her left."

Darcy then scratched a finger in a careful line along Sandy Curran's right arm. "See this stippling?" Darcy waited for everyone to follow the imaginary line she'd drawn on the screen.

"So the body had been moved." Syd stared at Darcy.

"Well, at least repositioned. It could have been the shooter but that wouldn't explain the livor which wouldn't even start until the heart had stopped beating for at least twenty minutes."

Parker watched Darcy as she spoke and was momentarily distracted as she tried to place the beautiful woman's name in the archives of her lover's past, realizing that despite their time together, she hadn't learned any names at all.

"Pretty risky for a cop killer to hang out or return to the scene," Mack remarked.

"Right. And why? They didn't even take her weapon," Syd offered rhetorically.

"Maybe they figured a police weapon would be too hot to hold on to?" Parker made a concerted effort to participate instead of focusing on the alluring presence of Darcy Dean.

"Maybe," Darcy replied absently.

"They still haven't recovered her cell phone, right? What about the GPS?" Syd looked at both Mack and Darcy.

"Yes. Weapon was still there but phone was not. Maybe that's why they moved her body?" Darcy looked to Mack, the seasoned detective, for confirmation.

"Possibly. But why do you want to take that kind of risk? You can't get into it without some hacking skill, if then. More importantly, it's useless as soon as someone turns it off remotely or, worse, uses it to track you. A gun I can turn into cash inside of twenty minutes." She shook her head and continued. "Tell us about ballistics."

"It looks like the gun was a Glock 20, ten millimeter automatic. A ton of police departments use them but so does just about every gun freak in America. The bullet was a ten millimeter lite or FBI lite round—they make the gun weigh less in the field." She focused on Mack once again. "SLPD will be using those after the equipment upgrade next year. Thousands of rounds are sold every day."

"So what you're saying is we have a law enforcement victim no one is paying attention to who was killed by one of the most common guns shooting one of the most common bullets." Mack stared at her and rubbed her fingers across her forehead.

"That's what I'm saying. I'm sorry I don't have better news."

Parker watched Darcy lock eyes on Sydney for no particular reason since she was speaking to Mack. Her silky blond hair fell in chunky layers around her face as she talked, and Parker tried to imagine Syd with her intimately, until she realized she didn't really want the image in her head.

"What about her cell phone GPS?" Jen asked cautiously.

Darcy regarded her appreciatively. "Good question. Unfortunately, that usually comes from a detective and I haven't seen anything from the new detectives yet."

"These guys are so green, they're probably still looking for their cars," Mack grumbled.

Darcy nodded and flicked her hair behind her shoulders. "Her MCT was still running but the location record said her car hadn't moved in over three and a half hours. The phone GPS is the only thing that could confirm that Sandy's whereabouts may have been different from her car's." She looked at Mack.

"I requested those records before I was booted and never got a callback from the division."

"Did it look like someone tried to take the gun? Maybe if the killer came back?" Darcy asked.

"I can't say. It was snapped into her holster, and her right arm was lying next to her holster on the seat."

"Maybe it was someone just walking by who saw an opportunity but got scared when they had to move a body." Parker avoided qualifying whose body it was for Mack's sake.

"Another possibility but you would think if they got that far, they would just take it," Mack replied.

"What's the VBCI's say?" Syd asked. "They were on scene, right?"

"Jonas." Mack looked at Syd, who made a disgusted noise and ran her long fingers through her military short hair.

Mack rolled her eyes. "Exactly. Jonas was standing there shooting the shit like someone just stole a street sign." The outrage in Mack's voice was clear. "Williams told me he would get me a supplement and then I get transferred before anything ever came through. I wonder if it ever got written. Jonas pretty much said that he would just translate what the major told him."

"Stellar police work," Syd commented sarcastically.

"Tell me about it." Mack sat and shifted to lean on her knees. "I waited until they both were gone and I sort of snuck into the building over here, facing the car." She spoke quietly about what she had done without authorization, leaning back to point at the image of the warehouse. "I put the footage on a Jumpdrive I gave Syd tonight."

"What made you want to go in?" Parker said what she imagined everyone was thinking.

"First, because Williams said it was locked up tight and there was nothing to see. Which turned out not to be true. Second, because it looked like there were fresh deep tire tracks near the loading dock on the street side of the warehouse that bordered the lot." Mack stepped over to tap the front of the warehouse now pictured on the screen. "Since it was supposedly under construction and vacant, I wanted to be sure that it had nothing to do with Sandy. I couldn't find anything obvious to do with the shooting, but I tend to lack the trust I should have for this situation. I took some quick video scans and got out. Right after I was transferred, I was denied the warrant to make official entry."

"How can they stop you from coming into their warehouse?" Parker was confused.

"They didn't. I mean, it never made it to a judge. Someone stopped it in transit before it even left the PD."

Jen said quietly, "You don't really think someone from the department killed Sandy, do you, Mack?"

Everyone heard the worry in Jenny's voice.

"No. I don't." Mack answered quickly. "I just think everyone's incompetence is covering someone's tracks, maybe intentionally or maybe not. Maybe we're just all perfecting doing crappy police work. Either way, leaving this case in the hands of two rookies ensures that we'll never know what really happened."

"Darcy, are you okay with being part of this unofficial inquiry?" Mack glanced over at the lab manager. "You're new here and, let's be honest, if anyone figures out I'm still looking…"

"Look, I think we probably have some extremely lazy cops here. But if we have dirty cops? It doesn't seem likely, but I want to know. Most of all I don't want some scumbag to get away with murder because we did a shoddy job. The latter seems like what we're looking at if we don't do something." Darcy sounded suddenly angry.

"I agree." Mack looked defeated for a moment. "This has already left a stain on the department. If we can't protect ourselves, it's not a long leap for the public to think we can't protect them."

"I'll see what I can do on the cell phone stuff. I'll have to tread lightly since I'm new here," Darcy said as Syd began saving files and closing the stacks of computer windows. "The official photos should be back in the morning, although I can't imagine seeing anything new."

Syd glanced over the room. "Obviously, this meeting never happened."

Parker heaved herself up and broke the tension. "Would everyone like another drink? Maybe we could sit in the living room and talk about rainbows and butterflies for a while so I can sleep," she joked to the group who seemed to be relieved by the change of topic. Sydney slid an arm around Parker and moved a lock of hair away from her eye.

They migrated downstairs. Jen settled against Mack on the sofa and closed her eyes. Syd guided Parker to sit next to her on the opposite corner and drew her legs over her lap. Even if Parker didn't need the intimate connection at that moment, Sydney did. She watched Darcy shift into a club chair opposite them and slide a foot casually over the ottoman.

"So." Darcy grinned as she broke the awkward silence. "Guess you haven't got my picture up anywhere, huh, SyFi?" She pretended to scan the large room.

"Okay, first, stop calling me that, and no, the life-sized portrait of your ego was just too big. I think the ceilings in here are only twenty-five feet." Sydney's wry tone was soothed briefly by Parker as she massaged her fingers down her neck.

"Got it," Darcy replied tensely. She seemed to be searching for a new entry into a conversation. "Well, I guess I'll answer the burning question since SyF—*Syd* must not have mentioned me. A few years ago Sydney and I were together, you know, in a relationship." She glanced at her audience as if anticipating a reaction she didn't get. "It was about a year and half, right, babe?"

Syd felt Parker's fingers twitch against her neck at the term of endearment. Sydney placed Parker's other hand into her lap and drew lazy circles over her wrist with her fingers.

Then she turned to address only Parker, instead of returning the volley in the uncomfortable verbal tennis match with Darcy. "Darcy Dean is the person I told you about, Park. You know, my only other long-term thing until she cheated on me with her drunk ex-girlfriend?"

Syd didn't bother to look at the woman who had wasted nineteen months of her life many more years ago than Darcy wanted it to seem. All of it a distant memory as far as she was concerned. Sydney often wondered how her universe was suddenly so different, unrecognizable from this time last year, let alone from the time she'd lived with Darcy Dean.

Darcy's mock pout was intended to be cute, Syd supposed, but she thought it transparently forced and superficial. She could respect her as a colleague, but after this case was done, she had no intention of inviting her to tea. She briefly considered how an inch had once seemed too much distance from Darcy, but now a mile seemed too little.

"Sydney, we were young, I was still finding myself, and you were just starting out in the business. In fact, you didn't even officially have your own business. What does DRIFT stand for anyway?"

Parker straightened as she addressed her lover's ex. "Digital Reconstruction and Independent Forensic Technology. Syd does remarkable work. She was an expert witness for the Walters trial last year. Did you see it?"

Darcy tapped her chin as if to store the information away. "Huh, I'll have to Google you, Syd. I don't do that nearly as much as I used to right after you left." Darcy looked carefully at Syd.

Syd thought about the Darcy who had captured her heart more than a decade before and wondered now what she had seen in her. When she had come home early to find a boozed-up Darcy hosting an intimate night in their bed with her ex, it had been enough for her. Despite admitting to carrying on for a while, Darcy had sworn it was Syd she really loved. The next conversation they had was through the bedroom door as Syd packed everything she owned. After she drove away from DC, Darcy simply became a part of her distant memory that, until tonight, had faded into the grays of her past.

"Ready to head back, Darcy?" Mack seemed to sense that it was time to break up the reunion. "Jen and I need to get the baby home before it gets too late."

"Sure. Thanks. I guess we'll all meet somewhere when we have something new to report."

"I think it will be better to just meet here for a while," Syd said. "If it starts to heat up we may need to have a plan B, but for right now I'm good with this, if Parker is. This is her home, too." She looked at Parker who nodded her okay. "As soon as I finish integrating Darcy's pictures and the video from Mack's phone, let's regroup." Syd walked toward the door with a possessive arm around Parker's waist.

Darcy moved toward them and dragged her body against Syd's. The move was meant to look like a hug. Syd didn't react and she was relieved to see no response on Parker's face. They'd be alone soon.

❖

"Love you guys," Parker called after their friends, sliding the door closed quickly, intentionally avoiding eye contact with Darcy. As the latch engaged, Sydney spun Parker until she faced into her. Capturing her in a deep kiss, Sydney lifted her against her chest and Parker folded her arms around Syd's neck, returning the kiss.

"What was that for?" Parker breathed quickly as Syd returned her to her feet but did not release her hold.

"I just wanted you to know how much I love you. And that I'm sorry you had to deal with Mean Dean in our home."

Parker laughed at her lover's concerned face. "Do I have anything to worry about with Darcy?" she asked lightly, already knowing the answer.

"Not a thing. You know you are my world, baby." Syd's tone conveyed that she meant the words with every cell in her body.

"Then you don't have to be sorry. She does, however, still have feelings for you, just in case you didn't notice."

"It's been years, Parker." Syd looked dubious.

"Let's go to bed and I'll explain the competitive lesbian I-want-what-you-have disease to you. Think of it as a bedtime story." She smiled up at Syd who followed after her.

"You know I respond much better to live demonstrations."

Parker turned and walked backward as she lifted her shirt over her head and tossed it at Sydney. She caught it as Parker reached behind her and snapped open the clasp of her bra exposing her ample breasts to her lover. "Do you now."

"I think I'm feeling much more enlightened." Syd was looking at her intently as Parker stepped out of her remaining clothing and cast them in a heap onto a chair.

"Show me." Parker's voice was intentionally seductive when she felt the backs of her knees skim the mattress.

Syd reached a hand to hold her firmly at the waist and kissed her languidly before removing her own clothing and pushing Parker back on the bed. Syd heard Parker take a ragged breath as she knelt over her. Gently grazing her fingertips over Parker's smooth skin, she grappled with the rush of her own hunger for Parker. She bent to course her tongue over the path her fingers had just drawn, stopping to slowly pull a now taut nipple between her teeth.

"You mean like this?" Syd sealed her mouth over the puckered point making Parker moan in response.

"God, you're good at that," Parker breathed. Syd felt Parker's nails scrape against her scalp, tensing suddenly when she circled her tongue around Parker's nipple once more.

"I'm also interested in your opinion of my other talents." She moved her mouth down Parker's ribs and nipped at the skin covering her hip, relishing the guttural sounds Parker made in response. "Like maybe this one."

Parker arched against Sydney's mouth when she glanced her tongue over her burning core.

"So...very...good," Parker managed as Syd slid her tongue along the sensitive flesh. Syd looked up to watch Parker's expression change as she gradually buried her fingers inside her and increased the friction of her mouth around her charged center. Moments later, Parker ground her body against Syd who slowed her movement in order to temper her building intensity.

"Damn it, Syd. Don't stop." She scraped her fingers over Syd's hard shoulder as she rolled her pelvis against her.

"What do you need, baby?" Syd teased her with varying rhythms and patterns as the layers of Parker's arousal began to consume her completely. "You want to come for me?"

"Yes. Now." Parker fisted the tangled sheets and thrust against her.

Her response nearly pushed Syd to her own peak as she felt Parker's body suddenly contract around her, but she was too focused on the experience of guiding and driving her lover through hers to give in.

Hearing her name being called over the deafening sound of Parker's whispered surrender spurred Syd to coerce Parker's body further, resulting in a second even more intense explosion.

Syd moved to capture Parker's mouth in hers as Parker rode the splinters of her shattering release.

Parker kissed her ravenously before guiding her hand between their bodies. Syd knew Parker would instantly feel the searing heat between her thighs.

"I know you're close, love." Parker's voice was ragged and needy in Syd's ear as she ghosted her fingers tenderly over Sydney's hard center. Syd gasped at the touch, and pressed reflexively into her hand.

"So close." Syd barely finished the words when Parker's tormenting strokes breached her resolve. Her body jerked as the sweeping force of the climax poured through her, the sensations coating her like warm wax.

She pressed Parker to her and floated on the ebbing waves of ecstasy, not ready to experience any distance between them.

"You are everything to me." Syd barely achieved audible sounds.

"I love you more than anything, Syd." Parker folded into Syd's embrace. Syd dissolved into the bliss of sleep and comfort of knowing Parker would always be completely hers.

Chapter Nine

Chief Jayne Provost stalked on high red heels into a tall mirrored glass building overlooking the lake. She wondered if her new office would have a view of the water. She would make sure of it once she took the reins. The company was a powerful player in the business world, having landed some pretty large government contracts in the last several years, but like most big corporations, security was a necessary evil someone always thought about a little too late. While the incumbent CSO had made a mark for the corporation, she knew she could and would do more to make a name for herself.

The selection committee was meeting for the last time with the two final candidates for the job. She wasn't worried; she had this in her pocket. Her competition, Major Dawn Turner from Raleigh, might hail from a much larger department than the SLPD, but Provost sported the chief title on her resume. Regardless, these people would be lucky to have her.

A dark-haired, middle-aged man strolled down the hall in an overpriced suit and too much jewelry for a guy who wasn't a pimp or a Mafioso. He smiled at Jayne who thought the feelings behind it were as genuine as the ones she returned. They stepped inside his large office and he swung the door closed behind them.

"How nice it is to see you. How have you been?" Provost asked. She couldn't have actually cared less but she could play the game…hell, she'd perfected the game. She just wanted the opportunity to sit in front of the committee to seal the deal.

"It's great to see you, Jayne. Ready for this?" He sat behind his desk, affirming his power. "Thank you for helping me out when we needed it."

"Of course." Her voice was too sweet. "I've told you, I can handle anything you throw at me. Emergencies have been my life since I was twenty years old." She felt smug. "Let's just make sure that Junior spends more time baking cookies with Great-Aunt Bessie instead of causing his parents so much concern, understood?"

He nodded knowingly.

She continued, "Favors are what friends do for each other, right?"

"Absolutely, Jayne. And they aren't readily forgotten."

"I'm counting on that. You might want to make sure he starts learning from his mistakes so he isn't in trouble anymore, okay?" Jayne reclined in her chair allowing her skirt to subtly slide north as she watched the CSO eagerly attend the show. She had no intention of dipping her toe in those waters, but donning the bathing suit often came in handy. She also thoroughly enjoyed the sport of leading men around by their dicks; unfortunately, it never presented much of a challenge.

The man nodded, his eyes scanning her toned legs intently before he suddenly cleared his throat. "Well, I think they should be just about ready for us." He checked his watch and stepped around his desk. "This office should be yours in a few weeks."

She appraised the lake view and the sleek wooden paneled desk. She would make sure she turned the desk to face the water so she could appreciate her achievements as she worked. "Count on it." She offered him a knowing smile and slid past him out the door.

Her Louboutins clicked loudly on the shiny marble-tiled floors. The heavy double doors of the conference room swung open just as they approached. A uniformed Dawn Turner exited the room, shaking hands as she went. Jayne thought the police garb was a mistake since, in her opinion, the board needed to see how she could assimilate to a corporate culture, not just coast on the legacy of a public sector job. She didn't feel bad. Turner had no shot at the position anyway.

Jayne breezed into the room, smiling and shaking hands as the selection committee rose to greet her. "Gentlemen, thank you all so very much for meeting with me. I've heard such good things about each of you."

She thought the committee members were suitably impressed when she returned their softball questions with aplomb and efficiency. After all, she had studied each question at length and had prepared her answers weeks ago, thanks to her mutually beneficial relationship with the outgoing executive.

The questioning quickly began to feel like a casual conversation with some familiar colleagues. She didn't see the point in working too diligently to get a job she already had.

A scant forty-five minutes later, she stood to shake each man's hand. She thought that the lack of women on their staff would also be an advantage for her. Women were often difficult to assess and were less easily managed.

She clicked back to the lobby and out to her city-owned vehicle, never thinking twice about using government resources for her personal business.

❖

"Where the hell are you? I expected you an hour ago," the CSO bellowed into his phone.

"So sorry, I didn't realize I was punching a clock for you." His son spat the words. "It's not like I haven't been working my ass off, you know."

"And being paid very well, don't forget," he grumbled in response. "How many units are left at our disposal?"

"Three hundred and twenty, give or take a supplemental shipment I might be able to liberate by next week." He sounded proud of his accomplishments.

"Don't push it. We have to be careful. Another $180k would be nice gravy, but we'll have plenty of time later." He pushed back from his desk as he disconnected the call. He imagined what it would be like not having to share his take with anyone. He had always been averse to sharing.

His ex-wife was living on the Cape with her antiques dealer boyfriend in the house he had bought and paid for decades ago. She had soundly screwed him in the divorce. He pictured the bleached blonde that his wife had convinced to testify about their brief affair. He had reasoned that he deserved all the sex he could get since she certainly hadn't been attending to his needs. Years after that failure, he had determined that money and sex were all any red-blooded American man needed, and he made sure he always had plenty of both.

If he ever again allowed another woman to share his home, he would make sure they left with nothing when he was through with them. He'd thought he was marrying for love all those years ago. She had expected him home for dinner and to assist with child-rearing instead of building his career and fortune. He had made the right choices in his professional life, and sadly, the wrong choices with women whom he regarded as opportunists poised to pick the flesh from his bones given their first opening. No, sharing was not appealing.

He walked to his AMG Mercedes. He had custom ordered the $150,000 car in a deep green, the color of money. At one p.m. his admin called his cell. He hit *ignore* before walking in to have his weekly manicure and massage. He was a busy man.

Major Williams sauntered up the walk leading to an impeccable colonial in the tony Fishers Gate neighborhood. Before he could reach for the doorbell, the large red door swung open and a well-dressed woman in her early sixties greeted him. She handed him a Jack Black on the rocks, shutting the door behind the senior law enforcement officer.

"Well, Damon, to what do I owe the pleasure of your company? It isn't Wednesday and I assume my daughter hasn't done anything else to disgrace this family." Her expression was always pinched and artificial but he pretended not to notice.

"Not yet, Pamela, but give her some time." He chuckled about the woman's obsession with Sydney Hyatt's every move in Silver Lake as he took his favorite seat in her stuffy living room. He was careful to sound sympathetic. "I'm certainly glad I never had any kids, seeing what you have had to go through. I know she was provided every opportunity, given your pedigree, Pamela. Still she acts so...classless." Major Williams was raised in the worst part of town by two neglectful and abusive criminals; the term *classless* to describe anyone else was ludicrous and he knew it.

"Yes, it's particularly trying when I'm attempting to do so much for the people of this city. I am constantly reminded of her notoriety through that little business of hers." She sounded condescending as she referenced DRIFT. He wondered how everyone seemed to think Silver Lake was in existence simply because they were. He considered that the sour woman perched on the settee in front of him and his bossy chief should have been best friends but then decided their competing egos would have spelled disaster.

"It's really too bad the city council won't move her off the approved vendor list. Then I could at least *pretend* not to know who she is, and I would stop being worried about what she's doing to embarrass me this week." She pursed her lips and recounted the story of seeing her only child in the restroom with her mouth on another woman. She sounded horrified at the display of impertinence by the daughter she had raised. "She flaunts her sexuality in public. What would they have done in there if I hadn't walked in? I think she's intent on embarrassing me every chance she gets."

"Well, your seat as chairperson of the Concerned Citizens' Coalition should prove valuable, Pamela. Perhaps as your close relationships with the heads of key government sectors develop, it will help decrease her market share, so to speak." He watched as she nodded enthusiastically.

"Ah, yes. The CCC certainly has increased my profile with local decision makers already." She spoke formally. "Speaking of which, apparently our esteemed chief is looking to create a vacancy, Damon." She delivered the statement as if she was innocent of any nonpublic knowledge and was simply discussing city gossip with an old friend.

He nodded and raised his glass as he shifted his gun belt and hoped Pamela couldn't see it cutting into his bulging belly. Rather, Pamela Hyatt seemed to be relishing the thought of her increased influence in Silver Lake because of his potential promotion. All from a cushy chair in her living room. He had other plans, but if she thought that her relationship with him would help her run for city council as well as her campaign to keep her dyke daughter out of the news, he would be happy to let it endure.

"I just happen to be meeting with Chairman Franks for breakfast at the President's Club next week, and I'm sure he would love to hear my recommendations for the next appointment to the chief's office. I believe he very much values my opinion, Damon."

"As do I, Pamela." His conciliatory tone was almost as insulting as the condescending one she bestowed upon him. Theirs was an alliance of reluctant convenience, mutual benefit, and mild disdain.

"I'm sure you do, Damon. Would you like another drink?"

"Please." She moved to the bar to refill the glass.

"Just so you know, Pamela, I'm old-school. I find this entire open acceptance of homosexuality just as disgusting as you do. Being in law enforcement, I'm forced to deal with it, like you have been." He knew his words would cement the affinity between them. "It's a blight on the department and this city. I've tried not to let it affect my job but the politically correct bullshit is getting on my nerves. When I am chief, this department will stop being a dyke farm."

"From your lips to God's ears, Damon." She seemed to brighten with a fresh charge of energy.

He leaned back and crossed his legs at the ankle. "Is there anything else I can do for you while I'm here, Pamela?"

She looked mildly repulsed at his inference, but stood to lead him down the hall. The SLPD watch commander turned off his radio as he began unbuttoning his shirt. Pamela shut the bathroom door as she traded her expensive suit for a silk robe and walked back to the bedroom.

CHAPTER TEN

Parker kicked off her shoes in the loft she had barely finished renovating in January. She carried her heels up the
black metal stairs to the bedroom she had come to love but rarely
spent much time in, now that she slept across the hall every night.
She was happy to stay at Sydney's as it was bigger and the hub of
her business. She mused that Mia would do well in her carefully
decorated space, not to mention that she would be close to friendly
faces if and when she needed them.

Parker's long day had ended with a screaming match between
client and contractor in an office building her property-develop-
ment company was managing. After standing between the two
grown men in a ten-million dollar development, she'd actually had
to duck when the contractor threw a roll of plans at the client and
told him to go get his contractor's license since *he* certainly wasn't
finishing the job for the conceited bastard.

She repeatedly shook her head at the behavior of two adults
who regularly fought like children and then shared a beer at the
corner bar after it was over. The only person with a shorter life and
higher blood pressure as a result of the argument was Parker. She
slid off her jacket and draped it over the chair against the wrought-
iron loft rails.

She threw herself down onto the platform bed and stared at
the seed glass light fixture above it. She had taken forever to decide

on the decor but had finally gotten used to the rough floors in the funky space and had chosen a soft green paint to complement the bathroom tile her friend Allen had selected for her. A glint of metal caught her eye as the air conditioning blew a long silver object in a circle.

She stood to balance on the bed and grasped the silver lightning bolt that hung from a transparent cord above her window. She braced on bare feet and locked knees appraising the piece, which had appeared as if from nowhere. Turning it over in her hand, she read the inscription: *Thank you for loving me—SH.*

The small gesture from her no-nonsense lover caught her off guard. The woman who had orchestrated the sentimental gift wouldn't have even considered a second date with her a year ago, making it even more significant.

"You okay?" Syd's husky voice jolted her out of her thoughts.

Parker barely grabbed the window frame in time to stop her tumble from the bed. "You about gave me a heart attack. I didn't even hear you coming up the stairs," she replied, her voice breathy, as Sydney laughed and walked toward the bed. Stepping gingerly to the edge, Parker wound her arms around her lover's neck as she tried to pull her up onto the mattress.

"How about you come down here," Syd said, glancing at the ceiling perilously close to her head. "One wrong move and I'm out cold."

"When did you do this?" Parker kneeled on the mattress and reclined onto the bed at an angle as Sydney lay back with her. She looked up at the gift spinning in front of her bedroom window.

"Before I went to the gym today. I know you'll kind of miss this being your place and I just wanted you to know that I knew." She winked at Parker and ran her fingers through her thick dark hair, skimming a thumb over her cheek.

Parker grazed her hand down Sydney's muscular arm and squeezed gently. "You're too good to me, you know." Parker rubbed the platinum lightning bolt charm at her neck, Syd's first gift to her. Parker surveyed her angular face and slowly moved toward her. She hooked her thigh between Syd's. "I can't get enough of you," she offered in Syd's ear and slid her mouth to find the very sensitive zone behind it, kissing carefully.

"This is very good news." Syd gasped as Parker abruptly found a path under her shorts and claimed her solidly with her fingers.

Submitting to her lover, Syd reclined farther into the soft comforter as Parker pushed her toward surrender. A slow rhythm built as Parker nipped along her neck and turned to suck each of Sydney's long fingers slowly and seductively into her mouth. Parker locked her eyes with Sydney's now cloudy focus and moved to whisper in her ear, "Show me how much you love me, Syd."

The release was almost instant and incredibly intense. Parker was overwhelmed by the sensations finding her as she watched her strong lover fall over and under for her.

Sydney shifted Parker into her arms and held her as Parker curled against her. "I love you, Park."

"I love you."

They lay together quietly until Sydney stirred them both from the stillness. "Our meeting of the Lesbian Mystery Solvers Guild is starting soon, you know."

"How could I forget," Parker replied sarcastically. "The head of the Sydney Hyatt Fan Club will be there, too."

"I thought you were the president of that club," Sydney joked at Parker's mock pout.

"Apparently, I was voted out during a one-woman coup." She batted her eyes dramatically, lifting herself to straddle Sydney. "But don't worry. I don't plan on giving up my seat. I like it here." Her eyes danced as Sydney looked at her carefully.

"I wouldn't give you up, not for anything in the world." Her tone was sincere as she brought Parker's mouth to meet hers.

❖

Darcy Dean arrived first and looked over the black Porsche with the *DRIFTER* license plate. She was impressed with Sydney's success, but then again, Sydney had impressed her in many ways. The past few days had kept her reminiscing about her one true love, wishing she could craft an opportunity to talk to her alone. Parker was nice enough, but she wondered if they were as solid as they seemed. Sydney had been an insatiable lover a decade ago and she pondered if her new girlfriend provided the same electricity for Sydney that she once had.

She briefly thought about waiting in the car but decided to walk slowly toward the lobby and press Sydney's buzzer. A file was pressed under her arm as she waited for entry. Parker answered the door in brown shorts and an old T-shirt with *Hyatt* printed over the pocket. *I guess someone's staking their territory.*

"Hi, Darcy." Parker's voice was cheerful as she led Darcy through to the living room where Sydney was tending a makeshift bar on the kitchen island.

"Hey, Dean. Beer or wine?" She didn't look up. Darcy wanted to look in her seductive gray eyes.

"Um, beer is fine, please. I'm a simple girl, SyFi." She winked at Syd when she looked up at the mention of her old nickname.

"Stop. Please."

Darcy shrugged. "You used to like it." She stared over at Sydney.

"What does it mean?" Parker ventured since the conversation couldn't get any more awkward, or inappropriate, for that matter. And she was curious, dammit.

"Well, Sy, for her name—I used to just call her that—and then when she started all of this freaky science fiction reconstruction stuff, it just kind of morphed into SyFi." She shrugged again as if she knew now that the name held no significance for anyone in the room except her.

"Just Syd will work fine." Syd's tone was flat and dismissive. Parker thought that Darcy looked dissatisfied at being an outsider in Sydney Hyatt's world.

The buzzer rang again and Parker was happy for the job of retrieving the rest of the guests. She tried to let go of her tension as she let them in through the lobby door.

"You okay?" Jen held Parker in the hallway while Mack continued into the loft with Olivia.

Parker offered in a stage whisper, "How about, next time, we have a secret work party and invite over all of the exes still pining for Mack and serve them cocktails?" She pursed her lips and shook her head.

Jen giggled at Parker's sarcasm. "Does Syd have any old feelings for the crafty Ms. Dean?"

"I don't think so. She acts like she can barely stand to be in the same room with her. However, our friend Darcy would certainly ride that ride again if she had the chance." She chuckled, knowing their absence would be obvious by now.

"Does Sydney know that?"

"Not before the other night. We had a talk about what she would take from me if she had the chance. There might have been visual aids." Parker's delivery was bone dry.

Jen laughed out loud. "I love you. You crack me up."

"Let's go watch the drama." She caught Jen's fingers in her own and led her inside.

Parker could see Syd already in her chair through the studio windows as Mack and Darcy were halfway up the stairs.

"I'm going to steal that baby—she is too adorable!" Darcy cooed as she made faces at Olivia Grace in Mack's arms.

"Just no end to what you're willing to steal from here, is there?" Parker said, loudly enough for only Jenny to hear as they followed behind.

Parker and Jen dropped into adjacent chairs settling the baby carrier between them.

"I'll go first," Mack volunteered. "I sweet-talked the admin in the patrol division to rush me the phone records for Sandy. I told her that I forgot to include them in the file for the rookies and didn't want anyone think I was guilty of sabotage. She seemed to buy it and gave me the last two months'. So I haven't looked at all the numbers yet, but the last ten calls were to the station and Mia. The interesting thing I learned from the cell company is that her phone was on and pinging the general vicinity until twenty minutes *after* the call to 9-1-1. Then the battery was removed or destroyed because the phone was never in service again. Someone there, a crime scene tech or a uniform would have been the only ones with access unless our killer hung around for the show. And you know for a fact it was gone when you arrived, right Darcy?"

"Absolutely."

"I hate to say this out loud," Syd said, "but you and I both know that the triangulation is weak on cell towers. A lot of courts are barring the use of that as stand-alone evidence. The shooter could have had the phone nearby before he took the battery out." Syd braced her foot on the counter in front of her computer as she addressed Mack.

"I know, but at least it's *something*." Mack sounded desperate for any lead.

"I brought the 9-1-1 call if you guys want to listen," Darcy offered as she held out a disk to Sydney. Parker watched her fingers graze over Syd's for just a second as she released the CD.

"I would do anything to know who made that call to dispatch, wouldn't you?" Mack looked resigned.

"I know. I think it could maybe tell us if someone is pulling strings here or it's just what it appears to be." Syd looked doubtful.

"You can clearly tell this is a guy trying to sound like a female and doing a really bad job," Darcy offered.

Syd piped the sound through the room's speakers.

Dispatch: *Fairfax 9-1-1, what is your emergency?*
Caller: *I think an officer is dead at Forty-Sixth and Lincoln.*
Dispatch: *How do you know it's an officer, ma'am?*

Caller: *Uh, I looked in the window of the car after I heard a gunshot.*

Dispatch: *Where were you?*

Caller: *Uh, walking by.*

Dispatch: *Did you see anyone else there?*

Caller: *No.*

Dispatch: *Any other cars?*

Caller: *No, just her unit is there. It's number 2-3-4. All black, no markings.*

Dispatch: *Can you stay on the line with me until police reach your location?*

Caller: *I don't want to get involved.*

Dispatch: *What is your name in case the police need to reach you?*

Caller: *I want to remain anonymous.*

Dispatch: *Okay, can you tell me anything else?*

A dial tone roared into the speakers.

"Bad, right? That was clearly a guy," Darcy declared shaking her head at the poor impression everyone had heard.

"Wait, wait." Sydney excitedly spun back to the computer and enhanced the audio, driving the audio slider on the screen back about ten seconds.

"Listen." She hit play and everyone strained to hear over the background noise.

No, just her unit is there. It's number 2-3-4.

"Did you hear that? Her *unit*—civilians don't say that, *cops* do. Civilians say *her car*, *the car*, or something like that."

"You're right." Mack stared at the screen as if she expected the answers to be written there. "The background noise was brutal."

"That was the helicopter looking for the home invasion suspect that went out right before we got there. We had to resort to yelling at each other a couple of times."

Both Mack and Syd shifted around to look at Darcy. "What did you say?" Syd asked slowly.

"A *police* helicopter was still there?" Mack asked impatiently glancing back at Syd who was grabbing her cell from the clip on her belt. Parker noticed her gun again. She also noticed Darcy watch Syd intently.

"Fairfax County or State?" Syd asked enthusiastically. Darcy seemed captivated by watching Syd work.

"Well I didn't see it, but it had to be county. State was putting on the dog and pony show with their bird at the fairgrounds all weekend," Darcy responded. "They had one of my scene team vans out there until Monday."

Mack looked at Syd, obviously understanding her new train of thought. "Williams told me we had a double at Parkside Manor. I assumed that's why no one was available for Sandy but me and David."

Syd's fingers started flying over her telephone contact list. "Zander Young is the newest pilot for Fairfax County. He and I did a long investigation together last year," Syd replied in answer to the rest of the room's curious stares. "He owes me one."

"For?" Parker looked over to Syd.

"Let's just say I have information he doesn't want made public."

"Blackmail?" Jen stared incredulously at Sydney.

"No, nothing like that. He just owes me for not reporting the slap and tickle session he was conducting with another member of the flight center staff...*in* the new helicopter."

Parker laughed out loud and then smacked her hand over her mouth as the call connected.

"Zander, Syd Hyatt, how are you? I need you to check back in your log for me as a favor...A really quiet favor, okay?" Sydney slid a large paper clip back and forth in her fingers as she described her request. A smile broke over her face as she high-fived Mack and did a victory dance in her chair before she disconnected.

"One full-reel video coming up. Zander *was* flying that night and made a pass over the warehouse district at least once because they got a report about the possible shooter in the Parkside case." The group cheered as Sydney started tapping away at the video she had been working on.

Everyone got closer to the screen and Parker leaned against her lover while the newest evidence began to play. Mack dropped a kiss on Jen's fingers as she tilted her back against her. Parker felt a pang of jealousy stab at her and forced herself to refocus when Darcy brushed her thigh against Sydney and took up position on her other side.

"I've uploaded all the pictures Darcy sent and integrated them into Mack's cell video to get the best 3-D images I could approximate without using any presumptive data. Meaning I wanted to be careful not to add or assume information where there was none just based on our conversation. If we need to do that later, I can."

The rough video from Mack's phone began to find focus, a morph somewhere between a cartoon and a movie. A shaky tour of an open expanse showed an empty industrial space in the midst of some sort of transformation. Mack narrated the tour through the warehouse adding approximate distances.

"Was the warehouse being remodeled?" Parker spoke first breaking the silence in the room. "I'm noticing what looks like fairly fresh Sheetrock mud. Is that just an effect on the video or is it really new?" She leaned to look closer at the image.

"No, it's fresh," Mack responded. "I called the property's registered owner and he said that construction crews had been working all week. The new tenant plans to store textiles in their warehouse, so they wanted the environment to be as clean and dry as possible, hence the expense of finished walls. He said that they were planning to paint the Tuesday after the holiday. The crew doesn't work Mondays as a rule. I asked him about loading-in construction materials and he claimed that, as far as he knew, they used pickups which aren't high enough for that dock. He gave me the contact at the construction company but I didn't have a chance to follow up before I got yanked off the case."

"What makes you ask about the walls?" Sydney asked.

Parker rested her hand on Syd's shoulder and she entwined her fingers in response. "Well, first of all, unless they have the worst construction manager ever, that place isn't ready to paint."

"Why?" Mack stared at the now frozen image.

"Look at this knee wall." She pointed to the place on the image. "The panels have been torn away from the floor strips and the screws are missing." Parker felt Darcy look over at her when she held Syd's hand.

Sydney leaned closer and enlarged the image. "Actually, I don't think they're missing, Park, look." With the mouse, she hovered over two screws that had been wedged against the corner and gleamed as the light of the video passed over them.

"Yeah, those are Sheetrock screws. They weren't unscrewed either, the rock is all torn away and crumbly. Something hit that corner. I don't know if it means anything, but if you're remodeling a space and preparing it for finishes, that should be the last thing you let happen." She was pointing at the screen as everyone else followed her finger.

Syd began clicking windows as new pictures were laid over old and layers became 3-D renderings. "I think I can enhance the shot of this section."

The images skimmed by. Syd played the video at regular speed first and then replayed it two additional times at half-speed before Jen whispered, "I think I know what made the break in the wall." Mack raised an eyebrow at Jenny.

"Time out, Syd." Mack said quickly, and Syd clicked the mouse and the view of the wall froze again.

Jen leaned toward the screen. "I think this may be useful… maybe. It looks like there was a pallet jack here. The floors are clear and smooth. But look at the worn path in the dust, how it kind of shines like metal. If someone isn't very experienced at using a jack, they won't pick their load up high enough and the forks skid along the ground. If you follow the trail of the skid marks"—she waited as Syd zoomed the video out and dragged her finger along the pattern that only she had noticed until then—"the marks go straight from the dock leveler and toward that wall where the break is."

Mack looked at her wife and crinkled her nose. "How do you know about pallet jacks?"

"Mack, I wasn't always the mother of your child and Parker's favorite employee, you know." She smiled at Parker who laughed at her. Mack nudged her to go on.

"I was in a leadership program in college and spent two summer internships learning how to manage a shipping warehouse. I kept having to terminate workers because they were damaging product on the jacks or chipping out the ramps because they wouldn't raise the forks. It's laziness really, but it's faster to pull them up as they go and just enough to begin to move the jack, but that doesn't allow for uneven concrete, hazards, a dropped board, etcetera." Jen smiled satisfactorily, obviously quite proud of herself. Mack squeezed her cheeks and planted a loud kiss on her lips.

"So," Darcy continued the thought as she stood close behind Sydney once more. Parker saw her intentionally skimming her breast over Sydney's shoulder. She was sure any rush born of the contact was felt by Darcy alone. "If someone was loading or unloading a trailer, it obviously means a delivery truck would have been in the dock. Otherwise, they wouldn't have been able to reach this…stage? platform?"

Parker said, "It's called a dock plate. And no, if there was no truck there, no one would have walked on or off the dock plate from inside the warehouse." She looked at the group to see if they were following. "If you were just using the door for ventilation, you wouldn't get that close without worrying about falling off, right?" Syd nodded at her.

"So why are there half footprints leading on and off the plate, if a truck wasn't there?" Mack chimed in.

"And there would be no reason for equipment like a pallet jack or a forklift to be there, since this was supposed to be the finish week and the guy says they reportedly haven't been using it," Jenny continued Parker's thought.

Mack was taking furious notes in a spiral pad as the brain-storming continued. "So let's say Sandy drives up on a truck being loaded or unloaded in the middle of the night at a supposedly vacant warehouse. She thinks maybe kids or vagrants or maybe a stolen truck. She tries to get close enough to see which it is before she calls it in, and someone makes her." She was talking almost as fast as she was writing before giving up the pen and staring again at the screen.

"The subject or subjects get spooked and shoot her when they figure out who she is, see the uniform, or the government plates. Even though she drives an unmarked, it's pretty obviously a police issue."

"She wouldn't have tried to approach the warehouse." Syd picked up the thought. "There are too many ambush points. She would have observed from the side lot and gotten a good look at the operation from back here before picking up her phone or requesting a check-in. She wouldn't have confronted them unless she had backup, and her mic was never keyed, right?"

"No, never," Darcy confirmed. "I asked someone from dispatch to go back over their records looking for random squelch or broken transmissions around that time, and nothing."

Parker squeezed Syd's shoulder as she leaned even closer to the screen. "Can you zoom in on this part?" She pointed to a tiny red square tucked under the knee wall that had been hit.

"Here?" Syd looked at her for confirmation.

"Yeah, see it?" Parker pointed at a thin item that looked like a piece of colored paper sticking out of the wall at the floor. "So, if construction was being fast-tracked, Sheetrock would have only taken a week for this size area." She circled the space on the screen. "If that paper was there before the stud runners were bolted into the concrete, they would have moved it or kicked it into the void space behind the wall. You should see what gets left back there.

This item looks like it just got wedged under the metal runner which means it happened recently. And maybe, just maybe"—she looked to Jen for confirmation—"if it's a pallet tag, it would give us an idea *what* was being loaded and unloaded. Of course, if it's not just construction materials."

Jen nodded. "It could be a pallet label that got jerked loose when whoever hit the wall. They usually only use one industrial staple to affix it to the base or side run of boards on the pallet. The wood face can be really soft, so they can come off fairly easily," she explained, and Parker leaned to offer a triumphant slap on Jenny's shoulder because they were too far away to hug.

Mack stared at both women. "I don't know what just happened but I'm very turned on right now." The room erupted into much needed tension-dissolving laughter.

"Nice job, Park," Syd whispered to Parker who was still standing behind her.

"So," Mack said with new focus, "now we need to figure out what truck was there when, and what happened to the merchandise if there was some. I guess we can rule out a party or a drug deal."

"You mean because drug dealers don't usually have pallets of weight dropped at a warehouse they don't own?" Syd said sarcastically.

"Exactly. And we can't be sure that the owner of the property isn't involved somehow, so I'm leaving that alone for the moment."

Darcy held up her phone displaying an email. "Williams just sent me a message asking about the scene photos." Darcy looked at Mack. "I haven't had a chance to make any copies of them yet. What do you want me to do?"

"Send him the pictures from the lot just like you would on any other case. Just interoffice them to the wrong mail code. Address them to him, but at South District. Hell, they can't find their own station half the time, let alone misdirected mail. That way you've done what he asked and he can't get too bent out of shape. I just want a little extra time."

"We need to get in that warehouse, Mack," Syd said. "Sooner rather than later, in case someone notices it. The construction crew could just sweep it up and not think anything about it, assuming they aren't involved, of course." Syd was picturing evidence disappearing and it made her nervous. If this was what they thought, it could really help to have that tiny piece of paper.

"Syd, I can't ask you to break into a privately owned building with me. That's too much."

"You aren't asking," she replied quickly. "Maybe I like long walks in the Warehouse District, and I happen to hear a dog whining? I would have to look into it in case the poor thing got locked in, right?" She flashed an innocent look at Mack.

"Let me think about this. I have to know who I can trust if we need backup, and right now, everyone's running scared of being the next one transferred into Siberia."

"I can help," Darcy offered to the group as Mack shook her head. "Come on, I can drive you and stay in the car as a lookout. Ask Syd, I can defend myself."

Syd nodded as she remembered being tackled by Darcy one night when she came in late from work without calling. Darcy had put Sydney on the floor in roughly five seconds. While Syd tried to get her breath back, Darcy finally realized she wasn't a machete-wielding burglar. She had apologized for a week afterward. "Yeah, she could probably defend herself."

"Let me try and get the lay of the land before we make a plan," Mack said. "Syd, call me when you get the aerials, okay? Let's all get some sleep and meet back when there's something new. I know you're right—we can't wait too long."

The baby voiced her opinion right on schedule as Jen collected the bundle and headed down the stairs.

Syd pushed the door closed after everyone had filed out and observed Parker sitting on the kitchen island. She walked to her and wedged between her knees, "What?" She studied Parker's furrowed features as she gripped the countertop instead of pulling against Sydney as she would have expected.

"I don't like this," she said in a matter-of-fact way that made Sydney pause.

"The case? You don't have to be invol—"

"Being jealous. I don't like being jealous." Parker frowned at the floor as if considering her words carefully.

"Of Dean?" She hadn't noticed that Parker was upset during the meeting but her girlfriend was very good at laying low in certain situations. That made her good at her job and often confounding in a relationship.

"Yes, of Darcy. She looks at you constantly. She puts herself in a position where she touches you all the time—like tonight, dragging her chest across your arm." Syd remembered it and had hoped Parker hadn't seen the blatantly tacky move. "She brings up things from your past together any chance she gets. She does it to push her way back in with you and to push me away. She loves to recount your history that I know nothing about."

Syd had never ever seen Parker pout before and thought it was adorable. She silently congratulated herself on mentioning neither of those things out loud.

She placed her hands around Parker's hips and touched her forehead to Parker's as she prepared to fill in the blanks of her history with the devious Ms. Dean. "Okay, here it goes. First of all, I was twenty-two when we met. I had never had a girlfriend and my only female role model was my mother. The fact that I didn't move in with a drunken murderer seemed pretty good as far as I was concerned. She was older and she knew how to manipulate me—like I told you when we first met, remember?"

She tilted Parker's chin so she could see her eyes before she continued. "I did what she said, when she said it, because I thought that was what relationships were. That was certainly what my mother demonstrated them to be, one person in charge of the other. I was going to parties with law enforcement types who could, and did, help me professionally, and I was getting regular sex."

Parker's eyes got huge. Sydney kissed her soundly and continued, "Not great sex but good enough for twenty-two. I learned a lot in a year and a half, mostly what not to look for in a relationship. Truth be told, how to not get in a relationship to start with. And it was a bad one, not at first, but certainly later. It was a bad place to find myself. Nothing I would ever even consider being in again, and certainly not with her. However, had it not happened, I would not have spent many years picking up strangers in a bar."

She took a breath and winked at the now decidedly less pouty Parker. "And I wouldn't have needed to meet my lightning and change my evil ways."

Sydney slid a finger down the charm at Parker's neck and smiled. She'd presented it to her last December at the Pride Lounge, a place Parker had rarely gone at all and Syd had rarely departed from alone.

"You're too damned charming for your own good, you know." Parker's eyes watered at her lover's heartfelt speech. "I don't think I can let you go out alone anymore—it's too dangerous for us mere mortals."

Syd smoothed a hand over her shoulder. "Now who's being charming?" Syd whispered huskily. She moved Parker's long hair behind her shoulders as she locked her eyes onto Parker's. "I couldn't imagine being in a relationship last year, but thanks to you, I can't imagine *not* being in this one. I love you more every day and don't forget it." Syd kissed her on the end of her nose and then on her cheek. "I can't breathe when you're hurt or sad or even just away from me for too long. Darcy Dean is my past, my very distant, unpleasant past. Don't let her manipulate you because only then does she have someone to play her little game with her."

"You're mine," Parker declared soundly, the jealousy fading away.

"That I am." Syd kissed her again. "Now, hold on to me so I can prove it to you five or six times."

Parker laughed and snaked her arms and legs tightly around Syd's torso as Syd swept her off the counter and down the hall to bed, slapping off lights as they went.

❖

Chief Jayne Provost reclined naked on the fine cotton sheets of the best hotel in Silver Lake. She turned lazily to pick up her ringing cell phone from the nightstand. An over-Botoxed face grinned up from the contact display.

"Good afternoon, sir, to what do I owe this pleasure?" She knew exactly why he was calling and she rested her head back on the upholstered headboard while he spoke, stroking the sheets with the palm of her newly manicured hand.

"Well, this is really just a formality, Jayne, but after my glowing recommendation and your last panel interview, the committee has made its decision. Welcome to the company, Chief Provost. We're very lucky to have you." He rattled off her new title as she pictured the lake view through her new office window.

"Thank you, the pleasure will be mine. Shall I assume a formal offer letter will be sent?"

"Already on the way, Jayne. The sooner we can wrap this up, the better."

Jayne knew he was eager to claim his platinum retirement package and start enjoying his freedom. "I shall turn in my resignation as soon as I receive it, then. I imagine there will be some press coverage. Just a heads-up. Have a great weekend." She ended the call and smiled.

"Looks like we can quit meeting at hotels, Luke. I got the job." Her smile was more like a satisfied smirk when she imagined her powerful new role and pushed her twentysomething companion back into service between her legs.

Chapter Eleven

"Hi, Mia. It's Parker. Do you have time to talk for a minute?" Parker cradled the phone on her left shoulder as she cleared off her desk. She noticed the clock read six thirty p.m. and a renewed wave of fatigue found her.

"Hi. Sure." Mia's voice was much stronger than the last time Parker saw her, but she still sounded weary.

"How are you?" She listened carefully.

"Compared to what?" Mia attempted a laugh but her words sounded angry. "Sorry, I mean, I'm okay, I guess. I took vacation from work until I can get things organized. I just can't imagine moving without her...doing anything without her, Parker. I still don't even know where I'm going to go."

"That's kind of why I was calling. Don't feel any pressure to say yes if you don't want to, but Syd and I discussed it. I practically live in her loft now and mine's vacant. I just redid it last year, secure building, fully furnished, on Meridian Street, close to town, and right across from Sydney's in case you ever needed anything or wanted to talk. Only if you're interested, that is." Parker stopped for a breath as she realized the words had come out like a hard sell she didn't intend.

"Wow. Okay. That's...I mean, wow." Mia seemed to be trying to adjust to the idea. Or perhaps guilty for leaving the home she had shared with Sandy.

Parker was still stunned that Sandy's family had acted so insensitively. She wondered if Mia was looking for an excuse. "Mia, you won't hurt my feelings if you say no or want to live somewhere else. I wasn't trying to pressure you. I just wanted to put the offer out there."

"No. Sorry. I just didn't think that I would feel okay about moving, but this kind of feels okay. Like the next step, you know? It's not as scary if I'll be near friends, maybe. Are you sure?" She sounded relieved.

"Very. I can show it to you whenever you want. Take your time and think about it. We aren't putting it out for any other offers right now, so you can sleep on it, okay?"

Parker had packed her briefcase and now rode down in the elevator grateful that her cell signal had held steady on the trip down to the parking lot. Throwing her briefcase into the trunk, she was happy to be finally steering toward home.

"I told her mom I would be out by the end of the month, so maybe I could even get away earlier."

Parker thought about how Sandy's mother had discounted their relationship like college roommates splitting up at the end of a semester. The sooner Mia could be away from them the better.

"Sandy is in every square foot of this house. I need to go but I feel like I'm holding on to her too tight. I know moving will never stop me feeling like this, but maybe I can do it a little better from a distance."

Parker steered her black Audi convertible into sparse late-evening traffic and was grateful to make the light at the corner. She could almost feel the sadness as Mia talked. "You have my number, Mia. Syd and I will be here for you if you need us, okay? You just let me know what works for you. There's no commitment either. If you decide you don't want to stay, you can just tell me. You've been through enough for right now."

"Thank you. Tell Syd thank you, too, okay?"

"Sure. Let me know when you feel up to it."

"Thanks, Parker. It means a lot."

She made the final turn into her parking spot and noticed no light from the windows of the loft. She collected her briefcase from the trunk as Sydney's text scrolled across her phone.

Going to run the errand with Mack. Be back soon.

She replied, *Please be careful. I don't like this. No cowboy stuff.*

Don't worry. I love you.

Let me know as soon as you're done. I love you.

Parker dialed Jen as she walked up the steps.

❖

Syd finished the text and returned her phone to her back pocket. Mack drove Darcy's car while the blonde reclined in the back.

"Let's just get the damn thing and get out." Mack exhaled the words.

"Agreed." Syd no more wanted to be this far outside the law than Mack did.

"I never realized how completely uncomfortable this car was in the back seat. I'm glad no one's trying to make babies back here."

"Really, Dean? That's what you're thinking about right now?" Syd shook her head and glanced into the side mirror to monitor anything behind them. The streets were deserted—no one usually spent a Friday night in the industrial part of town.

"What else should I be thinking about, Hyatt?" Her seductive tone grated on Syd as she thought about how the exchange would have made Parker feel.

"Can we focus, please?" Mack cut off the barely civil banter. "Darcy, as soon as we get out, you drive over to the side but keep the engine running. Watch for anyone suspicious driving or walking. Keep the doors locked until you see us. Okay?"

"Got it. You guys don't really think anyone will be there, do you?"

"Doubt it," Syd grumbled. "But we don't know what may be going on in there, so we have to expect anything." She noticed Mack was staring intently out the window. "You okay?

"Yeah, but Jenny's panicking. I just want this over with."

"Parker isn't overly fond of this either. In and out, let's just do this fast." They both pushed on thin black latex gloves.

Mack drove slowly into the dark grid of warehouses and extinguished the car's headlights. Syd scanned for ambient light at or near any structures as Mack stopped behind an adjacent warehouse visible only to the train tracks.

This wasn't the first unorthodox situation she and Mack had been in together, and somehow the trust they shared was inexplicably instinctive. Mack had come through for Syd when Becky was holding Parker hostage last year. Good instincts and Mack's quick response saved Parker's life that night. Syd knew Mack trusted her as a de facto partner.

They bailed from the car and ran in a crouch until they stood at the side of the square metal building. Mack pointed at the door. Though Syd had been prepared to force the lock open, she found the door unsecured. Syd knew that also meant someone else could already be there, but she was still grateful they wouldn't have to do any breaking before the entering part of their questionable endeavor. Mack drew her weapon and nodded Syd through the door in front of her.

The space was dark but for the street lamp shining through a plexiglass vent window near the roof. Acutely aware of the circumstances that brought them there, Syd thought of a fallen officer's last watch that had gone so wrong as she moved into the shadows. Mack checked the lot once more and moved in behind Syd allowing the door to all but close. Syd and Mack scanned the empty space when Syd pointed to the floor where a red tag was lodged.

Mack nodded and looked over the warehouse for anything else that might tell them who had been there the night Sandy was killed, or since. Syd snatched the red tag up by its edge and signaled by waving the item in front of her and dropping it into a bag. Mack quickly rescanned the building for anything else useful before jerking her head toward the door, signaling back to Syd for them to get out.

They stepped from the door and pulsed a penlight to signal Darcy to pull across the lot. The sound of a shot pierced the silence and glanced off the metal of the warehouse wall. They both dropped to the ground and crouched behind the shadowy corner of the building. Weapon leveled in the direction of the shot, Syd squatted on her heels with her back pressed to Mack's.

"Wait until Dean pulls around closer," Mack whispered to Syd. No footfalls followed the shot, no more noise at all.

Darcy coasted and circled to a stop. Syd followed Mack in a run for the car, each jerking open a car door.

"Go!" Mack ordered. Darcy left the lights off until they hit a main thoroughfare.

Syd glanced at Mack in the back seat. "Shall we assume that was a warning or a coincidence?"

"I think we should assume a truck backfired in the area, don't you think?" The caution was clear in Mack's voice. Darcy didn't seem to be listening and apparently hadn't registered that the noise was likely a gunshot.

Syd laid the plastic bag with the pallet tag on the center console and turned on the center lamp. They tried in vain to read it.

Mack said, "Let's wait until we get back to the studio, it's too faded."

"Agreed." Syd texted Parker, *On our way back.*

A quick reply came: *So glad. ILY, Jen's here with me.*

Syd held the phone up for Mack to read and she nodded. "Darcy, head for my place, okay?"

Parker and Jen met the trio at the front door and Syd locked it behind them quickly. Once inside, Mack produced the red tag which was dusty and faded but, under bright light, clearly stated the date of manufacture and *XC9023, Silver Lake, VA, CacheTech, Inc.* Syd knew they were closer but none of it made sense yet.

Syd photographed it with a pay-as-you-go phone and sent it to an anonymous email address Mack had set up. The address wouldn't be impossible to find, but someone would have to know where to look, and she had made sure it wouldn't be obvious.

❖

"Hi, it's Gilbert." The man shifted his backpack as he perched on a railroad tie overlooking Logan Street. "You, uh, wanted me to call if there was any visitors out here." He liked having a phone and wondered if the nice man would let him keep it. He already said he could have the gun and all the bullets. He felt safe sleeping under the overpass for the first time since he left the halfway house in North Carolina a few months ago. He had made a pillow from his duffel bag and slept with the weighty pistol beneath it.

"What'd you see, Gil?"

"Some people. They were driving a four-door car, a dark color I think, and two people got out an' went into that building that you told me to watch. I was watchin', sir."

"I appreciate that, Gil, you did a great job," the man offered in an encouraging tone. "Can you tell me what they looked like?"

"Well the one drivin' had pretty long blond hair, so I think that one was a girl. The other two had short hair but they kinda didn't look like guys. Big, but not like a guy. I know that don't make much sense, but it was dark. You kinda just get feelings about stuff, stayin' out here, y'know?" Gil was struggling to explain. It would have been nice to have pictures but he wouldn't go back there again.

"Dark hair?"

"I think so but it was real dark, sir."

"That's okay, I think I know what you mean. You did good, Gilbert."

"Can I keep doin' it? Watchin' for ya and have this phone?" Gilbert was desperate.

"Anything else you want to tell me?"

"Um, well, I didn't mean to but the gun went off when they were there. I didn't mean to shoot the gun, I was holding it and it just went off. It was sort of funny to see them run." Gil laughed.

"Yeah, I'll bet. Hey, I'll bring ya some food next time I'm around that way. You did a good job."

Gil's information seemed useful. He couldn't have cared less about the burner phone he had given Gil. The minutes would run out eventually and no one could trace it back to him since he had paid cash at some random convenience store. The gun had been bought from a junkie in an alley, probably stolen, but that wasn't his problem either. He didn't spare Gilbert another thought after they hung up.

❖

"We need to get inside CacheTech or at least get to someone on the inside." Mack addressed the huddled group as they reviewed notes from the past few days. "Someone who can tell us if this pallet tag is a coincidence or if it actually belongs to product."

"Can we get a list of their employees from anywhere?" Darcy looked at Parker and Jen. "I know HR is in your wheelhouse."

"We might not need to if we just want to see a sampling of some employees." Jen pointed to Parker's tablet and she passed it over. "I look at people's previous job history and company colleagues all the time on LinkedIn, Facebook, or other social media sites when we're hiring. We just need to search for people who list their company as CacheTech or CTI. Then I can see if their profile is accessible. You can't imagine what some people put on their public profiles." Jenny looked serious as she scrolled through potentially relevant matches.

"Okay, on Facebook, I have two warehouse associates, an admin, accounting, inventory manager, inventory clerk, warehouse manager." She swiped through the results. "The accounting woman is locked down, can't even see her friends."

"She's less likely to give us any information if she's that conscious about privacy, anyway," Mack ruminated.

"The administrative assistant works for the meetings director. She's wide open but she probably wouldn't be part of the knowledge base from that department anyway."

Mack rubbed Jenny's shoulders while she worked.

"Warehouse guys...but you run the risk of them knowing nothing or being part of it."

"I'm thinking that whoever would be in this would need some higher-level knowledge about controls," Syd offered.

"Surprisingly, not always. A major electronics retailer lost a ton of money in one year, all because one warehouse employee took a small bribe from a vendor. Between the two of them, they managed to siphon product and payments of nearly fourteen million before they were caught," Jen said as she clicked on another profile.

"I stand corrected."

"Status changes every Sunday morning..." She skimmed quickly and read from the page. *"Finally done, ready for my two day break."* She clicked another warehouse clerk's profile. "This guy is partying every Sunday night and posts about sleeping until noon on Monday. So it looks like maybe the warehouse doesn't work on Sunday and Monday." Her fingers flew across the virtual keyboard, mentioning bits and pieces about each employee she found. Darcy dragged her chair closer to watch the operation.

"Warehouse supervisor. I would guess that someone in his position would either be involved or totally oblivious, so probably not useful or too risky, right? Anyway, no pictures to show."

Parker mouthed "I love you" to Syd because she felt it, and because Darcy was sitting too close to her lover.

"Inventory could be sticky. The team presumably would count and report up to management. At least that's how it should work. If they're part of it then they could be fudging numbers and no one would know. When I was at Sexton Building Supply that's how it worked, anyway. Once you knew what you were doing, you would simply ghost count what you knew was missing every time." She kept scrolling and clicked on the inventory manager's page. "Here we go. Here's a Taylor Westin."

"Is his page open?" Syd lobbed toward the small huddle that was now Jen, Darcy, and Parker. Mack was studying her notes and added more as her wife rattled off names.

"That would be *her* page. And definitely open." Jenny showed Darcy and Parker the profile picture of an androgynous woman straddling a platinum Harley Davidson motorcycle.

"And definitely family," Darcy delivered as she whistled appreciatively. "Come to Darcy, baby."

Syd looked at her ex and shook her head.

Parker wondered if Darcy ever thought of anything else but was mildly afraid of the ensuing reply.

"Yes. Definitely family," Mack said, glancing at the screen. "That cover picture is at TPL. I recognize the neon signs from behind the bar."

"Maybe Syd knows her. I mean, she practically lived there once upon a time," Parker blurted out before pinching her lips shut when Syd shot her a look and threw a stress ball at her, connecting with the top of Parker's head. It bounced onto the desk where Parker trapped it and stuck out her tongue at Syd.

Then, conceding the distinct possibility, Syd motioned for them to hold up her profile picture. The girl had short light brown or blondish hair cut into a blended faux hawk. She had an angular face and a sturdy build that would have made her stand out. Syd had known all the regulars at the Pride Lounge, especially anyone presenting potential competition as this woman would have.

"Nope, must have been after I became pastor at the Church of Parker." Syd laughed at the collective groans that fell over the room. Parker lobbed the stress ball back at Syd which she caught easily as she winked back at her. "Steve might know, though." She snapped a picture of the screen with her phone and texted it to her friend who was the longtime bartender at The Pride. *Hey babe, know this girl?*

Yup, Taylor, comes in every Sunday night like clockwork. Doesn't seem like your type, Syd. She likes the girly girls. Thought you did, too.

Just the one, Steve. Thanks for the 411.

Come visit soon, Syd, miss ya.

Will do.

"Okay, he says she's a Sunday night regular. Maybe we could see if we can get a conversation started. She apparently has a taste for the very feminine, so that lets me and Mack out."

Mack smirked at Syd's comment.

"You kind of weren't ever *in*, just so you know." Parker gave her a disapproving look and stifled a laugh.

"My love, it's for the greater good. Mack needs us." Sydney looked innocently at Parker and she folded her clasped hands over her heart.

Not looking up from the tablet, Jenny mumbled, "Uh, Mack, you were never an option either, by the way." Darcy looked like she was enjoying the banter as the two women were reined in by their partners.

"Well, okay. If I must tart myself out to that tasty little treat, I will. But I won't like it. At all. After the first day or two." She laughed and rubbed her hands together.

"Someone better call and warn her to wear body armor and a garlic necklace." Syd looked at Darcy.

"Not nice, Hyatt." Darcy smiled broadly at her.

Parker seemed thrilled that Darcy would be hitting on someone else for a change. Syd couldn't help but notice how fast Darcy had moved targets.

"According to her profile, she's single and yesterday's post says, *Ugh, please no more blind dates! Where is my perfect blonde?*" Jenny read the update to the group.

"Right here, lover," Darcy cooed at the screen, fluffing her blond locks.

Jenny clicked through her pictures. "Okay. She drinks beer, goes to the gym, plays softball and basketball, and drives an SUV. Apparently someone cut her right out of the *Lesbians for Dummies* manual." Jenny laughed. "In fact I think I just read the profile of my own wife."

"What's wrong with that?" Mack feigned hurt.

"Absolutely nothing, sweetheart," she replied as she blew her a dramatic kiss.

"Are you up for this, Darcy?" Mack asked.

"Gee, you want me to offer myself up to a very hot chick in a gay bar and get her to spill her life's story before falling into my soft, waiting arms? I just don't know if I can stand the pain."

Syd watched Parker laugh at Darcy's theatrical presentation, in spite of wanting to dislike her.

Mack looked exasperated. "Actually I want you to gently coax information about her job out of her before you drain her blood."

"You people are just no fun," Darcy sighed and smiled.

The sweaty man dragged three pallets from a white box truck he had parked at the storage facility. The machine wobbled as he awkwardly pushed and shoved them into the large room. He briefly considered this location not appearing as professional looking as the other place, but he couldn't risk the heat. The good part was that he could conceal the inventory in one spot and leave it. A total of twelve pallets sat in the unit waiting for the anxious buyers to come around with their $300,000.

He was being forced to share the proceeds on some of it, but with the extra product he was moving, that was small change. His partner thought small, just moving consumer goods, but he knew he could sell some commercial gear, too. The last units he sold brought $50k a pallet and he had liberated two. No one even knew they were missing.

It amazed him how stupid rich C-level employees could be. They got so used to people kissing their asses and telling them what they wanted to hear, they hadn't missed the crap load of product disappearing over the last six months.

At this rate, he planned to pay off his condo, buy a nicer Benz and settle onto easy street. He would make sure to keep his head down and be ready in case he could move more merchandise no one was paying attention to.

After the last of the pallets was tucked in for the night, he stopped by to pick up his car. His luxury vehicle was always a hit with the ladies at the bar and he steered toward the Silver Lake Country Club. He had no intention of dating these women, just convenient playthings to pass the time. Women were all the same, he'd learned. Socialites weren't any harder to get—they just dressed better.

CHAPTER TWELVE

Syd pushed open the lobby door to let Mia inside. Parker thought she looked thin and pale. Mia smiled at them both as she followed down the hall and into Parker's apartment. She only managed to hold it together for a second after Syd had gathered her in for a hug. Mia's body was shaking against Sydney who simply rubbed stilling hands over her back. Finally Mia backed away and pressed her hands down the front of her shirt to smooth out imaginary wrinkles.

"Sorry. I don't know why that happened. I'm probably just tired." She hugged Parker before straightening her shoulders and looking around the open room. "So, it's really great in here, and it really couldn't be more convenient to work. I can't wait to see it all." Her enthusiasm appeared genuine but Parker imagined being anywhere without Sandy felt like a new punch in the raw places she was collecting in her stomach.

"I keep having to remind myself that Sandy's gone." Mia answered the question no one had asked out loud. Parker wondered how long she would have to endure the pain that must keep renewing in her mind.

"I can't imagine how much it hurts." Sydney pushed her hair behind her shoulders. "We're here for you if you ever need to talk."

"I know," was all Mia managed.

Sydney put a steadying arm around her shoulders and guided her farther into the loft behind Parker. Mia looked around making appreciative remarks about the polished concrete floors, the sparse modern furnishings, and the open industrial kitchen that sat under the bedroom. Then she walked toward the stairs. Parker caught Sydney's eye and they stood at the bottom instead of following her up, giving her a bit of space to adjust and contemplate.

They heard her footsteps circle the room, pausing at the closet and bathroom, before she leaned over the railing to address her friends.

"You did an awesome job up here as well, Parker." She turned to come back down the stairs and glanced back again to take in the sleeping area. "It's so different from the house. Maybe that would help." She shrugged and seemed to fight new tears from spilling down her face. "I have a bedroom set that's mine—well, it was ours. I would like to bring it with me if I could. It might not be healthy and all that, but I guess I'm not ready to give up where she and I slept together just yet."

"Of course," Parker said. "Jen was just saying that they needed a bed for their extra room. I'll talk to her about it."

"I really don't have any other furniture to speak of. I just have our clothes...*my* clothes." She couldn't fight back her tears any longer and Parker wrapped her arms around her. Parker was struck by how fragile she seemed and couldn't fathom processing the grief that Mia was.

"You can take as much time as you want to think about this, Mia," Syd said quietly.

"No, I like it, I really do." She spoke to Parker as she rubbed the heels of her hands against her eyes. "Can I move in next week? I mean, if that's okay. Maybe just a few odds and ends to start with."

"Of course." Parker took her hand when she stepped back. "We can move the rest of my things out this week and it will all be yours. Anything you need, we'll be right over there." She pointed toward the hall and Sydney's loft.

Mia looked around again and, almost to herself, said, "Yeah, I can do this. I'll be fine."

Parker's heart broke for Mia as she clasped her shaky hands together and walked toward the door.

"I can give you a check right now," Mia said suddenly, rummaging through her large shapeless shoulder bag.

"No. Don't worry about it until next month. We'll deal with the lease when you start moving your stuff over, okay?" Parker wanted to make the transition as easy as possible despite her inner businessperson screaming to get it all in writing first. "Call me whenever you think you want to start and we can help." She glanced over at Syd who nodded in agreement.

Mia hugged them both again before she walked to the lobby door and looked back. "You're good friends. Thank you. I'm going to be okay."

The door clicked shut behind Mia. Parker linked her arms around Sydney and walked back into their living room. Parker stood quietly in the embrace, grateful for the foundation they had.

"I have something for you," Sydney spoke softly as she handed over a folded packet of papers she had balanced on the back of the sofa.

Parker looked curious and she unfolded them. "What is this for?"

"It's so, if anything happens, you aren't ever battling *my* mother for property. It will automatically be yours. My lawyer said that it was ironclad."

"Is this about what Sandy's family did to Mia?" Parker refolded the documents and stroked Sydney's cheek.

"Yes, and because it's smart and because you deserve to be taken care of. We already have the medical POA and since you're going to be with me forever…" Sydney winked at her and turned to kiss the hand grazing her cheek.

"I love you. It's not necessary since you aren't going to go anywhere until I've been dead thirty-five years," Parker joked.

"And I wouldn't survive if I ever lost you, Syd." Her voice was serious now. "Let's do mine then, too, okay? Make sure you don't ever have to live across the hall from *my* mother."

"Anything you want, always."

"You're just saying that because we're going to a bar with your ex."

"Actually, I mean it but I do have great timing." Syd smiled, withdrawing her key and pushing Parker toward the car.

❖

When they arrived at TPL, Steve came from behind the bar to kiss Parker on the cheek. "You are lovely as always, my dear."

"Great to see you, too, handsome. We've missed you." Parker smiled and returned the kiss.

"Hey! You barely even stop making drinks when I come in," Syd teased her oldest friend, feigning indignation.

"That's because I do not enjoy fondling *you*." Steve shot Sydney a scornful glance.

"First of all, yuck. And second of all, you actually have no desire to fondle her either, which saves me from breaking your fingers." Syd sent a mock scowl to the very gay bartender.

"Parker, how can you be with such a brute?" Steve said with an exaggerated lisp while he fanned himself which made Parker laugh even harder at the two of them.

"Could we please have a cab, a ginger ale, whatever light beer you have on tap, and my—"

"Scotch? Like I didn't know that one." He rolled his eyes at her. "Quite the little party back there, hmm?"

They teased each other but Syd missed visiting with him as often as she used to at the bar. Once upon a time, she would hit the Pride at least three days a week before selecting some random female companion for the evening. That was all before she started seeing Parker and couldn't make herself touch another woman.

"We just came to watch you *work*." She made air quotes.

"I used to watch *you* work. Now I have to watch Paula Tucker scoop up all the women, Tequila." His pet name for her referenced her talent for separating women from their clothes. It always made her laugh and Syd knew it had long stopped making Parker jealous over her lover's dubious past.

Steve handed over the drinks and Parker carried three of them to the back table.

"Thanks, Steve, I miss you, too." She was handing him her credit card as Darcy walked in wearing tight jeans and a very revealing ribbed tank top. It barely covered her assets which struggled to remain inside the all but transparent white cotton. Her hair was down and blown out into a carefree blond mass across her shoulders. She had lined her eyes heavily and dusted some shimmering powder across her chest. Coral gloss made her lips look full and shiny.

Darcy, locking eyes with Syd, blew an exaggerated kiss in her direction. She stepped next to Sydney and pressed her chest hard against Syd's bare arm.

She spoke quietly with her back to Parker's table. "You know we could skip all this and find a place to go, just the two of us." She flashed her eyes and pursed her lips almost imperceptibly as she spoke. "We were good together once upon a time. I miss you and I really miss how you used to make love to me." If she knew it was inappropriate as hell, Syd couldn't tell, since the words continued to rush from her lips unchecked. "I remember the way my body responded to you. I recall some pretty exquisite nights in our past. I know you do, too, right?"

Syd scowled at her, leaning away. "What goes through your mind, Dean? I know you realize that my girlfriend is sitting right over there. Have a little class." Syd couldn't wait until this case was over.

"What she doesn't know…" Darcy skimmed a finger over Syd's hand, a move which was blocked from Parker's view by

Darcy's body. Sydney jerked back roughly as she fired a territorial stare at her. She then stepped closer to the predatory blonde who seemed to care little about what Sydney wanted.

"Not if you were the last woman on earth." Syd glared and snatched the receipt off the bar, folding it into her wallet with her card. She shook her head, catching Parker's watchful eye from the back booth.

Syd walked quickly to the table. "Drinks okay?" she asked, attempting to change the subject when she noticed Jenny staring at her, too. She kissed Parker very gently and held her mouth to hers for a bit longer than necessary. "Remember, I love you more than anyone ever has, please."

"I do," Parker replied, issuing a contented sigh. She pushed her hand over Sydney's firm thigh and turned to watch Darcy settle herself at the bar. Syd noted that Darcy was seemingly unfazed by the less than pleasant exchange. She perched on the edge of the barstool and arched her back. She planted a straight, shapely leg that ended in a high-heeled boot anchored onto the wood floor, hooking her other foot around the silver leg of the stool. She looked poised and tragically practiced at the art of planned seduction. Syd briefly wished she could choke her.

Shortly after eight p.m., a woman Syd recognized as Taylor Westin cruised into TPL wearing black jeans, heavy black boots, and a gray Silver Lake Fitness T-shirt which stretched tightly over her sculpted arms. Her short dirty-blond hair was spiked over her multipierced ears. An array of heavy silver rings adorned her fingers.

Syd watched Steve slide her a bottle of Coors Light. Knowing what all the regulars drank made Steve very good at his job and filled his tip jar, often more than once a shift.

Tilting the bottle in salute, she rocked back on her heels scanning the array of familiar faces, none of whom seemed to interest her. She looked over the dance floor before heading for a bar stool.

As if waiting for her cue in a choreographed dance, Darcy spun her stool, nicking Taylor's leg with her shoe.

"Oh! I am so sorry." She giggled playfully and covered Taylor's arm with her coral tipped fingers.

"Quite all right." She calmly took a sip from the amber bottle, running her eyes over the lean, leggy blonde. "I'm Taylor, and you are?"

"Darcy." She put out her hand in greeting. "Do you want to sit down and have a drink with me?" Darcy was obvious about finding the dashing Taylor Westin very appealing and did nothing to hide that fact from her.

Taylor took the hand in a very light grip. "Love to."

The foursome watched the exchange as Syd shook her head. "Amazing how easy that was for her." She could still feel Darcy's fingers on her arm and longed to wash the experience from her skin.

Mack chuckled. "Compared to that, I'm not sure I ever had game."

"Oh, you had it, sweetheart. I just had it surgically removed after our second date." Jen nudged Parker who smiled and gripped Syd's leg tighter.

"I'm letting you keep yours until you stop using it on me," Parker whispered playfully to Syd.

"It doesn't work on anyone *but* you anymore." Syd sent her lover a sexy smile.

"Good answer." Parker kissed the words hotly into her girl-friend's ear. Apparently, Syd's shivered response had been what Parker desired as she turned back to the show.

❖

"So, what do you do besides kickboxing with unsuspecting bar patrons," Taylor flirted. She had leaned an elbow onto the surface and stood close to Darcy rather than sitting on the vacant stool, for which Darcy looked unreasonably grateful. Taylor casually dangled her beer from long fingers as she spoke.

"I work in a lab. How about you?" She refocused her offhand response into a return question, using her sexiest voice. "When you're not charming unsuspecting bar patrons, that is." Taylor seemed to be enjoying having a woman so blatantly flirting with her.

"I work for CacheTech. It's a computer company on the west side. I just took over as inventory manager."

"You mean it's your job to know how much stuff they have at all times?" She made sure to sound genuinely fascinated, and then she realized she really was. Darcy watched Taylor's mouth glide over words. Her teeth were white but the bottom row was slightly crowded.

"Yeah, we have a system, so it's usually not too hard." Taylor looked pensive as she lifted the bottle to her lips.

"Usually, huh? That doesn't sound good." Darcy leaned a little closer to her target and suddenly forgot to think of her that way.

"Yeah, I'm just taking it over and we're bleeding inventory like crazy," Taylor said. "And I don't know why I'm boring a very beautiful woman with work stories."

Darcy watched Taylor pick at the corner of the label on her bottle before staring through the heat she felt forming between them.

"Do you want to dance with me, Taylor?" Darcy knew she had a job to do but she felt immensely attracted to the woman with all the answers. She decided she could extract them from her later. The feel of strong arms around her waist might make her forget that Sydney Hyatt and her new lover sat just a few feet away.

In her heels, Darcy looked almost straight into Taylor's eyes. She happily allowed herself to be moved over the floor by the delectable target of her investigation. Darcy leaned her head on her shoulder and closed her eyes, steadied in Taylor's grip and breathing in the scent of her.

After two dances, Taylor led a reluctant Darcy back to her seat, never releasing her grip on her narrow waist. "I think we might need more drinks." Darcy was unwilling to let Taylor go and it had nothing to do with the case.

"Or we could go have a late dinner and talk some more." Taylor held her hand and stroked her skin as she spoke.

"I would really like that." Darcy stared into Taylor's sharp features. "I'm ready if you are." She guided a light hand over Taylor's bare arm, dragging her fingernails behind.

"Give me a minute to make a pit stop and then we're out, okay?" Taylor tapped a finger on Darcy's chin. "Don't go anywhere."

"Right here when you're ready." Darcy watched her lanky frame disappear into the bathroom.

She was shortly joined by Mack, who ambled up to the bar, pretending to drink from her long-empty beer bottle. "Well?"

"It's a start. I'll get something by tonight. We're headed to dinner. Call you later."

"Be careful."

"Yes, Dad."

Mack chuckled and shook her head leaving the empty bottle on the bar.

❖

Taylor Westin overtly appraised the curvy blonde in tight jeans as she slid into the booth across from her at Cadillac Jack's.

"What can I get you?" Taylor asked Darcy, seemingly captivated as she never moved her eyes from Darcy's.

"Beer is fine, light please." Darcy actually had butterflies in her stomach when she looked over the table at Taylor.

"It seems we have some things in common...perhaps." It should have sounded like a line to Darcy, but it didn't. Taylor's delivery didn't make it seem like one either.

After dinner and a variety of conversation subjects, they strolled into the parking lot hand in hand. Darcy had collected the requisite information, enough to get them to a new place in the investigation anyway. She couldn't ask anything more without sounding like she was conducting an interrogation. Besides, she couldn't stop herself focusing on the way Taylor was making her feel. The way Sydney used to, all those years ago.

"I'm having a really nice time, Taylor. I hope I can see you again," Darcy said as she sat in the passenger seat and slid her fingers across the center console tracing the pebbled pattern of the taupe vinyl. Taylor turned toward her and covered the hand with hers.

"I don't want to let you go just yet." Taylor stared at her and smiled briefly.

"Then maybe you shouldn't." Awkward silence was replaced by a tiny whimper when Taylor delivered a ravenous kiss that Darcy thought she would remember for a long time.

CHAPTER THIRTEEN

As she returned from a punishing workout, Syd's phone rang from the slot in the console of her car.

"Sydney!" Zander Young's loud nasal voice made Sydney flinch. "Miss having you riding my jump seat!" The awkward young pilot had landed the county job just out of flight school. Sydney imagined that someone in his well-connected family had pulled some strings on his behalf in order to secure him the coveted position.

"I'm sure you say that to everyone, Zan. Got anything good for me?" Sydney glanced her fingers through her hair, still damp from the shower.

"Well, as a matter of fact I do. Three hours of uncut video of the darks streets of Silver Lake. Don't say I never gave you anything," the young helicopter pilot joked. "So, what's in it for me?"

"How about I don't call Captain Bevins and tell him what a bad boy you've been with his admin in the back of his new Eurocopter?' She was smiling, imagining the look on his pale face.

"Geez, Hyatt. That's just mean!" He seemed to know she was kidding...almost. "How do I get it to you?"

"Where are you? I'll pick it up now."

"I'm at the mall. I can meet you in the parking lot if you want."

"Perfect. I'll be there in ten at the food court. And, Zander, we never had this conversation, okay?"

"What conversation?"

"Thank you. I really appreciate it."

Syd raced back to her studio after collecting the disk and worked continuously until she heard Parker walk through the door at seven p.m. Sydney waved quickly barely breaking her focus on her computer. Parker headed up the stairs, thumbing into the studio. Syd spun in her chair, "I got it, I got it, I got it." She smiled and smoothed her hands over her hair.

"Going to share what you got?" Parker grinned as she was dragged into Sydney's lap.

"First, tell me about your day." Syd took in Parker's weary features and drew her hand down the sides of her structured raw silk blouse.

"Well, I talked to Mia today and she told me she definitely wants to rent the loft. She seemed really relieved, and I think she'll be happy to be close to some friendly faces." Parker leaned back against the arm of the chair. "It will seem weird to have someone else actually *living* there, but I'm glad it will be her."

"It will always be your place, though." Sydney tried to reassure her.

"True, but I much prefer our place, because it's where you are. Oh, and I kind of volunteered you to help her move some boxes next week and help her with the bedroom furniture. Mack and Jen are going to pick mine up tomorrow, okay?"

"Of course. You're doing a good thing, babe." Syd held Parker's hands to her lips, kissing her fingers.

"I think it will be good for her and good for us, not having to maintain two places. Are you still sure you're okay with this, me being here permanently, with no escape?" She smiled playfully.

"Let me think. The gorgeous woman I'm in love with will be here all the time where I can have my way with her at my whim. My libido won't know what to do."

"You have a one-track mind, my love." Parker laughed and inclined her head toward the computer. "Now show me what you got today."

"Okay. Watch." Syd whirled the two of them back toward the monitor and clicked the mouse to start the video. A nasal voice squelched through. *"Reference Signal 36 Team Alpha 22, no visual on suspect at this time."*

Parker crinkled her nose at Syd in question.

"Ignore that. They were looking for the home invasion suspect which is why they were up in the first place. It's here you have to watch." Syd pointed the end of her pen on a white square moving through some dark streets. Syd punched in some keys and a dashed outline framed the white shape and zoomed it to the center of the screen.

"Here's the warehouse." She pointed to a gray square. "Here is where the roll-up door would be. Now, watch the truck make a turn and back in, probably right before Sandy saw them. In fact"— she punched through another sequence and the picture zoomed out and refocused to show a different view—"there's Sandy's patrol car, and there's the truck pulling in. They probably wouldn't have noticed her, not at first, but she couldn't have helped but seen them." The image pivoted and marks on the side of the box truck were barely visible.

"Too bad you can't see the name on it, huh?" Parker looked disappointed.

"I'm insulted that my girlfriend has so little faith in me." Sydney pouted for as long as she could while she made the markings fly from the side of the truck into a new window and start to fill in.

"Well, now you're just showing off," Parker teased as she watched, obviously impressed. She tucked her toes under Sydney's thigh and stared at the screen. Suddenly the image of a computer plugging into a globe began to darken and spin onto the left side of a page. Seconds later, a tall building materialized onto the other side with the same logo and the name CacheTech, Inc., printed beneath it.

"Oh my God, Syd! You did it!" Parker hugged her neck and peppered her cheeks with kisses. "You're a genius. Did you call Mack?"

"I was just about to when you came home and I wanted to show you first. Besides, Mack won't kiss me and call me a genius." She smiled at Parker, but studied her face carefully. She saw dark shadows under her eyes.

"She better not. I'm going to change and meet you back here. I'm so happy to be home and to see you...and this!" She unclipped her cell phone from the waist of her skirt and handed it to Syd. "Call Mack before I do and blow the surprise."

"I love you, baby." She smiled as she watched Parker grin back at her from the top of the stairs. As Parker tapped down the metal steps, Syd called after her, "Let's go away together when this is over. I think we could both use a break."

"If there will be massages and lots of sex, I'm in," Parker called back.

Syd dialed Mack while she compressed the rough copy of the video and emailed it to Mack's covert account. She placed a thumb drive with the raw video next to the pallet ticket in a pocket folder marked *Recipes* and closed it into the safe drawer.

Mack answered the phone. "We're headed over there in an hour. I'll call Dean. Is that okay?" Mack spoke quickly at the prospect of some new investigative direction.

"Sure, see you then," Sydney replied and dropped the phone onto the counter. She had hoped to see the aerial video circle back to the warehouse but the final twenty minutes of footage showed only frames of a small neighborhood and a line of uniform backyards. By the time the video panned back to the warehouse area, the crime scene had already been discovered and the video documented only a burst of flashing lights. She grabbed Parker's phone and headed down to warn her of the impending visit.

❖

Syd had just dropped onto the couch next to her when Parker balanced on her knees and straddled Syd's lap. She pushed her dark lover back into the cushions.

"How am I supposed to seduce you if we always have company?" She bit at the tip of Syd's sharp nose and then snuggled against her chest.

"I guess you're going to have to quit your job and walk around here in negligees until this gets resolved." Syd sounded playfully resigned as she folded her arms around Parker's back.

"That doesn't sound like much of a challenge for you, you know." She wriggled around to feel more of Syd's body against hers.

"How about if you promise to turn me down at least once a day?" Syd arched back to look into her eyes and winked.

"I'd like to say I could do that, but I'd be lying." Parker rotated her hips into Sydney watching her eyes dilate at the unexpected sensation.

"Did I mention we have an hour?" Sydney breathed hard into Parker's neck as she ran her tongue along her collarbone.

"Can you ravish me sufficiently in that amount of time?"

"Twice," Syd teased.

At that, Parker jumped up and ran down the hall. Syd followed her heart into the bedroom.

"What do you want from me, Hyatt?" Parker purred as Syd carefully began sliding her mouth up Parker's body beginning from her toes.

"All of you, always."

Parker caught a ragged breath as Syd's tongue drew teasing circles on her sensitive inner thighs and her long fingers pinched at her pebbling nipples.

Syd delighted when every part of Parker's body responded to her touch.

"Yes. Please. There."

Parker's staccato demands whipped through Sydney and her tongue found and trapped her center in the exquisite prison of her burning mouth. Her fingers moved to stroke her drenched skin as Parker's guttural moans spoke of uncaged desire and an imploring need for her.

"Syd, please. I can't wait."

Those were the last words that Sydney heard before she sent Parker crashing toward her edge. She ground against Sydney and shuddered into a blissful release.

As Parker always did, she found her lover's neck and wrapped around her, savoring the bliss of being once again in her arms. "Don't let go." Parker heard and felt Sydney's sympathetic surrender. Syd regularly insisted that satisfying Parker created a sensation that abrogated her physical need to be touched.

"Never."

Within minutes, the jarring sound of the buzzer startled them out of their silent interlude. Parker groaned, rolling out from Sydney's arms. She moved to dress while Sydney walked to open the door.

"Tell them they're early," Parker called after Sydney.

Parker had managed to sufficiently wrangle her hair and clothes into their pre-ravished state and joined Mack and Jen in the kitchen.

"And where is my baby?" Parker noticed Olivia's absence immediately.

"Sorry. Baby fix will have to wait. We dropped Olivia with Richard and Allen in case the meeting ran late." Mack rubbed her hands over her neck as she answered. Darcy suddenly glided through the door behind them.

"I guess the official assembly has yet to begin?" All eyes focused on her as she dropped her purse onto the counter. Parker walked barefoot to Sydney and accepted a knowing glance and a chaste kiss. She knew the glow was likely still evident on her face.

"So?" Mack asked impatiently of Darcy.

"So? Can I have a chair, a drink, anything? Sheesh!" Darcy laughed as Syd slid a beer across the kitchen island and dramatically glided out a stool, sweeping a hand over the seat.

"Much better." Darcy took a healthy swig from her beer and placed it on the bar. "Okay, so she *is* over the inventory group—she was promoted to inventory manager last week when the other guy stopped showing up for work last month. She started digging and found out that the tally sheets that each one of the clerks turns in to the manager weren't matching with what was recorded in the system. The system looked like it balanced except for the odd one-offs for miskeys or breakage. So she started counting the warehouse herself, entering her numbers on a separate spreadsheet, and came up with a bunch of missing units. She didn't tell me how many, but she seemed to think it was a lot. She took a bunch of the records home to try to figure out why her numbers looked so bad and the other guy didn't seem to have any problems. When she asked about it, she was told to stick to reporting counts and not to worry about corporate numbers, since those were made up of more than her inventory counts."

Syd stared at her. "What did you do to get her to tell you all of this?" Her tone was wry.

"Nothing really. We just really hit it off and we hung out for a long time. We stayed out and talked and I pieced a lot of the stuff together." Darcy looked as if she got lost in the recall for a moment before resuming the account of her evening's assignment.

"I also found out that they track everything by model number, date, lot number, and serial number. It's on all the inventory sheets that the team uses to count every night and then on the automated ones that go up to management, which of course are supposed to match. She was able to estimate that over the last six months, about five to ten percent of the local inventory has gone missing even though accounting shows a relatively flat count. I'm not sure she really meant to tell me that part." Darcy paused to make sure everyone was still with her, then continued, "Tay says that the missing stuff was mostly just laptops and other high-end PCs until two weeks ago when a bunch of commercial switch gear went missing valued at about ten *K* each."

Mack wrote furiously in her notebook.

"And no, my skeptical little partners in crime solving, I didn't trade data for sexual favors." She managed to look slightly insulted. Parker thought she seemed mildly disappointed she hadn't compelled Taylor to explore more of her. "Anyway, all that's to say that if you ever need to get a warrant on this, ask for the CUPS for the dates that you want—the CacheTech unit production sheets. She uses them to introduce new inventory into the system when it's manufactured."

"Very nicely done, Darcy." Parker gave her a pat on her arm. Guiltily, she wondered if she was just happy that Sydney's ex was focused on another woman, at least for the moment.

Mack high-fived her. "Do you think she would cooperate if we ever need a witness?" Mack looked like she wasn't sure they would ever manage to get that far.

"Absolutely. It pisses her off that she finally got an opportunity to do the job and it's all screwed up."

Syd led the trip up to her office to play the helicopter video. When it was finished, she spun away from the screen.

"Can we review here?"

Parker watched the very linear thinker in Syd list the known data to see where the remaining holes might be. She started writing bullet points on a blank page.

"A: What if Sandy sees a truck, possibly with pallets of product in the warehouse being picked up or delivered by a guy that doesn't do much pallet jack maneuvering? There would be no other reason for a CTI pallet ticket to be in a warehouse rented by and under construction for a textiles company. B: So someone could be stealing or an employee is embezzling big dollars over a short period of time. They would have to eliminate anyone, especially a cop, who might have witnessed them in the midst of handling stolen goods to stop from being discovered."

Syd was on a roll, and Parker enjoyed watching her in her element.

"C: We have confirmed, by this video, that the truck belongs to CTI—meaning someone who is authorized to use the equipment is likely responsible for embezzlement. And D: If corporate honchos are reporting positive inventory, there seems to be a major cover-up, at least partly led by someone in the company with some clout. It sure would be nice to establish or refute any connection between the SLPD and, we assume, someone who is moving product from CTI. We also need to be sure we can prove that the SLPD connection was absolutely not Sandy."

Mack glared at Syd without comment and began reviewing the list. "We need to show exactly who else might have been there that night. Otherwise, it's just a lot of circumstantial bullshit and nothing to officially suggest that the two things are even related. Not to mention that I would just look like a bitter rank whore with a hunch who's trying to exonerate a dirty cop...or protect one if we make a link to someone inside the department."

"You got stonewalled, kicked off the case, and denied a standard warrant in the shooting of a fellow officer. A cop being involved or at least part of the cover-up is the only thing that makes sense," Sydney reasoned.

Mack replied, "Why would a cop even get involved in something like this? You have to assume that they're getting a cut. Who stands to benefit at SLPD and, of course, CacheTech?"

"We need to know why this warehouse and how they got access." Syd picked up Mack's train of thought. "Maybe the connection is more direct that we're giving them credit for."

❖

Back in the kitchen, Syd laid a block of cheese and French bread on the counter. As she bit a corner of bread, Parker started to tap away at her tablet. "So if I want a computer, I go to a big box store or order it online. If I want a cheap used computer I go to eBay or Craigslist, right? What if I'm trying to get a deal on a new one? I put in my search parameters to include the words *new* or *NIB* for *new in box*, right?"

Syd nodded and everyone watched her fly through the screens. "Why don't we just see if we can go buy one, or fifty?" She flipped the screen around and showed nineteen results for the words *new* and *CacheTech* sorted by highest to lowest dollar amount.

Mack started reading the posts and making notes. Several of them appeared to be related to the same seller location with roughly the same wording and, in most cases, the same amateur looking photo displaying refurbished units. The two highest priced and seemingly unrelated ones were $9200 each for 48-port switches which the seller claimed he bought for his business and then realized he didn't need.

"Yeah, I regularly spend eighteen grand out of my business account on shit I'm not even sure I need." Syd sighed at the thought. "My accountant would kill me. No one does that."

Parker looked happy with her contribution. "You know, my little friend from the Silver Lake Ball made a big deal about working for CacheTech. I could always arrange a business meeting with him. Or just call one of these sellers to see if he would clue me in that something fishy might be afoot."

"Absolutely not." Syd dropped the words on the conversation abruptly as if she had been lugging a heavy weight too long. She felt her heart drum loudly in her chest as a faint sheen of sweat glazed down her back. She fought the urge to move Parker from the room and them both from the conversation, instead gripping the stone counter of the kitchen island.

"I beg your pardon?" Parker turned to stare at Syd, her jaw set and tense. Syd had never seen Parker's current expression in the entire time they had been together.

"I said no." Syd's words sounded much more stern than she had intended.

Mack turned and spoke directly to Syd. "We just need a line to pull, Syd. Maybe this guy isn't the one involved, but Parker could just have a conversation on the phone. Parker wouldn't have to actually meet. Or she could talk to this Bryce guy like a potential CTI customer." Mack continued the planning as if to take the sting out of the statement.

Parker's eyes fired at her girlfriend as she ignored Mack. "Or you could please enlighten me on *your* plan, Ms. Hyatt." Her face was flushed. "I've been here every moment you have, in case you forgot."

When Syd didn't reply, Parker addressed the room. "Excuse me, I forgot I had some laundry going at my place." She turned and quietly left the apartment.

Syd knew Parker had been preparing the loft for Mia and there was nothing left in the small unit, certainly nothing in the way of laundry. She rubbed her temples and squeezed her eyes closed, fighting the alarms that sounded.

Jenny broke the silence. "It's not like she would be in danger, Syd. It's just a call. You let Darcy go with you to the warehouse. Besides, even if they did meet, it would be in a public place, not some dark parking lot. There's no harm in that." Jen was obviously trying to encourage Sydney to back off before she did major damage. Darcy was shifting uncomfortably; perhaps even she saw the inequity in Syd's response.

Syd could only focus on the dark terror that consumed her, the same feeling she had when she realized Parker had been hurt by Becky Weaver. Although that unstable woman was now committed to an institution, Syd had barely climbed out of the emotional well after that night. Mack, of all people, should understand her guilt and, even more, her fear, but she knew she was not handling this well.

"How about we all get back together tomorrow, okay? Everyone's tired." Jen handed the keys to Mack and nodded to Darcy. Syd was grateful Darcy wasn't given the option of staying there alone. She knew she had enough damage control ahead of her.

When the door shut behind them, Syd bent over the counter and dropped her forehead onto her hands. She was frantically searching for a stable island in the sea of her irrational panic. She wondered if she would always react like this to any possible threat to their relatively new connection. After a few minutes, Syd gathered a precarious grip on her emotions and made the long walk across the short hall.

She heard Parker throwing laundry, piece by piece, into the washer. Syd caught the slam of the washer door as the rumble of the industrial door announced her arrival. Parker was fumbling with the controls when Sydney's unsteady voice found her.

"Can we talk please?" She was miserable as she watched Parker jerk her hamper to the side of the laundry closet and shut the doors. Sydney's hands jammed in the pockets of her worn jeans.

"Haven't I already heard what you have to say, Sydney? As my personal decision maker and given my obvious cognitive handicaps, it's just so lucky for me you were there." Parker's voice was not quite a yell but she seemed to vibrate with anger.

"Parker, please. Will you listen to me for a second? Please?" Sydney's breath caught and her voice faltered. She had never seen the look currently on Parker's face, certainly not directed at her. She bit her lip in a weak effort to quell the emotion that pounded over her body.

"Of course, but be sure you get me flash cards in case I miss something. I can study while I'm up in my padded room." She crossed her arms defiantly and stared at Sydney as if daring her to speak.

Sydney walked toward her and Parker leaned back against the kitchen island. She held out her hand to stop Syd from reaching her.

"Stay there." Parker seemed to be planning to stay furious.

"Baby, I didn't mean it to come out like that." She raked her fingers through her hair, a habit usually inspired by deep thought or abundant stress. Despite the roaring river of adrenaline coursing through her veins, she forced her unsteady voice to continue.

"The thought of you being hurt again makes me crazy. Do you not understand that I have a picture of you bleeding or standing there with a knife to your throat flashing through my mind a hundred times a day, even now?" Sydney pointed to the doorway where she first saw Parker that night. She forced herself to continue. "I have nightmares about not being able to protect you from that crazy woman, and the fact that she got to you at all was *my* fault. Do you not understand that?" Her words escaped in a rush.

"I'm not made of glass, Sydney." Parker thought how many times she had told people that in her lifetime. For some reason someone was always trying to insulate her world and it made her feel like a child.

"I *know* you're not, but what if something happened to you and I couldn't stop it? Or I didn't do anything to protect you before something happened and I knew I should have?"

Parker suddenly screamed at Sydney, more out of frustration than anger now. "The Becky thing wasn't your fault and it's not your job to take care of me!" As soon as she finished the sentence she willed the words back. She knew they had been wrong. She hadn't meant to sound so callous.

Sydney's face leapt from sadness and hurt to all-out fury. She moved toward Parker, this time not waiting for permission.

"Then whose job is it, Parker? If something happens to me, whose job is it to take care of me?" She locked her arms against the counter and around Parker, still not touching her.

Parker fought the urge to let Syd cover every inch of her with her body.

"Mine." Parker's voice was quiet and measured now. She suddenly felt small and petty but she still wasn't ready to surrender. "It's just that you told everyone that Darcy could take care of herself. But as soon as I said that I wanted to help, you shut me down like some misguided kid who doesn't know the bike is too big or the wall is too high. You embarrassed me in front of *her*." Parker's voice trembled involuntarily as she searched for the words to further explain.

"Sydney, she's already hitting on you behind my back. Hell, in front of my face at the Pride. And it just made me feel humiliated and…insignificant, I guess." The fight had left her voice but the core foundation of the combat still lingered. "Maybe I can't bench press a person or engage in mortal martial arts combat, but I'm not insignificant, I'm not weak, and I am not helpless." A bit of her anger rose again as she bunched her fists at her sides. Her cheeks felt hot and she battled the warring emotions.

"Are you kidding me, Parker? First of all, I wouldn't touch Darcy Dean with someone else's hand. I told her about that bullshit stunt at the Pride, by the way. If it happens again, she's done. I can't wait until this is over so she isn't in our home anymore or around you.

"And for the record, I think you're the most resilient and capable person I know. But these people dropped a veteran officer with one bullet over some stolen computers. Do you really think they'll hesitate to end someone else if it feels too hot for them? I couldn't live with that, Parker. I couldn't live knowing that I did nothing to stop it, because I *can't* live without you. You and I both saw what it did to Mia. I don't think I would handle it even *half* as well as she is." She looked directly at Parker now, her eyes welling with tears.

Parker watched her resolutely refuse to let them spill.

"Every time we're together, you curl into me and tell me not to let go, yet every time you could be hurt or could be in danger, that's all you want me to do—to let you go—and I can't." Syd's jaw clenched as if she was trying not to lose control of the precarious hold she had on her emotions.

The last time she had seen Sydney cry was when Parker was being wheeled into an emergency room. She knew the pain from that day would never be far from her soul.

"It sounds cliché," Syd said quietly, "but even the thought of you being hurt...I told you, I can't breathe, Park."

She stared at Sydney for a few seconds before she took the step that closed the remaining distance between them. "I'm sorry. I just let her get to me." Parker gripped Sydney's shoulders and pressed her face against her chest.

Sydney crushed her into an almost painful embrace and pushed her mouth near Parker's ear. "I cannot lose you. I just can't. Please don't ask me to not try to protect you."

"Okay." She looked up at Syd and wished she could take everything back. "I guess it was just her." Her tears came in earnest as she laughed. "I'm being ridiculous."

"No, you aren't. It wasn't my finest moment. I'm sorry I embarrassed you." Syd kissed her and said softly, "I may not always say things the way I should—my heart just took over my brain. I will fix it tomorrow."

"You don't have to." Parker tilted her head onto Syd's arm which was still locked around her shoulders.

"Yes, I do. I love you with everything I am. I should have seen the potential fallout from this and fixed it before. I never expected to see Darcy again, let alone have to host her every other night in our home." She was still visibly angry. "There is no excuse for me not handling this sooner."

"I love you, Syd." Parker wanted to wash the past few moments away as she buried herself against the person who had become the touchstone of stability in her life.

"Please come home with me," Sydney nearly whispered the words, not holding her quite as tightly. Her fingers were tangled in Parker's hair as she spoke.

"Okay." She gripped Sydney's waist as they walked.

"What about your laundry?" Syd looked down at her, taking in the sheepish grin Parker fought to hide.

"It's three dust cloths and some pink boxers I wore when I was painting the bedroom. I think they'll be okay." Her serious matter-of-fact delivery made it harder not to laugh. "Tomorrow I'll be washing a rusty towel and the hamper liner."

Syd laughed until they slid the door closed and headed to their bed. Syd wrapped her body over Parker protectively as a peaceful sleep washed over them.

CHAPTER FOURTEEN

Finally home from a long shift, Darcy twisted the sheets around her red-tipped toes as she dialed the phone. She worried the drawstring on her blue cotton sleep shorts as she listened to the phone ring in her ear.

Taylor Westin's voice sounded happy as she answered, "Hey, you."

"Is it too late to call?" Darcy felt her pulse race at the charming sound of Taylor's voice.

"Not for you. I was hoping I would hear from you today."

Darcy stared at her bedroom ceiling and corralled the stomach flutters courtesy of the breezy first weeks of a promising relationship. They had seen each other for a brief coffee date only the day before but she couldn't stop thinking about the enchanting woman who'd fallen into her life at a bar.

"It's just been a crazy day and this is the first chance I've had to call you." She breathed heavily into the phone before she noticed it. She hoped Taylor hadn't heard it. "I wish I could see you."

"What's stopping you then? I'm just lying here watching TV," Taylor answered coolly.

"Is that an invitation, Taylor?" Darcy worked hard to quell the eager tone in her voice and hoped she didn't sound as if she was rushing things.

"Indeed it is. Want me to come pick you up?" Taylor asked.

"No, I can find you, you aren't far from me—just text me the address. See you in fifteen minutes?" Darcy danced out of her sleep shorts and replaced them with a black miniskirt and flip-flops while raking fingers and then a brush through her long hair, hoping for a miracle. She thought of trying to dust some makeup over her face but opted instead for the natural look. She hoped Taylor would see it one morning soon, anyway.

"I'll be here." Taylor's voice sent chills over Darcy's skin as she walked through a light spray of perfume and collected her keys. She sped the few miles to Taylor's and talked to herself reassuringly, hoping to calm her nerves.

Darcy rang the doorbell and could hear the hems of Taylor's jeans dragging along carpet before she stood there, barefoot, at the open apartment door.

Darcy breathed in the sight of a casual Taylor Westin leaning on the door before she reached to pull her inside.

"Hi," Taylor offered.

Darcy exhaled as electricity pricked over her arms.

"Hi." Darcy stepped to slide her fingers up the side seams of the black tank top stretched taut over Taylor's chest, and Taylor placed a firm kiss against Darcy's mouth in greeting.

Taylor pushed the door closed behind her guest and abruptly pressed Darcy's body between hers and the door, apparently unwilling to temper the desire that burned between them. The next kiss was deep and hot and thirsty. Darcy couldn't have pinpointed who had started it. She dropped her bag at her feet and scraped her fingers up through Taylor's hair as she felt the fascinating woman press her wiry frame harder onto Darcy's torso. The pressure was glorious and tantalizing, stirring a smoldering heat that spread through her. They spent another few fiery minutes exploring each other when the kisses became more desperate.

"Want something to drink?" Taylor breathed the offer between the kisses she delivered near Darcy's ear.

"I want you." Darcy watched for Taylor's reaction which came in the form of a low growl. She allowed herself to be led into Taylor's bedroom. Darcy heard a whimper escape her throat as Taylor pushed her smoothly onto the mattress.

"We don't have to..." Darcy couldn't pull her bruised lips from Taylor's mouth but wanted Taylor to be certain about the lengths they might travel on only their third evening together.

Taylor responded by smiling seductively at her before reaching for the bottom of Darcy's T-shirt and pushing it over her head. Darcy grabbed the button on Taylor's jeans, jerking it open.

She gave Taylor Westin free rein over her body.

Taylor skimmed her mouth over Darcy's naked flesh. Darcy fought to maintain control over her building emotions, and over the writhing figure that was burning a path across every inch of her pale skin. Taylor locked eyes with Darcy as their tongues glided over each other hungrily, demanding satisfaction.

Darcy pushed Taylor's hand lower as she was suddenly consumed by the need to be owned by the figure above her. "I need you to touch me now."

Taylor wasted no time claiming her new lover. She drove her to a punishing climax until Darcy begged for a breath and then begged for more.

Darcy briefly considered the neighbors when she screamed Taylor's name for the third time. How would she would tell Taylor about the calculated ruse that placed her in the bar and in Taylor's life in the first place? Darcy further drowned the thought by greedily compelling Taylor's surrender with her eager mouth.

❖

A short five hours later, Darcy heard an alarm sound and pressed an unfamiliar pillow over her face. The smell of heady cologne found her nose and she moved sleepily toward the middle of the queen mattress. She shifted the pillow off one eye and found Taylor smiling down at her, propped onto her tattooed right arm.

"Morning."

Darcy thought Taylor's voice sounded like velvet and melted chocolate as she recalled the aerobic night of naked bodies and lustful proclamations.

She curled against Taylor and angled her head into her neck, noticing three parallel scratches her fingernails had undoubtedly left there. "God, you're so sexy." Taylor seemed to feel every syllable as Darcy brushed a lingering kiss over her smooth shoulder and pushed her body still closer to Taylor's, skimming a teasing finger over Taylor's breast.

Taylor combed her fingers through Darcy's hair and returned the kiss lightly. "I'll give you a year to stop telling me lies like that."

Taylor's smile made Darcy realize that she wanted to find herself in Taylor's arms over and over. She hadn't felt like this about anyone since Syd.

"Are you going to regret this later?" Darcy was cautious about letting herself hope this was more than a casual romp to Taylor.

"I'll only regret not seeing you again when we both get off work tonight." Taylor cupped her chin as she delivered a rough kiss below her ear making her groan into Taylor's ear.

"Can we talk later, too?" Darcy was guarded as she hoped to stem the tide of a potential disaster as soon as possible. She had found her because she was the CacheTech inventory manager, but Darcy wanted to hold on to her for many different reasons, none having to do with stolen computers.

"Anything you like, Darc."

Even the way Taylor casually shortened her name made her sigh a contented breath. She suddenly felt terrified by the impending conversation. But not enough to stop desire from overtaking her one more time as Taylor glided her naked body over Darcy's willing flesh.

❖

"So, do I need to help you move the body or does Sydney Hyatt still have a pulse?" Jenny sauntered into the office and plopped into her boss's guest chair, waiting for what she knew was the rest of the story and having nothing to do with laundry.

Parker's best friend and colleague let a black microsuede pump dangle casually from her tiny foot as she waited for the answer. Parker addressed her formally, "Well, I've decided to let her live another day, pending a regular review of the case and her commitment to never repeat such egregious acts again."

"I see. Will there be punitive consequences?" Jenny looked just as seriously at Parker, biting her lip to keep from laughing.

"I've requested nightly groveling followed by mind-blowing sexual favors."

"Well played, Ms. Duncan."

"Thank you, Mrs. Foster. Shall we get some coffee?" The pair laughed at their inside joke until they returned from the break room together.

"So"—Jenny spoke carefully in spite of the earlier levity—"what's going to happen with the sleazy Ms. Dean? I spoke to Mack on the way home and she thinks she can meet with her separately if that's more comfortable for you." Jenny crossed her legs and sipped her decaf coffee. Parker knew she longed for real coffee and an occasional glass of wine but she wouldn't risk it as long as she was nursing her daughter.

"That's not necessary, really, but thank you. I think it would be worse if it looked like I was so insecure we had to banish her from the house." Parker chuckled but seemed far away for just a second. "Anyway, Syd's going to talk to her about it, and if she agrees to stop, then we leave it alone. Sydney can be very persuasive when she wants to be." She recalled the run-in with Bryce Downing at the ball. Sydney Hyatt could look dangerous and be dangerous in the right circumstances.

"She was just trying to protect you, Park. Mack says she still thinks about the Becky thing all the time," she said quietly. "I think she still feels guilty about it and we all saw you that night. It was pretty terrifying, Parker. I can't imagine what Syd saw when she came in. You were bleeding and shaking and…"

"I know. And I know what it was. I just wasn't ready to hear it that way, not in front of Darcy. And that's *all* it was." Parker allowed the flash of memory when Syd had held a gun to Becky's head. Parker had to drag her out of the blind rage to stop her from killing the woman who was intent on winning Syd at all costs.

"I told her that last night, after you walked out. She knew it was the *way* she said it, too."

Parker pushed away the memory of the night they'd returned from the hospital. "Does she talk about it a lot with Mack?" Parker was suddenly worried that Syd had been hiding her demons too well.

"I don't think they talk about it *a lot*, but Mack likes to check in with her, and she knows she still feels some responsibility." Jenny sounded apologetic for betraying confidences.

"Jen, it wasn't her fault. Syd didn't know Becky was crazy. I don't want her to be guilty about it forever." Parker wished she could slide her arms around Sydney at that moment. The tender underbelly of her tough-woman persona broke Parker's heart every time.

"Your knight takes her job seriously, you know." Jenny smiled.

Jenny often referred to Sydney that way, and Parker thought it was incredibly accurate. She had seen Sydney make it her job to be there for her. As if it was as much a part of her as breathing.

"Yeah, I know."

Parker smiled to herself as Jenny walked back to her office. She tapped out a text to Sydney who was unaccustomed to hearing from her during the workday. Both their schedules made it difficult.

Thank you for loving me like you do.

What did I do to deserve that? Syd replied.
Everything, all the time. I love you.
Love you, baby.

❖

"Hi." Darcy's nerves were close to the surface when Taylor answered.

"Hey, you." Taylor sounded very happy to hear from her new lover.

"I want to see you tonight." Darcy spoke with her forehead on the steering wheel scraping her fingernails along her thigh nervously.

"I'm glad to hear it. I hated leaving you this morning. It was hard to pull myself away."

Darcy took a deep breath and launched into what she needed to say. "You have no reason to trust me, Taylor, but I might need to ask you to take me somewhere tonight. Would you do that, if I asked?" Darcy now plucked at a tiny string on the seat upholstery in her car as she sat in the parking lot outside the lab.

"Should I be worried about this mysterious field trip?" Taylor sounded perplexed as she answered carefully.

"No, it's nothing crazy. I just…want you to meet some friends with me, okay?" Darcy moved the phone away from her mouth so Taylor wouldn't hear her heavy, anxious breathing through the microphone. She wondered if she should attempt further explanation but was fairly certain it would just make her sound crazy.

"Okay." Taylor delivered the word slowly and cautiously.

"I really want to see you, Taylor. I really…I really like you."

"Me, too. Are you all right?" Taylor was clearly worried.

"I will be when I see you." Darcy thought it was absolutely true.

"What time should I pick you up?" Taylor asked.

"Give me an hour?"

"See you then."

Darcy recalled the sensation of Taylor's body pressed against hers just hours before and hoped her pending revelations wouldn't dampen any burgeoning feelings she had for her, regardless of the puzzling request she was making.

"Bye, Tay." Darcy was a combination of wistful and nervous as she threw the phone onto the passenger seat and scrubbed her hands over her face.

CHAPTER FIFTEEN

Darcy was the last to arrive at the studio when Parker opened the door for her. Parker looked at her judiciously, trying to assess what was different about the woman who until now seemed so focused on inserting herself in her relationship.

"Hi." Darcy stared at the floor as she addressed the group, already assembled around the bar.

Sydney watched the uncharacteristically sedate Darcy Dean bring down the energy in the room with a single word. Syd slid the amber bottle of beer to her, and she picked at the label rather than suck down the alcohol.

Sydney found Parker's ear. "Trust me to be right back?"

"I trust you with everything, love," Parker said matter-of-factly.

"Excuse us for a minute?" Sydney pushed two fingers into Darcy's back and directed her away from her intrigued guests and toward the end of the hall.

Darcy looked puzzled as Sydney turned her less than gently to face her.

"What are you doing?" Darcy spun away from Syd's grasp with a smirk.

"Okay, Dean, here it is," Sydney continued without further preamble. "I don't know what's going on with you right now but you need to listen to me carefully. I spent a lot of years working through our relationship. I can handle what happened. I fought the legacy of whatever that was a long time ago."

Darcy looked shocked as Sydney continued pointing a rigid finger at her chin.

"I can manage you and whatever the little game is that you're playing, but Parker isn't going to be some collateral damage in the process. Do you understand that this isn't some bar challenge to see who takes home the most women? It isn't for me anyway." Darcy stepped back reflexively at Sydney's ferocity.

Sydney noticed Darcy's reaction and broke her stare. She suddenly turned away, roughly grazing her hands through her hair before she turned back and allowed herself to continue. Her only thought was fixing the things she'd allowed to make Parker un-characteristically insecure.

"Dean, I've truly loved one person in my life and she's standing in that kitchen. If I ever have to choose, you won't be any consideration at all, clear?"

Darcy nodded. The words had obviously stung. She looked at Syd as if trying to find an appropriate moment to enter the conversation.

"I hear you. I get it. I really do," Darcy said quietly staring at the floor. "Honestly, Syd. I loved you and it took forever to not want you back. When I saw you again, I just felt the old feelings. But I get it. It was a shitty thing to do at the bar and I owe Parker an apology."

Sydney was dubious.

"I'll take care of it, really." Darcy shifted her gaze and Sydney watched her gather her composure before she spoke again. "While we're here—and believe me, I realize this may not be the best time to ask—but I might need your help. I know you don't think I deserve it, but I feel stuck." Darcy pushed the pieces haphazardly into place. "I spent last night with Taylor Westin. I think I really feel something for her. I'm terrified that if I tell her how we met or why, actually, she won't wait for the whole explanation or believe that I really could care about her."

Sydney paced along the narrow hall and played the scenario in her mind before she spoke. "Here's the deal. I'll help you. As long as you don't ever ask me to hurt Parker or overlook you doing it again, deal?"

Darcy nodded and smiled at her old lover. "You really have it bad, don't you?"

Sydney shook her head and fought the grin that sought to overtake her mouth. "You have no idea." She hoped they had arrived at a place where they could begin again as friends.

The group was quietly offering theories and next steps to each other when Syd and Darcy walked through the kitchen. Darcy stepped over to Parker and urged her gently into the living room.

Syd watched them move toward the wall dividing the spaces. Darcy began what Syd hoped would be the last uncomfortable exchange with Parker. "So, I've been kind of an asshole, huh?" Parker shrugged, then flashed a wry smile at Syd. Syd nodded at Parker and hoped the awkward moment would fade quickly.

Darcy cleared her throat, and Syd gave her the floor.

She looked at Mack first. "I've been giving this a lot of thought, and I think you need to talk to Taylor Westin. She can give us some help that we can't get otherwise." She rushed the words out when Mack started to shake her head. "I know she'll help us. She loves her job and all this missing inventory is making her look bad. She wants the answers as much as we do." Darcy glanced at Sydney as if hoping for some assistance.

Syd was speaking honestly when she backed Darcy's suggestion. "I kind of agree, Mack. We don't know who the players are over there and she does. I know it's a risk, especially in light of Darcy's new feelings"—she paused and watched the group focus collectively as a rare blush found Darcy's cheeks—"but if we're going to push this over, this might be the best way."

Syd watched Mack process the latest risk to her career.

Mack absently fingered the relief carved into the brass of the badge clipped to her belt as she responded. "I suppose if you look at it from the outside, I have a picture of a truck and weak circumstantial evidence linked to it. Until I can prove that inventory is missing and that it was likely in that warehouse, then I have nowhere to even start. I couldn't even report this. All the evidence I think I have wouldn't get a second look from the DA. I know that, on its face, all this amounts to is speculation." Mack sighed and sent a warning look to Darcy. "This would burn us both with the city."

"I know, Mack. I trust her. I don't know why, but I do."

After a few seconds, Mack nodded. Darcy dragged her cell from her back pocket and walked out to her car.

The fateful phone call could end a lot of things that were just starting and Darcy secretly prayed she could stop a runaway train with her words. She sat on the concrete landing outside her door and watched the headlights from Taylor's Highlander sweep over the lot. She felt a flush wash over her when she saw Taylor scan the building and smile over at her.

"Hey, sexy," Taylor offered and Darcy wondered if she would have the chance to always feel Taylor's voice the way she did now.

"Hi." Darcy stood and fell solidly into Taylor's embrace. She thought about how they fit together and struggled against the urge to drag her inside instead of having the conversation she dreaded starting. "Before we go, I need to explain something. Please hear me out before you get mad, okay?"

Darcy folded back onto the step and patted the space of cement beside her. Taylor looked nervous as she sat next to Darcy and laced their fingers.

Darcy squeezed Taylor's hand and launched into the speech she had practiced to herself all day. "I work for the city...in the crime lab." She paused as Taylor nodded silently. "A cop was killed recently, and my friends, including a police sergeant, were friends of hers. They were finding some things that didn't make sense. So they started working on it, you could say...unofficially." Darcy watched as Taylor leaned into the railing reflexively creating distance between them. Darcy held out her hand for Taylor again and felt reassured to continue when she took it.

"So we got some evidence about a truck that was seen in the area on the night she was killed." Darcy exhaled and felt Taylor's hand close more tightly against her clammy skin.

"Darcy, I don't understand what this has to do with me or us." Taylor leaned in perhaps to study her and Darcy pressed her mouth onto Taylor's quickly, musing that it could be her last opportunity.

"I know, I'm getting there. I want you to know how much I love being with you and want to see where this goes." She took another deep breath. Darcy brushed her thumb over the back of Taylor's hand.

"I do, too." The question in Taylor's voice still lingered.

"Okay." Darcy began and squeezed her eyes shut as if she could summon extra courage if she didn't have to look at Taylor. She spoke quickly. "I knew who you were before we met. I intended to meet you that night, but I didn't expect to fall for you." She forced the sentences out in a rush and winced when Taylor let her hand drop.

"How? I'm obviously missing something." Taylor's expression clouded as she processed the conversation.

"The truck at the scene of the shooting was delivering something. We believe that whatever was in it was stolen or somehow intentionally misdirected. Then we found out that the truck belonged to CacheTech."

Taylor jerked up and walked a few steps away from Darcy, seeming to try making sense of the scenario. Taylor wheeled on her as the realizations flowered. "So you picked me up in a bar to pump me for information?" Taylor's tone was suddenly angry and hurt as she turned to confront Darcy now standing helplessly on the step.

"No, I mean, I didn't *intend* to pick you up. I just planned to talk to you and then I didn't want to leave and I forgot about all the other stuff." Darcy knew the disclosure made Taylor feel deceived and used.

"You realize I could lose my job for telling you what I shouldn't have." Taylor laced her fingers behind her head and stared out at the parking lot. Darcy hoped she wouldn't choose to just drive away from this craziness.

"I know. But you won't. I wouldn't burn you. We're all risking too much in this…whatever it is. That's why I wanted you to meet them."

"You can't be serious. I don't know them. How do you expect me to trust them or even you?" Taylor studied her. "Be honest. If the roles were reversed, you wouldn't be any more willing to do this."

"Probably not. But I swear the information won't get out. This hits too close to home for us." Darcy took a step and forced herself to reach out to Taylor, risking the certain rejection she expected to find there. Darcy circled her arms around Taylor's long waist and watched her expression.

She sighed as Taylor's body softened and she dropped her arms around Darcy. "It's a pretty long leap from missing inventory to murder, Darcy. I can't imagine anyone I work with being involved in the murder of a police officer."

"I know this all seems crazy." She tried to ignore how much she felt when Taylor was touching her…despite the struggle not to.

Taylor looked at Darcy warily. "What would you have done if I didn't agree to go out with you? What if you hadn't even liked me?"

"I saw your picture and I volunteered," Darcy said as she looked hopefully into Taylor's eyes. "I thought you were hot."

Taylor shook her head and let Darcy kiss her. Darcy had every intention of resisting the urge but failed miserably when her mouth betrayed her mind.

"Syd and Mack can explain everything. Please don't leave without going with me to hear them out." Darcy hated that she sounded as if she was begging, but she was.

Taylor regarded her carefully. "You better be worth it." Taylor kissed her again and warily allowed Darcy to pull her to her car.

"I am. I promise." She silently vowed to be everything she was promising Taylor she was.

❖

Darcy led her through the large oak door of Syd's loft. Taylor was visibly unprepared for the crowd that greeted her. Darcy knew that Taylor had likely planned to spend a quiet evening with a new woman, not listening to a bizarre conspiracy theory from a gaggle of strangers instead.

At the awkward look on Taylor's face, Mack stepped from the kitchen to offer her hand. "I'm Sergeant Foster, Silver Lake PD, but please call me Mack." She was doing her best to legitimize the odd meeting by trying to let her know they weren't all lunatics. "This is my wife, Jenny."

Taylor looked over the badge hooked on Mack's thick black belt and shook her hand, moving over to Jenny before she spoke. "Taylor Westin...but I guess you all already know that, huh?"

Parker walked around to take Taylor's outstretched hand as the newcomer's eyes swept over the group. Instead of a hand-shake, Parker offered her a casual hug and smiled. "I'm Parker. It's nice to finally meet you, Taylor. It seems Darcy here is quite a fan."

Syd watched as Parker adeptly warmed the room and reas-sured Taylor that she hadn't been manipulated quite to the degree she thought. Parker had succeeded in finessing the situation in less than thirty seconds.

Sydney clasped Taylor's hand firmly and smiled as she placed her other hand on Taylor's shoulder, "Syd Hyatt. Beer, right?" Taylor smiled for the first time and nodded thanks to her host.

"Why don't you join us in the office so we can try to convince you we aren't all certifiable?" Syd saw Taylor relax by inches. "I think this is called trial by fire."

Darcy gently slid her hand into Taylor's, noticeably grateful when Taylor's fingers curled around her own.

"I think you're right. Sounds like I have some catching up to do."

Darcy led her up the stairs behind the others. The group, now of six, filled up the space as they listened to Mack run down the past weeks of investigation. Darcy sat cautiously on the counter near Taylor's chair and then moved onto her lap when she looked more interested in the unfolding story than angry at her. Taylor slid her hand around Darcy's hips and placed the other over her thigh as Syd began the video.

The final scene froze on the wall juxtaposing the aerial video still and the CacheTech logo. Taylor Westin stared at the wall screen and stayed quiet, her mind obviously sifting through the last two hours of her formerly simple life.

Still staring at the screen, Taylor said quietly, "I've spent many sleepless nights trying to figure out where three million dollars in inventory went. No one seemed to know or care, and now you're telling me that someone I work with is probably stealing it and could have murdered a cop?" Taylor rubbed her fingers across her forehead as if she was trying to stem an ensuing headache.

"Is this some of the product that's missing?" Mack handed her the plastic bag containing the red tag that they had taken from the warehouse.

Taylor looked momentarily stunned as she nodded and handed it back to Mack.

Darcy pushed against her and asked quietly, "Can you tell them about the schedule? You know, about Sundays and Mondays?"

"Yeah, I guess." She seemed curious to see why Darcy thought the information was useful. "So the warehouse is completely shut down Sunday morning about three a.m. and no one is scheduled to come back until Tuesday morning at four a.m. The inventory team works Sundays because we can get our static counts when the stock is frozen."

"Is anyone else ever there on Sundays?" Mack was tapping a pen on her knee and watched the new draftee adjust to the implications of the situation.

"Sometimes sales will come in to work on presentations or check delivery schedules if they have a big install. National sales handles those and the big retailers. Consumer sales does the one-offs for small businesses."

"Anyone else?" Syd rested her forearms on her knees and then leaned across the desk for the mouse.

"I mean, anyone who works there can come in after hours, if you're salaried, that is. The warehouse manager generally does paperwork on Mondays and sets up the route schedule for the rest of the week. We rarely see him otherwise. They keep our departments separate from a managerial standpoint so there's less chance for collusion on the inventory. At least that was the plan," she said sarcastically. "Sundays are the most deserted because even the office staff isn't there."

"Makes sense that the truck wasn't missed on Sundays then." Syd tapped her fingers on the counter in thought.

"July 4th was a holiday so pretty much everyone was gone that day." Taylor seemed overwhelmed at the thought that this had gone on so long.

Everyone turned as a tap on the glass in the door startled them. Mia was there, staring through the glass at the screen, a puzzled expression plaguing her weary features. Jenny opened the door and hugged the redhead who looked into the room and then back over to the screen.

"Hi, Mia!" Parker said brightly and hugged her as well. "I thought you weren't moving the rest in until tomorrow. We would have helped."

"I just dropped off some clothes. I wanted to let you know I was here." She again looked at the wall screen, her eyes fixed on the truck and logo frozen there. "I knocked downstairs but no one answered. I hope it's okay that I came in. I saw you all up here."

"It's perfectly fine, Mia." Syd wondered how she could have left the door unlocked—she was normally so careful. Mia was more than welcome but her security oversight wouldn't happen again.

"So I guess they finally found San's phone, huh?" Her voice sounded sad as she looked over to Mack.

"No, Mia. We haven't found it. Why?" Mack stood up and walked closer to their friend, taking her hand.

"Those look like her pictures from the warehouse investigation." The statement drew the air from the room as Mack stepped directly in front of her and took her other hand as well.

"Mia, what warehouse investigation? What pictures?" Her voice was edgy and serious as she stared at the gaunt woman's face.

Mia was quiet for a moment, seemingly sifting through her mind about revealing Sandy's last secrets in a room full of people, some strangers.

"Was Sandy killed because of that?" The weight of the question was heavy on her and she suddenly looked unsteady. Mack took her by the shoulders and placed her gently in the chair she had just vacated. She knelt in front of the chair looking desperate for the words to come out.

"Mack, I never even asked. They told me some drug dealer did it." Her lips trembled as she spoke. "I didn't want to know where it happened so I didn't have to picture it." Tears escaped to Mia's cheeks before she roughly scrubbed them away.

"Mia, you were right to remember her the way you last saw her," Mack said, obviously trying not to push her too hard, too fast. "What did she say about the investigation? Do you know where it was?"

The room vibrated as Syd took notes as Mack continued to kneel in front of Mia.

"She never said where it was, I don't think. She would just send me the pictures so she could delete them off her phone. That's what she was talking to Major Williams about at the ball." Mia looked far away as a sad smile stretched across her mouth. "She used to joke about sending me unsexy text messages and still getting lucky." Another round of tears cascaded from her green eyes and she struggled to regain her tenuous composure.

"Mia," Syd almost whispered as she measured her words, "do you still have the pictures? Can we see them?"

In answer, Mia dug her cell phone out of her back pocket and unlocked it. "I couldn't delete any of her messages, even those." She stroked the screen when Sandy's contact picture came up and offered it to Mack. She buried her head in her hands and sobbed quietly into Mack's shoulder. Mack handed the phone behind her to Syd while Parker and Jen found a place on either side of their heartbroken friend.

Syd quickly connected a USB cable to the phone and projected the images onto the screen. Mack watched over Mia's head as the photos scanned by. Parker whispered to Mia before she and Jen led her downstairs with the offer of tea and more benign conversation. Syd knew Mia had enough bad memories for a lifetime and whatever this was would likely make things worse.

"These are from that night, Mack. Just three." Syd tried to keep the excitement from her voice. Sandy's dark picture came into focus on the screen.

"Mack, that's CTI's logo." Taylor said what everyone already knew.

Taylor watched the screen without a word when the box truck with a dark fuzzy logo came onto the screen. Syd zoomed in on the front plate which read *CTI0071*, and Taylor interjected, "That's the spare. The company pays for customized plates on the trucks and we number the fleet accordingly to keep things simple. We have two spare trucks, seventy-one which has a logo and sixty-two which is blank. Sixty-two was down until two days ago, bad starter."

Taylor looked stunned.

"Taylor, who drives those trucks?" Mack demanded.

"Anyone. Usually someone who's running a hot shot—an unscheduled delivery, when something's been left off an order, or for an emergency like a failure on a critical unit in a hospital or something like that. No one is assigned to them."

Syd jotted down the plate number and clicked the last photo of the truck with a man walking around to the back. Taylor tensed against Darcy as she slowly stood, pulling Darcy up with her, still holding Darcy at the waist. She stood stiffly watching the image as Syd played with focus and zoom.

"That's the warehouse manager. That's Bryce Downing."

Syd bristled at the name of the man who'd attempted to strong-arm Parker at the ball. Now realizing he was also a possible murderer caused Sydney's fears to multiply. She bristled when she pictured the man pawing at her lover.

She quickly copied the remaining photos to her file and disconnected Mia's phone. The images went back months and it would take a while to catalog the evidence that Sydney believed was getting them closer to Sandy Curran's killer. The leap was still long but she felt the answers knocking at her gut. What was certain was that Sandy has passed the information to Williams, making his sudden assertion about some botched drug deal obviously bogus. He very possibly knew what had happened and why Sandy was there. The question now concerned why Williams was involved, and worse, potentially covering for Bryce Downing.

Mack looked deep in thought when she bent to thumb away a scuff mark from her shoe. She suddenly straightened and stared at Syd. "Pull up the official scene photos again."

Syd connected an external drive and began clicking through the deck of pictures Darcy had provided and that, as civilians, they should not be seeing.

"Stop," Mack commanded and approached the screen. "Darcy, what does that look like to you?"

"Um, the view from inside Sandy's car looking toward the warehouse." She looked, puzzled, at Mack.

"And the person outside the car. Who is that?" She pointed to a large pair of feet meeting the hem of black BDUs.

"Looks like our favorite major to me." Darcy caught Syd's eye as if seeking a clue where they were headed. Syd shrugged in reply.

"Correct me if I'm wrong, but didn't he tell you and then me, in no uncertain terms, that he did not enter the car and that the warehouse was inaccessible?" Mack spoke with excitement as if waiting to tell the punch line to a joke.

"That I remember clearly, yes." Darcy stepped closer to the screen.

"Look at the knee of his pants and the toes of his shoes," Mack directed and aimed her pen at the disembodied legs in the photograph.

"It looks like white gravel dust."

"Except it wasn't gravel dust..." Mack began.

"It was sheetrock dust," Darcy completed Mack's thought. "The kind you get on your black pants from inside a warehouse."

"And transfer to the seat of a police car when maybe you move a body over." Mack's jaw clenched.

"And steal a phone to be sure there isn't evidence on it." Syd was indignant at the mention of the major who was more than likely in this up to his flabby neck.

"There's your connection. We know who probably moved that body." Mack shook her head in disgust.

"And who took her cell phone," Darcy agreed. "All he had to do was tell the truth. If he had, we would all think this was routine."

"The last question is why." Syd noticed Taylor watching them carefully.

"We both know Williams isn't that smart. Someone's leading him around." Mack rolled her shoulders. "The only question left is who."

Parker walked back in as Sydney began closing programs. "Are you finished with Mia's phone? She wants to go home." Parker's voice was small and sad and she crossed to Syd and took the proffered device. She bent to kiss Sydney's cheek before she walked back to see Mia out.

❖

Syd found a somber contingent in the living room a few minutes later. Everyone was silently staring at the television. A press conference featuring Chief Jayne Provost blared from the speakers, a special cutaway feature on the community channel. Syd perched on the arm of the sofa next to Parker and watched as *SLPD Chief Resigns* was repeated on a crawl along the bottom of the screen.

"I just wanted to take a minute to thank the City of Silver Lake for this wonderful opportunity to lead and help grow this department as well as help to accomplish the goals it has achieved over the past five years." A smattering of applause from the department plants in the audience drowned out her words so she paused briefly and mouthed *thank you* several times.

"Arrogant much?" Mack commented snidely. Syd sighed at the television and watched the political posturing unfold. Jen moved closer and slid her hand into Mack's.

"The city gave her a dress uniform when she was sworn in," Mack said. "I'd bet you my paycheck that she has never even put it on. She wears designer suits and it makes me wonder if she's ever done street work in her life. Chief O'Brien worked at least two shifts a month in the worst part of town to make sure he kept in touch with real police work and with his officers. The rank and file won't be at all sad to see her go."

The chief adjusted the microphone creating what Syd believed was an intentional pause for dramatic effect.

"It is with a heavy heart that I announce my resignation. Per my contract, I've already notified the council chairman and have completed the five years of my contract in service to the people of Silver Lake. Because this is now my adopted home, I'm staying very close by, in this great city. I've long wanted to hone my skills in business and marry that to my law enforcement expertise. I hope to continue to work closely with my dear friends at the PD in my new role as vice president and chief security officer for CacheTech, Incorporated."

Everyone froze as the chief scanned the televised assembly room and smiled directly into the cameras.

"Son of a bitch." Darcy was the first to speak as she reached for Taylor's hand. Taylor looked suddenly uneasy about the company she worked for.

"I am also privileged to announce the appointment of Major Damon Williams as interim chief while the council finalizes the appointment of the permanent replacement."

"This is about to get really ugly from all aspects." Mack stood up and looked back at Taylor who nodded in agreement. "Let's talk in the morning, Syd. I'm thankful for all of you for helping me on this, but you might wish you hadn't." Mack clearly needed to process and plan. "Needless to say, no one breathes a word of this since we may have just figured out where the connection is." She delivered the order seeming to forget that she was speaking to her friends, not her squad. She strode angrily out the door and to the car with Jenny close behind.

Parker looked cautiously at Sydney. "Do you think the chief's involved with this?"

"I don't believe in coincidences, not ones this big. She's in this up to her nose. How much do you think she'll make in the new job?"

Parker was an HR expert. "Could be over 200k in this area, but the benefits are what seal it—company cars, stock options, a sign-on bonus, annual incentives, and retirement guarantees. It could net out to be 300k or so just in the first year."

"Who the hell is giving up that job?" Sydney asked drolly, looking to Taylor.

"Bryce's father, Lawrence Downing III." Her delivery was matter-of-fact as she was noticeably trying to process her day.

Parker clicked open a window on the tablet. "Lawrence R. Downing III apparently did a short stint as an MP in the Army many years ago and has parlayed that into a career as a security expert. He worked for some of the big computer companies in New York, San Francisco, and Seattle and then came out back out here ten years ago when he was forty-five. He grew up in New England."

"So this guy's going to retire at fifty-five?" Syd sounded bemused.

"Looks that way. The bio says, *He enjoys sailing and always looks forward to more time on the water.*" Parker read from the *Eastern Computer Times* where one could pay for page-long advertisements that were disguised as articles.

"I guess we don't have to wonder if there was a prior link to the PD since CTI was the major sponsor of the ball." Syd watched as Parker clicked on another link and expanded a picture of the CSO and his son flanking the beaming chief in a two-year-old publicity shot. "Looks like there are many connections going back some years."

Another link. "It says here," Parker continued, "that Bryce is eager to follow in his father's footsteps at CTI. The other picture is just the chief and Downing at a city council reception at the Marquee Dining Room."

Sydney was now bending closer to see the next shot. A dark-haired woman in too much jewelry was shaking hands with Bryce Downing. "Recognize that stain on humanity?" Syd asked Parker, pointing at the screen.

"Oh my God, is that your *mother*?"

"It sure looks like it." Her mother's alliance with the city council and Major Williams was bad enough, but even she couldn't imagine Pamela could be part of any of this.

Taylor stepped over to look at the photos. "Bryce tells anyone who will listen that he'll be in that job one day. I guess that day is going to have to wait." Taylor shook her head as if knowing not to wait for answers no one had.

❖

Darcy stood and picked up her purse from the counter. She looked weary as they issued their quick good-byes, knowing everyone needed a break from all this. Taylor followed her out.

When Taylor turned onto Darcy's street, Darcy looked at Taylor carefully and asked, "Do you want to come in for a bit?"

Taylor nodded and followed her from the car. It seemed they were both anxious for a tiny piece of normal as they continued to digest the insanity of the evening.

When Darcy keyed open her town house door, she half expected to hear Taylor say that she had changed her mind. She was more than pleasantly surprised when Taylor pointed the remote to lock her SUV.

Taylor was staring at her when she closed the door behind her but said nothing.

"I'm sorry about today, Taylor," Darcy managed as she looked down at her hands and she knitted her fingers together nervously.

"Just convince me that you're sure we're here for the right reasons." Taylor clearly needed one last round of reassurance before she moved toward filing the revelations away for later digestion.

"Completely positive, Taylor. I really want to be with you." Darcy took several tentative steps closer before Taylor closed the remaining gap between them and pressed her mouth solidly on Darcy's. The kiss was hard and long. Darcy surged against

Taylor who braced a muscular thigh between hers. She responded by tilting her hips against Taylor and pushing harder against her mouth.

Taylor guided Darcy toward the floor and onto the soft rug before unbuttoning her shirt and snatching her own from her body. Darcy scanned her fingers over Taylor's torso as she unclasped her bra and then Taylor's. Darcy gasped as Taylor lowered bare skin onto hers and ground against her heated core. Taylor appeared blinded by the rush of energy burning through her as she claimed the figure under her. A few minutes more and Taylor was loudly consumed by the fire stoked by Darcy's hand between her legs. A determined Darcy made it more than apparent that they were far from finished. She tugged Taylor's jeans away and drew a line across her ribs with her mouth.

Taylor shuddered as the intensity between them grew. "I want to taste all of you."

Darcy replied by pulling Taylor to her feet and toward her room. "Let's go to bed."

CHAPTER SIXTEEN

After hours of cataloging the photos Sandy had taken every Sunday for six months, they finally took a break.

"Do you think she got the job before or after Sandy was killed?" Jen folded her knees under her chin as she sat against the wall of Syd's studio.

"I have no idea," Syd admitted. "I have to think that Williams had some help with all of this. He's too stupid to go out on his own." Syd twisted Parker's hair loosely around her fingers as they sat together on the floor, Parker leaning back against Syd's chest, grateful for the steadying warmth she found there.

"I spent last night outlining the chain of evidence so I can explain it," Mack said. "I'll hand over copies of documents and preserve the originals for my personal insurance. This is bigger than any of us expected. I'm about to ask Major Cash for a fairly significant leap of faith. We're not only dealing with grand theft and murder, but I'm asking him to possibly add police corruption on top of it." Mack started the summary she would deliver to the major.

"We have regular Sunday night deliveries from CacheTech. We know that inventory counts were done before and numbers were fudged after. And since we can put Bryce Downing in that truck, it's a safe bet he was responsible for inventory adjustments. We can unofficially show three million in missing inventory thanks to Taylor, but I won't use any of those numbers until subpoenas are issued. We can reasonably prove, though, because of the pallet tag we found, that at least some of those missing units were in that warehouse."

Mack continued to connect the dots.

"Sandy had been watching this long enough to finally bring it to Major Williams, who not only didn't report the case Sandy brought him, but finds her murdered on the same property, and doesn't report it then either. Not only doesn't he report it, he makes up something to cover for what anyone who had connected brain cells would have linked together if they had stopped to think. Taylor identifies Bryce Downing at the warehouse and in possession of the truck that belongs to the company now paying our soon-to-be ex-chief big bucks. The only other person that stands to gain is now sitting in the chief's chair."

Syd handed a black-and-white yearbook photo to Mack. "I ran down the owner of Peticor Construction and I connected his son to Bryce. They were in the Silver Lake Christian Academy all the way through high school."

"I guess we know why he chose that warehouse. I think I have more than enough to bring it to Major Cash." Mack blew out a loud sigh.

"Do you trust him?" Jenny was obviously worried about Mack; she wore the stress like a heavy cloak.

"I have to. This is starting to look like we're the criminals here. I've trampled on every protocol known to man over the last few weeks." She kissed the top of Jenny's head as her wife stood to hug her. "Time to meet the brass."

She tried to smile but Jenny didn't look any better, and everyone knew that Mack was more than a little apprehensive.

Major Cash was a tall, lean cop just entering his fifties. He had been on the department for nearly fifteen years after a lateral transfer from McLean, but he had been in law enforcement since he graduated from college at twenty-one. Mack had worked with him since she was a rookie. She trusted his judgment. Of course, now she had no choice but to depend on it.

"Mack. To what do I owe the pleasure? We miss you over on the west side."

"I miss being there." Mack leaned over the table in the back corner of the coffee shop, off the beaten path on the north end of Silver Lake. "I think I finally understand why I'm not, though. That's why I'm here." She paused for a breath before continuing. "I need your help."

The major looked concerned and sipped his cooling coffee, never taking his eyes off Mack's worried face and whispered tone. "Shoot."

"What I'm going to tell you is not pretty, and I'm probably in some hot water here, but this is way bigger than me."

She looked around her, uncomfortable with her back to the door, but she trusted the senior commander to watch the entrance.

"This is about Sandy and about doing the right thing, Major. I'm prepared for the consequences if it comes to that."

The major set his mug on the table absorbing the warning in Mack's voice. "Okay."

"You know something was wrong in Curran's case. We talked about it." Mack began slowly reminding him of the concerns she'd had immediately following her transfer.

He nodded. He didn't interrupt her briefing or offer his thoughts about the disturbing facts in the case.

"I...got some information that made it look really bad. I found out that she probably did stumble onto something wrong at that warehouse that night, but it wasn't drugs, sir."

"How did you *trip* over this information, Sergeant Foster?" His words and tone subtly reminded her that she was a cop and this was sounding dangerous.

"Video, sir. There was some air traffic that night and there was video of the area where Sandy was shot. I didn't get it myself, but I saw it." She left the source of the information open for interpretation—after all, the media had helicopters, too.

"I saw the truck that was there that night. We know now that it was probably delivering stolen computer equipment. Sandy had been watching them for a while, six months or better. She told Major Williams about it several times before she died but nothing happened. It's reasonable to assume that she told him exactly where it was happening as well. A fact he didn't reveal when he ran the scene after the homicide. I can also be reasonably certain that Sandy had sent him photographs. I can show you a stack of them that she took from the same vantage point she would have had when she was shot."

Mack grazed her teeth over her bottom lip as she tried to frame her next statement carefully, "The second problem is, we...*I* think he's involved in covering for the shooter." There. She'd said it. The proverbial cat was out of the bag now.

"You really think that dumbass is in this?" His tone was dubious given his apparent low opinion of his colleague, but he lowered his voice and leaned closer to Mack.

"Up to his eyes, sir." She knew that Cash was aware of Williams's role as the chief's lackey. "If you could have seen that crime scene and the way he handled it, you would believe me."

"It's not that I don't believe you, that you believe it, but how do you plan on proving it?" He pressed a cheap teaspoon into his fingers as he digested the information.

"I'm not even as worried about proving it was him as I am about telling you the rest, which is, frankly, worse."

He blew out a breath and regarded her seriously. "You have never given me any reason to believe you are anything but ethical and by the book. Nothing you have said so far seems to have been garnered by *any* book."

Mack nodded and left the statement unaddressed. "The problem is the source of the stolen items. We traced them to the company and confirmed that one of their employees was taking the product or at least driving the truck that contained stolen product the night Sandy was killed. His father ranks pretty high in the company, Major."

"So we get someone to pick him up. We bring him in on suspicion of embezzlement and break him on the other." The major was obviously feeling more and more uncomfortable.

"The company is CacheTech, Major. The guy moving the freight, three million dollars' worth, is the son of the outgoing CSO."

He looked at her blankly when the dots seemed to connect in his mind. He hunched across the table and barely whispered incredulously, "You think Provost is in this?"

"Yes, sir, I do. I don't think she had her hand on the gun or any stolen property, but I think she has been feathering her own nest so she could get that cushy job. Otherwise, why would Williams be acting so off?"

She laid it out for the major. "The father is out and the chief is in. Williams is suddenly named interim chief. We both know you're a hundred times more qualified to do that job, and I'm not blowing smoke, sir." She meant every word she was saying as she handed him a folder full of evidence arranged chronologically. "This video shows the events in real time and lines them up against what we...*I* believe happened behind the scenes. Williams was aware of the suspicions that Sandy had because she had been funneling him evidence for months. Evidence, according to Mia, he claimed he was passing on to people in Investigations. I'm willing to bet no investigation was ever started. Maybe Williams saw an opportunity or Provost saw a way to cement her future. Whatever the order, a father managed to cover for his son who was the subject of Curran's suspicions, and suddenly two people got big jobs they wanted and my friend died."

"It's common knowledge that the major was recommended by Provost and no one can figure out why," Major Cash noted. "The guy's a joke, but letting one of our own go down for a job? Even I would have bet against that." It was the first time Mack had ever heard Major Cash speak poorly about anyone, regardless of his true feelings. "If you believe all this, why not go straight to the VBCI?"

Mack grimaced. "That's part of the problem. Jonas caught the shooting case and he's always been close to Williams. Williams basically told him how to write his report. He obviously believed it when Williams told him the drug deal theory without doing any independent work. You can read the report yourself. I need someone with clout to go there because Jonas has every reason to protect himself and the shitty job he did."

She pushed up the last bit of courage she had. "Sir, I believe if we could see cell phone records for the chief and the major since that night, maybe even before, it would tell us a lot. Some of my research indicates that the major was at the scene before the information started flowing through official channels."

Cash dragged a large hand down his face and looked wearily at Mack. "The less I know about how you got here, the better."

He tucked the envelope under his arm. "I don't know how to shield you from the shit storm that's about to come, Foster. If this goes bad and there isn't enough on those two, you know they'll try to fire you—if they don't prosecute you first."

The thought was terrifying. The various consequences had always played in the back of Mack's mind but she also couldn't imagine working for a corrupt department. She had never thought of being charged with a crime before the major spoke the words. "I totally understand. This is for Sandy, Major. I'll survive."

"I know you will. I'm going to see John." Mack nodded her understanding. He was going to the bureau, to see Supervisory Special Agent John Noles. "I need to be sure that I'm playing for the right team here, Foster. Do you understand?" Cash looked suddenly stressed and angry. His intent was obvious. She hoped the fact that she didn't protest told him volumes.

"I do." She was reasonably sure he saw what she did in the evidence or undoubtedly would, once he had more than a few minutes to digest it.

"I'm going to plant a seed, Foster. Call me at the first sign it grows, understand?"

"Yes, sir." She watched him stride purposefully toward the door with a paper grenade tucked under his arm. She felt like she had been holding her breath during the entire meeting. She drove her city car to the main station and tried to believe that doing the right thing wouldn't bite her soundly in the ass.

Major Cash hit the speed dial for Major Williams as he pointed his car toward the VBCI field office. "Damon, how's life as the chosen son?" Cash was embarrassed they shared the same rank. He hadn't seen Damon Williams do any real work since they were assigned to a common patrol squad fifteen years earlier.

"Looking pretty good, Mark. What can I do for you?" Williams sounded relaxed.

"Well, I know that the Curran case is still open, and I wondered if you were any closer. Mack Foster just came to me and mentioned that she had concerns about the two detectives on the case and wondered if I could let her work another angle. I told her that I would see what I could do. She's pretty adamant about a possible new lead, something about computers."

"This is getting out of hand, Mark." Cash could almost hear as the fury boiled through Williams's words. "I've told her what I needed her to handle and this is now approaching insubordination. There is no other angle. The detectives are about to make an arrest. I'll handle the sergeant, Major Cash. Foster is my problem. Don't worry about her little request."

Cash could hear the key tones of Williams's cell phone before their call was even disconnected.

❖

Twenty minutes later, Mack dialed the number. She closed her eyes briefly before Major Cash answered her call.

"Seed planted and growing, sir." Mack's voice betrayed her uncertainty.

"I see." Major Cash seemed to be digesting the statement.

"Suspended, pending the investigation of my alleged insubordination and a brand new anonymous citizen complaint. Apparently it's concerning my supposed harassment of a Silver Lake motorist, despite the fact that I haven't made a traffic stop in over a year. I was told I was a loose cannon and a risk to the integrity of the department, sir." She knew he could hear the weight that was descending on her now.

"I'm meeting now. Be available, Mack."

"It doesn't appear I have to work today, sir." She was trying to sound unconcerned but this could end her career and they both knew it.

He chuckled at her in spite of the gravity of what was happening. "Seems so."

"He took my badge and my gun, sir." The move had been punitive. The department never stripped credentials on a suspension unless the officer was accused of a crime.

"You have a backup at home, Sergeant?" He was clearly concerned for her safety.

"Yes, sir." She had a backup weapon in her gear bag but she hadn't been without a badge in twelve years.

"Be careful," Major Cash warned.

Mack disconnected her phone, walked outside the main station, and sat on the bench usually occupied by drunks and petty thieves just released from a night in lockup. Mack suddenly felt like she was walking far outside the lines. She had belonged to an exclusive club but now she was being made to choose membership over integrity. Mack believed she could only make one choice.

❖

John Noles stood behind his desk and shook Major Mark Cash's hand firmly. He held the documents that he had just read through. He ejected the disk from his computer and dropped it into the folder and then into a red glassine sleeve. He closed the flap with a tamperproof seal he initialed before passing it to Cash for his signature.

"I'll go as fast as I can, Mark. Tell her to lie low."

Mark Cash nodded as he headed for the door. He turned just before he stepped into the hallway. "I don't want to work any-where that makes this okay, John. I don't want any part of what we just saw. Hit it as hard as you can, so I can stop punishing her for doing the right thing."

"I'll do my best, Major. Thanks for trusting me with this." Noles slumped into his chair and stared at the red plastic scar on the Silver Lake Police Department. The warrant forms were going to take him hours, but he couldn't wait to serve them.

❖

She called Sydney, the only person she could think of who could possibly pick her up at four in the afternoon. Suspended de-tectives didn't get to drive their city cars, so she had to wait for a favor she hated to ask. It seemed that she had asked so much lately.

When Syd arrived, Mack dropped into the seat without saying a word and jerked the heavy door closed.

"Want me to buy you a beer or ten?" Sydney tried to make Mack laugh but understood her mood.

"Just drive, wherever. I need to clear my head." She fumbled with her keys before chucking them onto the floorboard.

"Want to tell me what happened? Was it Williams?" Syd's voice dripped with her distaste for the suspected criminal cop.

"Yeah, it was him. I'm officially suspended. He took my gun and my badge and handed me some bullshit story about a citizen complaint and insubordination. You could see even he didn't believe it," Mack grumbled and tapped out a text.

Interim Chief Williams was on the phone as he watched Victoria Hyatt pull up to the curb and collect the suspended sergeant. Hyatt's flashy car pissed him off him every time he saw it. Silver Lake wasn't that big and he saw that damned Porsche everywhere. He returned his focus to the phone call and recounted the events of the day and the case he wished would disappear.

Syd steered away from the curb and pointed the car toward a rural part of the county. She let Mack stew as she spun through the radio dials and pushed the Porsche past the speed limit, enjoying the rush she always felt when the powerful sports car responded to her heavy foot. She turned down Route 45. It was a favorite drive for Sydney, only forty minutes into the county. At the end of the road, a small lake was nestled in a grove of trees that sat just off a gravel turn. She often drove there to read or jog around the lake in cooler weather. Mack could use a peaceful place and Sydney would share hers.

A square of white eclipsed the back window as she glanced at the rearview mirror. She noticed the grille as the vehicle seemed to be attempting to pass them on the narrow road. "This guy is a fucking idiot!" Syd exclaimed.

Then she noticed the license plate in her side mirror. By the time the realization of what was happening found her, it was too late to avoid contact.

She gripped the wheel and attempted to steer against the skid caused by the right bumper of the huge truck. Sections of the steep embankment were bordered by a low guardrail which caught the small car's frame; the driver of the truck continued to push against the Porsche.

The Porsche overturned and teetered on the roll bars that shot up from behind the seats. The bars kept them from being crushed, and a fortuitous meeting with a thick stand of ancient shrubbery stopped them from continuing all the way down the very steep rocky hill to the dry creek bed below. Sydney felt a sharp stab in her side. She reached to feel for the cause of the pain when everything went black.

CHAPTER SEVENTEEN

Parker padded through the loft that felt strange with Syd still not home. She knew Syd had gone to collect Mack from the station, but that had been hours ago. She'd assumed further case discussion was keeping her at Mack's, but her calls had gone unreturned and texts uncharacteristically unanswered. She watched idly out the front windows waiting for the sweep of the Porsche's headlights to announce Syd's arrival.

Finally she called Jenny. "Are you ready to send her back yet? The two of them must be driving you nuts by now." She curled her feet under her on the sofa and sipped a fresh glass of wine. It was silly to miss Sydney after only a few hours, but she craved her nonetheless.

"What do you mean? It's just me and Olivia. I figured they were over there." Jenny sounded confused.

"When did you hear from Mack last?" Parker tried not to let her voice betray the mild panic she felt.

"I don't know, right before Syd picked her up, maybe? She was waiting outside the station about four this afternoon, right before we had the hiring meeting today. Oh, and she texted me when Syd got there."

Parker felt acid rise in her throat. "I'm going to check her phone. I'll call you back." Parker tried to sound unconcerned as she disconnected and ran up the stairs to the studio. She dialed

Sydney's cell phone number again, only to hear her voicemail answer. The biometric lock seemed to take ages to admit her into the loft and the wait to sign on to Sydney's computer was just as endless.

The GPS site had been saved as a favorite, a silly agreement they'd made to always leave the locator on their phone enabled in case of emergency. Parker had never had reason to use it until now. She highlighted Sydney's device, registered as *Drift 1*. The hourglass spun repeatedly and Parker rubbed her hand absently over her stomach, which swam with apprehension.

Sydney's phone, reduced to a lonely red orb, blipped steadily over Route 45 and Eisenhower Road: *idle time 1:53:45*.

Parker dialed Syd's number again and felt a stab pierce her heart when, again, she didn't answer.

Jen picked up on the first ring. "I called Mack and no answer."

Parker snatched her keys from the table. "Meet me at Richard and Allen's. They'll watch Olivia. Leave now."

❖

Parker waited in front of Richard and Allen's house, engine idling, while Jenny got the baby settled. Jenny had barely shut her car door when Parker jerked the gearshift into drive and hit the road.

Jenny said, "Richard's calling hospitals and the state patrol with the cross streets you gave me."

Parker nodded.

"I told them not to call 9-1-1, just in case, you know."

Jenny pulled out her phone, hit speaker, and dialed a number. Parker heard the call go to voicemail. Jen left a message: "Darcy, it's Jen. I think we need to call Major Cash. I don't know how to reach him. Something's wrong." She glanced at the GPS on Parker's dash. "We're headed to Route 45 and Eisenhower Road. Please call me back."

Jenny stared at the screen as if her mind could will the phone to ring. She looked at Parker whose tense fingers had turned white on the steering wheel. "They'll be okay, Park."

Parker didn't know who she was trying harder to convince. "They have to be. Sydney told me that she can't breathe when she feels that something is wrong with me." She caught a sob in her throat as it threatened to escape. "I can't breathe."

❖

Mack tried to push against the door before she recognized that the angle at which she was looking at the ground was inverted. She hung awkwardly from her seat belt as she craned her stiff neck to further get her bearings.

She pushed against the door at her side before searing pain burned through her forearm. She struggled to remember where she was. Drops fell against her neck and she reached up with her other hand to stem the water. Another drop deflected off her hand and she smelled the metallic odor of blood.

She heard a loud muffler rattle against its housing. She wondered if a car would stop for them, but the sound faded away too quickly. She shifted painfully to her left as Sydney's limp frame came into focus. A large gash had opened behind Syd's ear and a slim shard of metal protruded from her right side. Mack heard erratic and shallow labored breaths, and she strained against the confines of the seat belt that lashed her in place against the passenger seat. She searched in vain for her phone, leaning forward, attempting to avoid the stabbing in her right arm pinned to the door. She slowly moved the shoulder belt behind her head, so she'd have a modicum of mobility without dropping her onto her pounding head. At least, she hoped.

Mack gingerly walked her fingers along the ceiling of the dark vehicle and fumbled for the integrated phone Sydney had always used in the car. Her bloody fingers pressed every button she could find and she heard nothing. Mack didn't know if the phone worked when the car was off. Was the car off? She spent most of her time in an aging police sedan for which a keyless control was much too modern a feature. Still, she fumbled blindly over a myriad of buttons and tried to talk to Sydney.

"Syd? Sydney, it's Mack. I need you to wake up, okay? I need your help here, Hyatt. This car is like some kind of space age rocket. We need to call for help. Wake up, Syd." Her fingers still skimmed over the controls, now only barely reflecting in the dark. The road sounded deserted and there were no streetlights this far into the county. She racked her brain to remember where they had turned last. How long had they been driving, an hour, maybe less? She'd sat silently in her selfish funk for ages, not even saying much to Syd. A flash of light consumed her memory as she recalled a jolt before Sydney had grabbed the wheel and tried to correct the jerking and rolling sports car. Could it have been another car? Did a tire blow out? She couldn't focus a thought through the misty film of her recall.

The console where Syd usually stashed her cell phone was now suspended above her, empty. She tried to clear her thoughts and reason where the phone might be now.

She felt along the ceiling liner under her head, saw the fresh blood on her hands. She wiggled her toes and clenched her major muscles to be sure she could feel her body. She was weak but knew Sydney needed help much quicker than she did. Syd's skin was clammy and cold. She strained to hear her breathe now and wondered if the seat belt was doing more harm than good. She tried in vain to pull it away from Sydney's neck but it was locked in place.

Mack finally felt the heavy rubber of Syd's OtterBox phone case. She had given Sydney so much crap for arming her phone like a SWAT member, but Sydney swore she could kick it across the street and still be able to make a call. Mack whispered a quick thank you as the phone lit up. She'd known Syd's password once and fumbled through a few combinations. As she failed to enter the right code for the fifth time, she inadvertently hit the emergency call button which seemed to magically connect her to 911.

Her head pounded with every syllable she tried to speak. In her head, the words were screams but the dispatcher seemed to struggle to make out her pleas for help.

"What is your location?"

"I don't know, Route 45, I think." She strained to make herself be heard. "10-50 with injuries, two occupants. SLPD 1952." She managed a description of the car and requested an ambulance. She idly considered whether or not she could still identify herself as a police officer. Then she remembered that she didn't have her badge. She felt a strange sensation wash over her battered body, and the edges of her vision became dark before they overtook her completely. The phone fell back next to her head while the operator continued to talk.

❖

Parker felt a desperate knot building in her stomach as she turned onto Route 45. She'd held Jenny's hand until the twists of the road made it dangerous. Now she gripped the wheel until her fingers felt frozen around the vinyl stitching.

She heard a foreign sound escape her lips as a torrent of red and blue lights seemed to mound ahead of them in the middle of the desolate road.

Parker pushed frightened tears from under her eyes as the smears of light served to blind her. An ambulance overtook the Audi as Parker slowed her car to a crawl. A highway patrolman flagged them to the side.

"Miss, you need to turn around, the road is blocked." He shined his flashlight at Parker who held up a palm to stop the blinding assault.

"Can you just tell me if there's an accident? Is it a black Porsche 911?" Parker bunched her fists to her face, praying he would say no.

"I don't know, ma'am. I'm just working traffic." He attempted to stand back from the car and resume his duties.

Parker heard her voice growl out the next words. "Is it a Porsche?" She knew if he was there, he knew the answer.

"I'm just working—"

"The least you can do is tell me, or I won't leave." Parker's eyes bored into him. "You'll have to arrest me."

He stepped back from the dark vehicle and keyed the mic at his shoulder. He held the radio close to his ear as he walked away from them along the white line of the deserted state road.

He turned back as he released the transmission key on the radio. He seemed to weigh his words judiciously as Parker stepped from the car and looked at him intently.

He held up a swift hand and ordered her back in the vehicle.

"Tell me!" Parker bellowed at him.

Jenny ran around to hold Parker's arm.

"The car is black—that's all they could tell me right now. The license plate is *DRIFTER*." He said the words quickly, watching the information make things worse.

Parker felt her world go deafeningly silent as she saw Jenny speaking to the officer but couldn't make sense of their words. She thought she heard another siren approach her. The rough asphalt cut into her skin as she knelt on the side of the desolate road.

She saw Taylor Westin skid to a stop behind the police car as Darcy Dean bailed out of the Highlander. An older man in an SLPD raid jacket ran toward the highway patrolman. Jenny nearly toppled him when she left Parker and ran to grab his arm on the dark road.

Parker thought if this was a single car wreck on a dark country road, no one would be treating this as anything but a tragic accident, but the cop Jenny was with now seemed to know it was more.

Darcy reached Parker and attempted to pull her farther from the accident. When Parker realized they were walking away she plucked her arm from Darcy's grip and faced the scene once again. She could hear Jenny asking for information as she frantically stared into the riot of emergency vehicles. Each minute felt like hours as they waited for some news.

The reflective letters from the SLPD cop's jacket blazed against the nightmarish scene. Parker led the group that milled around him, waiting for him to speak. A sudden reverberation of helicopter blades beat against the inky sky and fired a spray of sand stabbing at her skin like a thousand tiny knives. Parker wondered briefly why she didn't feel anything.

He shouted to be heard as he angled to face toward Jenny. "Mack is intermittently conscious but she has a lot of contusions and abrasions. They think her arm is broken but she's talking. You can ride with her to the hospital—I told them to take her to General." He pointed toward the ambulance and Jenny nodded.

"Major, what about Sydney?" Darcy asked. As if to reply by proxy, the helicopter lifted and banked sharply over their heads. Parker felt her knees buckle as she squinted into the funnel of humid, dirty air that whipped her hair around her face.

The major waited for the noise to fade again slightly before he turned to stand where Taylor now steadied Parker against her.

"Parker? I'm Mark Cash. Sydney's in that helicopter. They think she's got some internal bleeding so they didn't want to take a chance. She has a pretty serious head wound and a piece of metal in her side which may be causing the bleeding. I'll take you there now if you want to go. You can see her when she wakes up."

Parker thought he had kind eyes as he tried to explain that the person she had made a perfect life with was in a helicopter where people were possibly trying to save her life. She felt the air slow around her and she watched Jenny climb into the back of an ambulance that screamed past them.

Darcy leaned into Parker in an effort to be heard. "Parker, go with Major Cash—we'll handle things here." Parker offered a tiny nod as she felt the major's hand guide her to his patrol car.

Closed inside, the cold blast from the air conditioning blew into Parker's face. The tight skin under drying tears froze instantly and she put both palms against the vents to stanch the flow.

Cash spun the fan control down to *low* in response.

"Thanks," she managed. She took in the console's extra devices and controls before she stared away blankly.

"The EMTs told me that she has some concerning injuries, but I think she'll be okay," he said.

His tires spun road debris into the air as he flipped on lights and sirens for the short drive to General. "Running Code 3 with a civilian passenger outside the city limits of Silver Lake is substantially thwarting regulations. And I don't give a damn."

Parker realized he wasn't really talking to her anymore. She felt numb as the jerk of the speeding car pushed her against the door. She checked the seat belt latch and tried to imagine a moment without Sydney, let alone a lifetime.

Chapter Eighteen

Parker paced the hallway of the surgery floor and ignored the now lukewarm coffee Darcy had brought her ages ago. She counted the steps between the doors marked *Authorized Personnel Only* and the elevator that had deposited her into the hell of waiting for someone to walk out and tell her this was all a horrendous mistake.

On the short walk to the elevator she counted only the black tiles; on the way back she counted the white ones. She half expected the compulsive activity to make the time move faster, but instead it only made the blurry squares shift in her swollen eyes. She made painful divots in her fingers as she pressed the edges of her necklace charm into them. It suddenly dawned on her that it could be all she had left of her improbable lover.

In the waiting room, Taylor held Darcy awkwardly on the patterned love seat. Parker watched Major Cash step away and take numerous phone calls. She thought he heard him say, "Thank you, Judge," once, but she couldn't be sure. She sifted through the memories of the indestructible Sydney Hyatt running an obstacle course outside her gym or sweating into the heavy bag that hung in the home they now shared officially. She thought of her leading her up the stairs of the restaurant on their first date and making love with her under the hot spray of the shower. She thought if she replayed every indelible minute of their relatively short time together she would find Sydney at the end, healthy and whole again.

At one a.m., a weary looking man in his fifties carried a chart into the waiting room. "Victoria Hyatt?" Parker scrambled to his side as Darcy and Taylor assembled just behind her. She stared anxiously at the official man wearing a caduceus patch on the sleeve of his dingy white coat. Parker felt her focus sharpen as she waited for him to speak. She hugged her arms across her body as if to armor herself against the unthinkable.

"Are you family, Miss...?"

"Duncan. Yes, I am. And I have medical power of attorney." She held up her phone displaying the PDF document. Sydney had insisted on drawing up the documents for both of them after the Becky incident. She was impossibly thankful to have them now.

He nodded and continued explaining the extent of Sydney's injuries. "We removed her appendix and managed her other wounds successfully. We should know if there are any complications in the next few hours."

"When can I see her?" Parker asked quickly while her mind processed the information.

"She's asleep and likely will be for a number of hours. You should go home and get some rest. She wouldn't know you were even here."

"Yes, she would." Parker's defiant tone was quick and bordered on angry.

He sighed and stared down at her. "She's being moved to a room now. Give the unit staff some time to get her situated and I'll have someone let you know."

"Thank you," Taylor said to the doctor, and Parker heard her breathe a sigh of cautious relief.

"Let me get you something to eat, Parker," Darcy offered. "How about some breakfast?"

Parker shook her head. "Not hungry."

"Please. Something. We'll bring toast and juice at least."

Parker just nodded as they headed for the elevator and she resumed counting tiles.

❖

Jen found Mack staring at her when Jen lifted her head from the bed near her wife's leg. Mack's right arm lay helplessly at her side in a heavy cast covered in blue gauze. Her eyes were black and a white bandage barely covered the thick line of stiches Jen knew ran across her temple. Her black hair was still matted from the injury and the blood.

"Hi, beautiful." Mack's voice was weak.

Jen tried to smile through a renewed flood of tears. "I love you. You're going to be okay." The words rushed out as she squeezed Mack's left hand.

"Of course I am. I have a family to take care of."

"Yes, you do." Jenny spoke through a new gale of emotion. "Mack, I was so scared."

"I'm sorry, Jen. Please don't cry." Mack's fingers barely reached Jen's cheek.

"I can't help it." She took a deep steadying breath.

"How's Syd?"

"I...I don't know. God, Mack, I haven't even checked on them. Life Flight came for her."

"It's okay, sometimes they just call it out as a precaution. Where is Parker, sweetheart?" Mack was stroking her wrist.

She shook her head. "I don't know. I stayed with you, I didn't even check on them, Mack," she said guiltily.

"I'm okay, go find her. I'll be right here." Jenny leaned over to kiss Mack softly over and over before her wife pushed her toward the curtain around the emergency department bed.

❖

Parker heard footsteps before she forced her eyes open and pushed up from the thin hospital pillow she had wedged against a corner on the floor. Jenny kneeled in front of her and pulled her into an agonizing hug. "Where is she?" The words rushed out as if Jenny was terrified of the answer.

"They just brought her out of surgery. Appendix and some internal bleeding, ribs and head injury." Her staccato sentences were all she could manage. "Waiting to make sure no more bleeding inside. She's going to be in a room and they said I could see her then." She paused to gather her thoughts. "Where is Mack?"

"She's still in the emergency room. Stitches, broken arm, black eyes. She asked about Syd so I had to come find you. She's going to be okay." Parker watched the relief spread over her face as she delivered the news. "Will you call me if anything happens, as soon as you know where Syd will be?"

Parker nodded. "Taylor and Darcy have been here. I'm okay, Jen. Go be with Mack."

She fervently wished she could go to Sydney, just to touch her or kiss her like Jenny could with Mack. She felt irrationally resentful but pushed the mood away quickly.

Chief Williams carried the last box to his new office and began weeding through the sad collection of dusty frames. The nicest one was of his nephew who lived in California with his new wife. They had visited once, but preferred a West Coast life to the small Virginia city he now commanded. He would text him to announce his promotion. He'd always hoped his nephew viewed him as a father figure since his brother's death. With his ex-wife long since remarried and his parents dead for nearly thirty years, somehow every victory felt a bit hollow with no one to share it with him. Pamela Hyatt had congratulated him when he showed up at her door, but he was well aware that her elation was self-serving.

He hung his certificate of promotion on an old nail Provost had left protruding from the narrow wall next to the window. A picture of the former chief presenting him with his major's credentials was matted just below the certificate in the same frame. He idly wished that the picture didn't speak volumes about the hard turns his career had taken, both because and in spite of the wretched woman.

Williams pushed Mack Foster's badge and gun into a drawer. He knew he would eventually turn them in to property for reissue, but for now they could stay in there. He opened the bottom file drawer and dropped a fat, unaddressed catalog envelope inside. He was sure he wouldn't need the insurance policy, but it would be a while before he would destroy the tapes of the devious Jayne Provost. He turned the brass key that stuck out of the lock and attached it to his key ring.

He had expected more of a fanfare when he took the chief's office. He expected visitors or congratulations from the city manager. It was still early; perhaps they would come in later or on Monday. A stack of reports and thick file listing open case statistics sat in the tray at the corner of his desk. He felt a renewed happiness as he signed on the line designated for the Chief of Police.

The jarring ring interrupted his train of thought and he groused into the phone, "What?"

He listened carefully before replying. "As far as I'm concerned, we're done here. Do not call me again." He wondered if the price he had paid was worth the return he had not yet been able to fully enjoy.

Vice President and Chief Security Officer Jayne Provost set the farewell card on the hutch behind her desk. She wrestled several boxes off the dolly and wondered whose job it should have been to move her into her official space. She found a list of Monday meetings her administrative assistant must have left for her. She glanced over the page and sighed, eager to discover the lay of her new land.

She spun in her chair and watched a huge boat sail past her window. Her new car was being delivered in an hour, and she imagined how impressed Luke would be as they cruised through DC. She considered how much she would love passing her old District haunts in the flashy gold Jaguar. She had briefly deliberated on ordering *CTI CSO* for a personalized tag. The dirty brass in DC could keep their badges; she had power and privilege no one ever bestowed upon public sector grunts, regardless of rank. She itched to flaunt her new power, with a lover half her age who was always willing to satisfy her needs.

She had managed to enlist some employees walking down the hall to help her move the desk so she could appreciate her lake view while keeping an eye on the door. They seemed perplexed when she pressed them into service so late in the day. Cops, even ex-cops, never sat with their backs to the door and she would never sit with her back to the view…a glistening monument to her achievements.

She wondered where the other executives sat. She wondered if their offices were bigger than hers. She wondered if she should call and check on the officer involved in a crash.

She felt a little sorry about it. She reasoned that one less dyke detective wouldn't hurt the SLPD. She stood to wander around the quiet offices and tested how many places the CSO's badge allowed her access. She discovered only one door that didn't budge when she presented her credentials; she planned to discover what was in there later.

Technically, she wasn't supposed to have her welcome meeting until Monday morning, but she was eager to get her office organized, so they'd created her badge early at her request. The security administrator had looked at her strangely when she'd reiterated the demand before she was even officially an employee. She might have to replace the impudent subordinate.

Bryce Downing nearly ran her down as he turned the corner to the hallway in front of her. "Perfect timing, I was just coming to say welcome."

"Well, thank you. I look forward to getting to know you better, Bryce." She didn't mean it, but he might prove useful considering she was responsible for his freedom.

"Would you like a tour?" He waited for her to follow. When she did, he continued. "I wanted to discuss some things with you as well." He looked conspiratorial as he waited for permission to speak about confidential matters.

Jayne smiled stiffly and spoke through her teeth. "Not here and not now. I will call you when I wish to discuss *matters*." He nodded soberly as he led her through large fire doors and into the dim light of the warehouse.

Taylor Westin swiped into her small office and sat heavily in her chair. She had hated to leave Darcy and Parker but she wanted to make sure she captured the latest figures. She had grabbed the night's unofficial tally sheets hanging from the clipboard outside her office. She checked them over, then added her summary sheet to the top. Bryce Downing would pick them up and process the numbers for the executives' weekly meetings and for accounting. Any abnormalities would be noted by the CSO and investigated if appropriate. Once she printed off the report she made another copy for herself, carefully folding the sheets and sliding the wad into her computer bag.

She then made copies of all the count sheets the clerks had turned in, placing an *X* on the corners of the sheets that contained the SKU from the pallet ticket Mack had shown her. She folded those pages into her bag as well.

She was looking intently at the waterfall of numbers across her computer screen when Bryce passed her office window with a woman she now recognized as Jayne Provost. He snatched the reports from the clipboard without looking at them, turning back out of the warehouse without so much as a cursory glance in her direction. She idly wondered how the warehouse manager didn't have to work in the warehouse. His father had scored him a cushy office on the first floor so he never had to visit the dingy space except to collect the reports. She was actually surprised he didn't just have someone bring them to him.

She drew another file from her drawer that contained manual calculations she had been collecting since she took over the job. Her accounting degree was finally paying off. She could clearly demonstrate the net loss of product now hovering over the three million mark. Taylor tried not to picture the feckless Bryce shooting a police officer, or anyone for that matter, but like her new friends, she couldn't imagine another explanation.

Her phone vibrated across the desk as Darcy's smiling face stared up at her.

Syd's in room 347—third floor. Thank you for staying with me.

She texted back, *Of course. I didn't want to be anywhere else.*

She hadn't meant to be so transparent. However, in the wake of murder, embezzlement, and general dearth of ethical behavior, playing hard to get seemed petty. She wanted to be professionally successful, she mused, but regardless of superficial success, she ultimately wanted to find another person who wished to come home to the same place, love the same way, and share the same goals. If Darcy could be that person, she certainly didn't want to risk it by being coy.

Taylor ticked off Darcy's attributes in the plus column: blond, smart, sexually compatible, fun, and most of all she didn't need someone to take care of her. In fact, Taylor laughingly imagined that she might have to fight Darcy for the right to make her soup if she had a cold. Definitely not a shrinking violet or any sort of wilting flower for that matter. Taylor clicked through her daily duties and imagined not seeing Darcy again. She didn't like that thought.

CHAPTER NINETEEN

Parker tried not to focus on the blossoming bruises that cascaded angrily over Sydney's cheekbones and followed down her long neck. Large gauze pads prevented her from seeing the multitude of black stiches beneath. The nurse told her that sixteen stiches were placed inside and over thirty externally. A large swath of tape and bandages covered Syd's stomach and ribs.

Parker held Sydney's hand to her mouth and she kissed her skin. She carefully stroked a warm washcloth over her fingers where dried blood remained. Everywhere she could touch Syd without hurting her, she did, with her fingers and then her lips. She ignored the incessant beeping of the machines and spoke quietly to her. The nurse said that it was just a matter of time before she woke up; her body was just busy healing itself. The nurse's smile had been kind. Parker rested her face near Syd's left ear.

"Love, I'm here. It's Parker, sweetheart. I need you to get well, Sydney. I love you."

Parker caressed Sydney's cheek and watched as her body twitched against an invisible force, as if she was dreaming. When she quieted again, Parker slid the chair next to the bed and placed her face on Sydney's palm. The exhaustion of the past hours consumed her. She heard Taylor's voice just outside the room before she closed her eyes.

❖

Darcy was dozing against the doorframe of room 347. Taylor sat down next to her and gently folded Darcy against her shoulder. "Why are you out here?"

A sleepy Darcy settled into Taylor and shrugged. "Didn't feel right. Not really my place in there anymore."

"Anymore?" Taylor arched an eyebrow at the new snippet of Darcy's life.

Darcy looked up at Taylor without moving from the comfortable place in her arms. "Syd and I were in a relationship a long time ago. I haven't been exactly mature about things recently, so I thought I would just be here if Parker needed anything, and not intrude."

"You're a very kind person, Darcy Dean." Taylor leaned down to kiss her briefly. "What do *you* need?"

Darcy chuckled and plucked her T-shirt away from her body. "Probably a decontamination chamber, I feel disgusting."

"Well, luckily, you look beautiful," Taylor lied as she stroked Darcy's haphazard blond hair which had seemed to develop corners and right angles over the past hours. "Why don't you go home and take a shower while I wait here. You won't be long, and I'll call you if anything happens." Taylor dangled the keys to the Highlander until Darcy closed her fingers around them gratefully.

Taylor stood, leaning against the wall, and pulled Darcy to her feet.

Darcy studied Taylor warily. "Tay, did you ever think that a week ago you had a perfectly normal life, and then Hurricane Darcy dragged you into this craziness?" She rubbed her stinging eyes with the heels of both her hands trying to refocus through the grit beneath her lids on the woman beside her.

"I'm not sure that anyone knows what normal looks like, certainly not me. And since you were missing from it, my life certainly wasn't perfect." Taylor slid her hands under Darcy's hair and dusted a kiss over her lips.

"Wow. That is one hell of a comeback." A warm flush of emotion flooded over Darcy, and she gripped the neck of Taylor's neatly tucked shirt. "You must have cleaned up in the bar."

Taylor smiled broadly. "I did," she responded knowingly.

"I'll be right back. Don't go anywhere," Darcy whispered, feeling oddly at home in Taylor's embrace.

❖

Mack found Jenny curled beside her, pressed awkwardly against the bed railing, when the nurse came through the curtain to check on her. Mack touched her fingers to her lips before the woman in Mickey Mouse scrubs looked down at Jenny.

"Isn't the patient supposed to be the one sleeping?" she whispered.

"I was—I just woke up," Mack replied. "This is my wife, Jenny. She says she's not leaving until I do."

"Sounds like you're pretty lucky." She smiled at Mack. "The doc should be by to spring you in a few minutes. Sorry we never got you to a room. Do you need anything right now?"

"I'm good. Killer headache, but I'm okay."

"He should send you home with something to help with that. I'm Cathy, by the way. I'll be here till five if you need anything before you go." She turned, her rubber soles making a horrific squeak as the curtain closed behind her.

A few minutes later, Major Cash poked his head through the opening and asked if it was all right to come in. Mack roused Jenny, who remained by her side.

"Sorry to disturb you." Cash stopped and took in the two women.

"Couldn't imagine two people looking comfortable on the glorified stretcher, could you?" Mack joked.

"Indeed. I'm sorry to intrude."

"You're not, please come in." Mack was happy for the distraction and at least a tenuous connection to her old life where she carried a badge and people still called her Sergeant.

"How're you feeling? You look like hell."

Mack laughed and felt the tired muscles in her back revolt. "Thank you, you're too kind." Mack fingered the bandage at her temple gingerly until Jenny guided her fingers away from the injury.

Major Cash's expression became serious. "You remember anything, Foster?"

"No, sir, Sydney started talking about someone trying to over-take us but I was looking down at my phone when it happened. What did they find at the scene?"

"A very twisted hunk of metal and some white paint transfer on the left rear quarter panel. We might want to think about you staying away from your house until this blows through…just in case."

Suddenly intensely alert, Jenny slid off the bed. "Are you saying this was intentional?" She held on to the railing with one hand and Mack with the other.

"I'm saying I want to be sure." He looked apprehensive.

"What about Sydney, Major?" Mack asked.

"Right now, I only have a civilian crash in a personal vehicle outside my jurisdiction. The warrants are dropping as we speak for the things we discussed, Foster. Noles was extremely impressed with your evidence. He expects the phone records by this after-noon. It doesn't look good for Chief Williams." Cash whispered the last words.

Mack shuddered at the phrase, disgusted. "That's a really hard name to hear."

"You should try saying it to his face." He delivered the words with disdain as he walked to the curtain and looked back at her. "Lie low and get better." She nodded as he disappeared behind the cotton drape.

"Jen, I need to go check on Syd when they let me out of here."

Jenny nodded. "I'll go find the doctor. Maybe they could speed things along."

After what felt like a hundred signatures, Mack had changed into her clothes again, choosing to zip her jacket over her bare skin and throwing away her bloodstained shirt. Mack walked slowly with Jenny who gripped her left arm tightly. Her balance was still a bit tenuous due in no small part to the medications and a day in the lumpy bed.

❖

Parker felt something tickle her nose and shook out of an uncomfortable sleep bent over Syd's bed. She raised her hand to rub her face when she felt warm fingers graze across her skin.

"Hey, Park." The barely audible words found their way through Parker's disorienting fog of exhaustion and worry.

She stared for a moment before she spoke. "You're okay. Syd, you're going to be okay. I love you. I have to get the doctor." She started to stand quickly from her chair.

Syd smiled at the cascade of words. "Wait. Can you just stay with me for a minute?" Sydney brushed her thumb over the rivers of tears now cascading over Parker's pale skin.

Parker dared not sit on the mattress in case she shifted Syd too much. Her normally physically daunting girlfriend looked more fragile and broken when Parker watched her try to talk. But her heart clutched at the blissful realization that they were going to come through this together.

"Can I kiss you?" Parker laughed and cried simultaneously as she bent toward Sydney's unscarred lips.

"You better." Syd winked at her and cradled her hand against Parker's face.

"I love you so much." Parker breathed in the relief she could finally allow her mind to experience.

"Love you, baby," Syd whispered. Parker thought those were the best words she had ever heard.

The door creaked open as Jenny whispered, "Can we come in?"

Parker motioned for them to come in and reluctantly took the opportunity to let the doctor know Syd was awake.

Jenny walked Mack near the bed and Syd croaked, "You look like a raccoon, Foster."

"Not exactly ready for prime time yourself there, Hyatt."

Syd smiled but made sure not to laugh. She hadn't tried it yet but considering the fact that breathing hurt, she didn't imagine that laughing was recommended. "Jenny," Syd whispered, "would you find out if I can have any ice chips? My mouth is a desert."

"Of course, sweetie." She left, seeming to realize that she had just been maneuvered out of a conversation.

"Okay, why did you want her out of here?" Mack asked.

Syd heard the door click closed before she answered, with effort, "Number sixty-one Mack, *CTI0061*. I saw the plate before the accident. It was a CTI truck."

Mack processed the implication of the information and lifted her good hand in resignation. "Even if it's a three million dollar score, are you really going to kill a cop, then attempt two more murders right behind it? You need to tell Cash everything you remember."

Jenny returned carrying a small Styrofoam cup filled with chips of ice. She stopped to read the text Mack was sending her commander. "They're going to fix this, sweetheart. You trust the major, right?"

"I trusted a lot of people. Not so sure I'm the best judge of character right now." Mack backed slowly into the side chair, suddenly a bit unstable. "But, yeah, I do, I have no choice."

"Syd and Darcy will back you up." Jenny stood behind Mack.

"I just hope that's enough." Mack sounded resigned and tapped her tight fist against her chin.

"It'll be okay. I believe that and so should you," Syd insisted in the strongest voice she could manage.

"Thanks." Mack read her return text and passed the phone to Sydney.

Within ten minutes, Major Cash pushed through the door and looked solemnly at Sydney and then to Mack. "Can the three of us talk?"

Jenny said, "Why don't I find Parker, and we go grab a shower and some clothes? I'm dying to get some fresh air."

"I would love some clean clothes, sweetheart. Thanks." Mack nodded and Jenny left the room again.

"You were right, Mack, cellular GPS records put Williams at the scene before the 9-1-1 call was made and at least near the phone it came from when dispatch got it." He shook his head and handed her a sheet with Provost's name at the top. At 10:24 p.m. she had received a call from a Silver Lake phone number. After one minute she made another call...to Williams.

"We need the Downings' numbers." Syd didn't wait to be invited into the conversation.

"Your friend Taylor already helped us with that. Their mobile phone numbers are published in a company directory." He pointed to another entry. "Provost spoke with Lawrence Downing ninety-eight times in two months, not including right before she called Williams. We should be able to track Junior's phone to the nearest tower if he was there."

"Oh, he was there," Syd grumbled.

"Major, Syd saw the plate. The truck that hit us belonged to CTI."

Cash shook his head. "This is either the dumbest group of criminals or one significant idiot that everyone is having to cover for. The sad part is that at least two of the people in this shit are—*were*—cops."

He turned back to Mack. "The bureau is going to work fast, Foster, which means you should be someplace safe in the meantime. I walked from my car to this door in less than four minutes and no one even approached me. I'm not saying they'll be that bold, but you should be careful."

Mack agreed. "Major, Syd prepared most of the evidence in the file I handed over to you." Mack nodded to Syd who knew that everything would come out soon enough.

"You do nice work, Ms. Hyatt." The major shook her left hand. He was evidently not surprised by the revelation.

"Syd, please. I'm talking to you while lying in a bed wearing the equivalent of a pale green handkerchief—I think you can call me by my first name."

Major Cash laughed. "What can you tell me about the vehicle that hit you?"

She glanced her left hand gingerly over her hair and swallowed slowly, "Large white Ford box truck, license plate *CTI0061*. Couldn't see the driver, my car sits too low, you know, by the time it got close enough. It pushed us off the side and then rammed us on the left rear bumper. That's how we ended up going off the road and, I have to assume, flipped over."

"When did you first see it?" He took notes by hand into a tiny pad from his pocket, then tapped some information into his phone.

"I don't know, I just looked in the mirror and all I saw was white." She closed her eyes and fought against the memory of the second she realized they were going off the road, being pushed off the road.

After a few minutes Syd looked up at Cash. "Did you see my car? Do you have a picture of the wreck?"

He looked uncomfortable and hesitated. "It's totaled, Syd."

"I figured that. I just kind of want to say good-bye." She attempted a smile as he drew his phone out of his jacket pocket and slid his thumb over the screen.

Syd let out her breath in an audible *whoosh* as the mass of black twisted metal came into view. "My insurance company is not going to be happy with me." She looked at the mangled mess she couldn't imagine two people escaping from.

"If this goes like I think it will, you'll be filing with another company." His smile was genuine.

"Major? Did they find my gun in the car?" Syd asked. "It's kind of my favorite."

"The traffic unit logged all the property while I was there. They found it and two phones along with two sets of keys and your duffel, Mack. I'll get it all back to you as soon as I can." He turned to Mack, who was draped uncomfortably in the blue vinyl chair. "You know, your black eyes would look a hell of a lot worse if you were pasty and pale like the rest of us."

Mack smiled for the first time since the conversation began. It faded again as she asked, "Major, will I get my shield back?"

"Damn right, you will. Trying to sanction you in the face of the damage control the department is facing would be political suicide. I will hand you your badge myself although the freaking mayor should do it first." He looked disgusted. The facts were all there but the reality still seemed hard for him to take.

"I won't hold my breath for that." Mack laughed weakly.

"Good idea." He walked toward the door after sitting with them for over an hour. He read a new message on his phone. "I have a feeling we might all want to watch the news tomorrow. They just towed a CTI truck to the state lab."

"That was fast." Syd smirked at Mack.

"They already had the warrant to match the trucks to the video, but your ID made it a bit more pressing." Major Cash stalked back to the hallway.

Syd pushed up awkwardly, wincing at the stabbing pain in her side. She looked hard at Mack as she said, "Come stay with us for a few days, okay?"

"That's fine with me, but what are we going to tell the girls? I really don't want to make Jenny any more nervous than I have to."

"That we deserve a slumber party and some time to regroup." Syd looked over the monitors and wondered if she could convince someone to spring her, too.

❖

Jenny returned, followed by Taylor and Darcy. The energy in the room felt lighter for the first time.

Jenny crossed to Mack and kissed her gratefully like they had been separated for weeks. "Syd, Parker's finding out when a doc will be back in for rounds. She'll be here in a few minutes. Meanwhile, Richard says Allen is spoiling Olivia rotten. He's working at the drafting table with the baby sling strapped to his chest. He doubts she has been alone since I left." Jenny shook her head as Mack laughed and Sydney tried not to. She pictured the fussy architect finding his inner motherly instincts.

Jen looked over at Sydney. "We borrowed some of your clothes, Syd. We don't need Mack looking like a flasher." Jenny jerked down the zipper of Mack's only covering. Mack grabbed her hand before it went any lower and grinned as she pried the plastic bag from her fingers.

"I agree, definitely not a good idea," Syd said. "So, we were thinking, we should all stay together for a few days." Sydney's tone grew dark and serious. "I'm going to sign myself out of here as soon as I can and you guys need to stay with us. We are, at least, in a secure building. Taylor, you need a few days off for sure—got any?"

"Fifteen of them to be exact. I can call in." Taylor obviously liked the thought of spending a few more days with Darcy, not to mention avoiding a face-to-face with Bryce Downing.

"Parker is going to *kick your ass*," Jenny said dramatically.

"She's right, you know," Mack said. "Parker isn't going to let you sign out of here AMA." She looked expectantly at the door.

"She will if it means keeping Jenny safe and the baby sequestered a little longer." Sydney had already devised a plan.

"Better argument is if it means keeping *you* safe," Darcy interjected. "I've never seen anyone look so scared in my life, Syd. That woman about took the doctor out when he told her to go home instead of staying with you."

Syd smiled and swung her legs tentatively over the side of the bed. She could imagine the look on Parker's face. "She is scary tough when she wants to be."

Jenny concurred, looking sternly at Syd. "She's ferocious when it comes to you. I hope you know that."

"I do. Believe me, I do." Sydney felt the words flush over her skin.

As if on cue, Parker pushed through the door and walked inside. She folded her arms over her chest and looked angry. "What are you doing, Sydney?" Syd opened her mouth to respond before Parker cut her off. "You just had fucking surgery, Syd. What are you thinking?"

Darcy stepped back and turned to find shelter with Taylor.

Syd heard Parker curse very rarely, only in the heat of passion and when she was beyond furious. The latter was fairly terrifying.

"I know you're mad, baby." She secretly hoped the term of endearment might soften her fury for a moment. "But I need you to listen for a minute, okay? Please hear me out. Everyone needs to stay with us until this all shakes out. We just don't know where all the players are or even who they all are, for that matter. It certainly isn't safe for Taylor to go back to work, and Mack's address is practically public knowledge as long as Williams is at the helm." Syd hoped she wouldn't have to mention concern for her own safety.

"We need to talk to the doctor, Syd, you aren't superwoman." Parker's worry for Sydney was palpable.

"Okay, then let's talk to the doctor." Parker shook her head when Syd readily acquiesced. As if on cue, a slight thirtysomething man in a white coat walked in with a weary look and a resigned constitution.

Five hours and reams of paper later, Parker helped a very weak Sydney, in loose cotton shorts and an oversized T-shirt, sit in a wheelchair. They headed for the exit where Jenny waited in her SUV.

"Don't let anyone see me like this, please." Syd smiled at a worried Parker and tried to ignore the throb of pain skidding over her right side. "I'm okay. Really. Let's just go home." Mack moved slowly to the passenger seat and Syd slid awkwardly into the back with Parker next to her.

The convoy of the three vehicles drove slowly down Meridian Street. Jen turned the SUV into Syd's vacant space, while Syd tried not to think of the scrap metal that was once her beloved Porsche. Darcy and Jen flanked Mack for the trek up the walk, and Taylor jogged around to the back seat to help Parker get Sydney to her feet.

"You should have stayed put, Hyatt," Parker grumbled and glided open the heavy front door, waiting for the group to file in. She slid the door closed and latched it, stopping to glance over their home where she usually felt safe. She longed for the day something made her feel that way again. No one had told her directly, but she could read Syd and even Mack well. Jenny hadn't needed to confirm that the *accident* might not have been accidental.

Syd leaned tentatively against a bar stool and offered the kitchen to whoever wished it.

"I'm going to lie down with Mack for a bit, if that's okay?" Jenny announced.

Parker nodded, straightening. "Do you need help getting the bed down?"

"Nah, I have the one-armed bandit." She thumbed over her shoulder at Mack who stuck out her tongue. Parker knew that Jenny wouldn't let her near the Murphy bed.

"We can always go to my place and get out of your hair, Parker," Taylor offered.

"No one's going anywhere. Couch or the air mattress?" Parker secretly thought the couch was far superior to the wretched thing she had slept on when she'd moved in across the hall.

"Couch is fine." Taylor was obviously uncomfortable being fussed over especially with people she still didn't know well.

"Pull the ottoman over, and it makes a nice bed." Syd's voice was still weak. "Sheets are in the hall closet, take whatever."

Parker walked over to hug Darcy firmly and then Taylor. "Thank you, both, you were amazing to me. To us."

Darcy walked to Sydney and placed her arms gently around her shoulders. "I'm glad you're okay, or going to be, at least."

"Thanks, Dean. Be good to that girl—she seems to like you a little," Syd whispered in her ear and winked at Parker. Darcy moved into the living room with Taylor's arm firmly around her waist.

"Can I make you something to eat, love?" Parker's voice shook as she bit at the inside of her cheek to steady it.

"I want a shower like you wouldn't believe."

"You can't. Syd, you heard the doctor say you can't get the bandages wet yet."

"I can sit on the bench and you can help me rinse off. I won't get the bandages wet. I just have to feel clean, please." Her gray eyes were weak and imploring as she walked carefully toward the bathroom.

Parker reluctantly agreed and turned the water to produce a trickling stream after she helped Sydney sit against the tile bench, angled away from the water. She tried not to react when she saw her lover's battered body. Parker cautiously stroked a soapy washcloth across Sydney's skin and rinsed the lather away with another. She knelt in front of Sydney who leaned stiffly into the corner of the shower. She crouched near Syd's thigh and wracking sobs overtook her.

"No, Park. Please don't. I'm okay." Sydney shifted to guide Parker to a spot on the bench near her. She lifted her left arm and folded Parker's wet body against her uninjured side.

Parker barely gathered the air sufficient to speak. She didn't intend for her words to sound so angry. "I could have lost you. You could have been killed." The last words died on a whisper as Parker felt physical pain at possibly losing Syd.

"I'm just fine, Park. I'm so sorry you had to go through this, that you had to worry about me." Another sob escaped Parker's throat, and Syd tightened her lopsided grip on Parker's shoulder. Sydney laid her lips against Parker's hair. "I get it. If I picture you in that hospital bed, it's terrifying."

"I watched them fly you out and I felt like I couldn't breathe. I couldn't hear. It was like wading through mud or something. Like I knew what was happening in my brain but my heart hurt—it actually hurt, Sydney." Parker had to get it out, to process the hours since the accident, the emotions she had buried until now.

Sydney tilted Parker's face toward hers. "I can't tell you how much I want to fix this, but I need you to look at me. I'm okay. We're safe and together. We will always be." Sydney looked desperate to take the memory from Parker, to erase her pain. "I told you I would never let go. I have never lied to you."

Parker nodded as she felt a chill over her arms having nothing to do with being cold, and she reached into the spray to stop the water.

They walked back to the bedroom, and Parker watched Syd push a towel over her hair and pat it over whatever parts of her body she could reach without too much pain. Parker pushed a long T-shirt over Syd's head and helped her lie back in the bed. She felt the wince of discomfort on Sydney's face as she reclined awkwardly onto the mattress.

Syd settled and tugged Parker toward her, gliding her fingers across Parker's hip. "We could, um…"

"Forget it, Hyatt. You're completely ridiculous." Parker inched toward her lover and fought the fear that still danced in her heart. "I love you so much. I couldn't imagine my life if you weren't going to be okay."

"I love you more than anything. Thank you for taking care of me."

CHAPTER TWENTY

Major Williams walked into his office to address his administrative staff regarding the changes he planned to make for the SLPD. He believed in his heart that the interim title was simply a formality, which meant that there was no time like the present to put his stamp on his department.

He passed two men in dark suits in the waiting area and was shocked to see VBCI SAC John Noles in his office.

"John. This is an unexpected surprise. To what do I owe the pl—"

"This isn't a social call, Damon." Noles stood and handed him a wad of folded documents. "I have warrants. We need to search your office and your house. This covers your cell phone and your computers." Noles was serious and dark when he spoke.

Damon Williams bowed his chest and stepped to the shorter man in an attempt to intimidate him. "You will do no such thing, John," he spat the words, displaying a bravado that began to fade as the implications of the agent's words began to build in his psyche. The two men from the lounge entered the office and stood behind him, plucking his weapon from its holster and the telephone from his belt clip.

"Damon, I'm trying to do this nicely. We waited for you to arrive before we went through your office. You need to understand that there's nothing you can do to stop this."

Williams sat in his own visitor chair and nodded, watching the agents dismember the dreams he had been building for years. The envelope was extracted from his bottom drawer, his last hope with it. He looked at his shoes that he had polished so well for his first full week on the job, then focused on John Noles who was cataloging evidence on a clipboard. "I believe I need to call a union rep and my lawyer."

"Probably a good idea, Damon," John Noles responded. "I have to know, when did you forget everything the job was supposed to be?"

Williams didn't answer. He suddenly regretted every decision he should have made and didn't. He knew there was no point in calling Jayne or even Pamela—he was on his own now and the best he could hope for was a deal. He blamed Bryce Downing and would make sure he paid. Jayne would pay, too. He wanted her to burn in the fire she'd set.

The agents waited as he arranged to meet his union lawyer at bureau headquarters. He thanked them for agreeing to walk him to the car without handcuffs. Damon Williams stopped to look at the photo of the day he'd accepted his badge, a long distance from being arrested inside the chief's office he had occupied for mere hours.

Jayne Provost collected her Tumi purse from beneath her desk. She planned on sitting down for a healthy lunch before returning for the remainder of the day's appointments. She glanced across the lake and idly watched a large trimaran amble across the water. She heard her door open as CEO Mason Bailey pushed through, leading a contingent of two men and a woman in dark suits. She recognized one of the men as a VBCI agent she had met at the Silver Lake Ball.

"Mason, good afternoon." The question in her voice was evident as she scanned his guests. "What can I do for you?"

Agent Angela Stall stepped ahead, her forearm resting on the weapon inside her jacket. "Ms. Provost, I'm Special Agent Stall. We have a warrant for your arrest. The charges are listed here if you care to read them. You also need to know that there are pending federal charges. We have a warrant for this office, your house and vehicle, your cell phone, computers, and corresponding records." Agent Stall watched her as if waiting for a reaction as she read from the paper.

Provost did not offer her the satisfaction. She was incensed at the circumstance that would decimate everything she ever hoped to possess. She stepped aggressively toward Agent Stall.

"Be very careful, Ms. Provost," Mason Bailey warned. "This is not the time to further embarrass yourself or this company. You and Lawrence have done enough." His words were weary and stoic as he seemed to process the fallout to come. "Do you have anything to say before you leave? Like where you put millions of dollars of my inventory?" He jerked the CTI badge from her lapel in disgust.

"Mason, I had nothing to do with that! We need to speak with Lawrence and Bryce. In fact, I was planning on coming to you with my suspicions this afternoon." Provost spoke as if she couldn't fathom the accusation and ignored everything she knew about remaining silent. She watched the male agents begin rifling through her bag and her desk.

Stall read her the Miranda warning and appeared to delight in the sound of the handcuffs as their teeth bit through the mechanism replacing her Tiffany bangle as the most prominent jewelry she wore. Provost knew the agents could have chosen to lead her discreetly from the building via some back door, but instead Mason Bailey held the front door open wide after they walked her through the busy lobby.

News vans were perched on the approach to CTI headquarters. Stall looked back at the CEO and rushed to speak. "The VBCI didn't call them, Mr. Bailey."

"I know. I did. The publicity on this is going to be hell, so I decided CTI should go first." He sounded unapologetic when he admitted to purposely humiliating his apparently short-term CSO." Bailey walked to the curb where a short man wielding a microphone began lobbing questions at him. It was only a few seconds before the CEO was surrounded by others.

❖

Parker and Jen worked diligently from the living room, trying to catch up from their missed work. Jen tapped away on the computer, handing Parker approvals to sign and resumes to review. Parker returned calls and apologized for delays while Mack hunted through the fridge, awkwardly lifting the tray of fruit Mia had left by the front door.

Parker heard Sydney call her from the bedroom. She ran to the bed, certain she would find evidence of a setback caused by a too-early hospital release. She was relieved to find a wide-eyed Sydney propped against the headboard and pointing at the wall-mounted television.

"Get everybody in here. They're going to want to see this." Sydney's eyes were fixed and staring at the screen. A tiny grin played over her lips.

All six of them crowded onto the king mattress and watched the *News 12 Special Report* banner covering the large screen.

News 12 was the first to bring you this story late last night and we are interrupting this morning's programming to bring you this special report.

Today, Silver Lake City Council confirmed that Interim Chief Damon Williams officially resigned from the Silver Lake Police Department. A confidential source inside the Virginia Police Union confirmed that criminal charges of tampering with evidence, collusion, and conspiracy are pending. The former SLPD commander is rumored to have cited direction from the former police chief, Jayne Provost, who left just last week for her new position as CSO of CacheTech. Ms. Provost refused to comment as she was led from the CTI headquarters in handcuffs by agents from the Virginia Bureau of Criminal Investigation. A brand new Jaguar, suspected to belong to Provost, was towed to the state's impound lot this morning. Preliminary court documents reveal that she will be charged with numerous felonies. A federal indictment is also expected. Neither Provost nor a representative was available for comment.

In related news, the former Chief Security Officer of CTI, Lawrence Downing, III, was arrested for embezzlement of over four million dollars in stolen property belonging to CacheTech Incorporated, Silver Lake's largest employer. CTI's inventory manager found the discrepancy and reported it to officials who launched an investigation. Downing was arrested while accepting delivery of a sixty-five foot sailboat at the dock of his Silver Lake mansion which has also been seized by agents.

Authorities tell us that Bryce Downing, Lawrence's son, is also charged with embezzlement and is being sought as a person of interest in connection with at least two murders, including the death of SLPD Sergeant Sandra Curran.

Sergeant Curran, a veteran of the Silver Lake Police Department, was shot and killed on July 4th and it is believed that she was investigating the delivery of stolen goods connected to the CTI thefts. Murder charges are also pending against Bryce Downing in the death of CTI's former employee Greg Matthews who police speculate may have also discovered the inventory thefts. Matthews's body was found hidden in the crawlspace of Bryce Downing's town home, also on Silver Lake.

Authorities declined to speak with us citing the ongoing investigation but a source inside the SLPD told News 12 that the younger Downing may also face attempted murder charges in connection with another police officer and a city contractor.

A CTI spokesman told this station that their records are an open book and the privately held company is planning to cooperate fully with law enforcement.

Finally, Silver Lake socialite Pamela Hyatt was removed from the city council Concerned Citizens' Coalition when she was charged with influence peddling and bribery. News 12 is unclear if the woman was connected to last evening's arrests but she was rumored to have been intimately involved with Interim Chief Williams and admits to having knowledge of the corruption at the SLPD.

We now return you to your regularly scheduled programming.

They all sat silently until Parker inched away from the crowd.

"I think I might throw up." Sydney spoke first as Parker dove for a trash can near the bed. Syd grinned and pushed it away. "No, I just realized there's one person I think is not good enough for my mother." Sydney was horrified at the mental image of her mother and the slovenly Damon Williams. Parker also shuddered at the thought.

"I think Jen and I should go see if Mia's home. She might need someone to talk to." Parker tapped Jenny's knee.

"Good thought." Sydney held her lips against Parker's as a little light dawned over their universe.

"Be right back." Parker turned and saw Darcy leaning on a pillow next to Sydney. She smiled at Syd who seemed to catch her bemused look. Parker looked at the wiry blonde holding Darcy's hand. "Taylor, you're in charge until we get back."

"Yes, ma'am." If Taylor caught the inference, she pretended not to notice, and Parker led Jenny from the room.

As they passed, they could see Mack outside the lobby door speaking with Major Cash. Jenny released a fortifying breath as he placed her badge in her hand.

Chapter Twenty-one

S ydney drew her tongue across the smooth plane of Parker's shoulder and slid the zipper of her halter dress toward the floor. "Like this?" Her fingers found the subtle curve of Parker's breasts as she skidded her fingers under the now loose fabric.

Parker spun away, pulling the dress around her hips. "Not even close, Hyatt. You're supposed to be helping us leave, not seducing me into a puddle."

"I like you in a puddle." Sydney's raspy voice gave Parker chills. She was momentarily lost in her girlfriend whose hands were now traveling slowly up her back. Sydney's silver cuff links, cut into lightning bolts, glinted at each of her wrists. The gift from Parker after her stitches were removed now claimed the cuffs of her starched white shirt.

"Dirty and impossible." Parker felt her resolve weaken as Sydney pushed a finger under her chin and captured her mouth excruciatingly slowly. "You make me incredibly hot," Parker managed when Sydney moved her lips a fraction from hers.

"I love it when a plan comes together." Sydney began moving her mouth down Parker's neck delivering chills in her wake. "How about we skip the reception and I'll kiss your entire body instead."

Parker struggled to fight the temptation to succumb to her lover's maneuverings. "Hey, Darcy Dean is madly in love with one of the guests of honor tonight. You know I want to keep encouraging her interests and, of course, make sure they no longer include you." Parker smiled into Sydney as she nipped her chin.

"Fine. Then I'll just kiss half your body when we get home." Syd zipped the dress and fastened the tiny snap at the top.

"Shortcuts do not impress me, my love. I want it all." Parker twirled away flirtatiously and dragged Sydney, who growled lustfully, to the door. They climbed into the Fosters' waiting Murano for their carpool to CTI.

Sydney glanced longingly over the shiny new black Porsche 911 that had been delivered yesterday. CTI had made sure that any shortfall in the insurance fell to them and not her. Sydney couldn't wait to drop the top and feel the power of that engine under her body again. She drew Parker against her, feeling the much more alluring power of her lover pervading her body instead. Sydney reminded herself that nothing would ever feel better than that.

The lobby of CacheTech was decorated for the grand event, designed, Syd knew, to turn the tide of bad press the company had endured over the past months. Metal folding chairs were disguised with white covers and a river of food and drink floated on long white tables that circled the perimeter of the three story lobby.

Taylor Westin noticed their arrival and waved across the expanse of charcoal gray marble before continuing her conversation with her new boss.

The mystery surrounding Bryce Downing's whereabouts had faded from the news within weeks of the arrests but was never far from the minds of the CacheTech executives who were still unraveling the forensic accounting nightmare. It was assumed that, despite his place on the FBI's Most Wanted List, he had used his ill-gotten gains to flee to Mexico and start the life of a fugitive.

Syd tried to fight the feeling that told her justice wouldn't be sufficiently served until the smug bastard was in prison where he belonged. Identifying the buyers of the stolen computers would have made CTI much happier, but they had settled for the recovery of the twelve pallets found in Bryce's storage locker and the seizure of the elder Downing's assets in a deal that saved him from any federal time.

Major Dawn Turner from Raleigh had settled into her new civilian role nicely. It had taken some convincing for her to accept the position and, if rumors were to be believed, some extra money as well. Turner's first task had been changing the rules and procedures for the handling of inventory, a review aided by their new operations manager Taylor Westin. Mason Bailey had promoted Taylor after she'd reconstructed the path of missing inventory and demonstrated safeguards which would stop future thefts from occurring.

Syd watched Darcy, dressed in white linen pants and a black A-line blouse, glide next to Taylor who draped an easy arm around her waist, never breaking the stride of her conversation.

Jenny swiped a glass of champagne from a passing tray as she confided, "I pumped enough for a week just so I could be a grown-up tonight."

"Cheers then. I love you guys so much." Parker kissed Jenny's cheek and reached for Sydney's hand.

A few moments before the end of the cocktail hour, Darcy dragged Taylor over to the foursome. She wore considerably fewer earrings now, having adopted a slightly more traditional persona for her corporate role. Parker offered Taylor a congratulatory hug. "Wow, what a year for you, huh?"

"Certainly not what I expected." The tall blonde caught Darcy in a kiss. "The best part is standing here."

"You already have my undying love, Tay. You don't have to butter me up anymore." Darcy joked, but her smile was electric as she looked at Taylor.

"I'm just ensuring that no one sweeps you away from me." Taylor gripped Darcy's waist firmly.

"Looks like you might have met your match, Darc. Don't blow it," Sydney mused.

Guests settled into folding chairs facing the makeshift stage while Mason Bailey introduced the executive staff. The last name was the most recent addition of the new CSO. Dawn Turner spoke eloquently about overcoming challenges and embracing obstacles. She pointed to the board's faith in her to set up best practices and introduced Taylor as her partner in the endeavor.

The speeches were long over and the revelers were thinning by 10:30. Parker enlisted Jenny to make the final pit stop to the facilities while Sydney and Mack were introduced to Provost's replacement.

Parker was impressed by the gleaming finishes in the ladies room. Onyx vessel sinks perched on quartz counters and brushed nickel faucets hung from invisible pipes in the walls.

"Maybe they could sell off some of this stuff and make up for Bryce's thievery," Jenny whispered to Parker.

"It's definitely a thought, but I think his boat and mortgage-free mansion should do nicely for starters. Allen would love it in here." She snapped a few shots with her phone and sent them off to her favorite architect.

Parker swept the lipstick wand across her mouth and thanked Jenny for relocating an errant strand of hair before they headed back. Jenny was admiring the giant canvases in the adjacent hall and wandered down a path leading away from the lobby. Parker followed, appreciating the works of modern art which rose over yards of rich cherry wainscoting.

Parker paid no attention to where exactly they were strolling until they found themselves in a quiet hall lined by ten-foot wooden doors. Jenny motioned for Parker to join her at the end of the long hall as she disappeared around the last corner.

Parker heard Jenny gasp and she watched a hand slip roughly around Jenny's neck. She was flattened against a grimy man in a stained white shirt. Parker could smell sweat and alcohol. She could see the small round hole that indicated the muzzle of a gun was now pointed at her.

"Well, if it isn't the dyke of the Silver Lake Ball. Where's your bodyguard now?" Bryce Downing looked pale and unkempt as he jerked Jenny against him more tightly and glared at Parker.

"What do you want, Bryce?" Parker attempted to keep her voice calm as she walked with her hand out toward Jenny. The adrenaline careened through her body as she fought to focus on the disheveled man.

"Well, first of all, I want the money you all stole from me, you bitch. Well, the money your dyke friends stole from me." He spat the words at Parker who fought the fear she felt watching Jenny struggle to breathe. Jenny was using her fingers to attempting to create a barrier between her neck and the man's ratcheting arm.

"The company just took back what they owned, Bryce. We don't have any of your money. This wasn't a good plan." Parker grasped at a logical attempt to snap Bryce Downing out of the madness he wore on his shiny, bloated face. It was a far cry from the well-groomed schmuck he presented at the ball.

"This wasn't even my plan. I guess I just got lucky." He laughed as he vented about the injustice he had suffered. "Do you understand how long I worked for what I had? Do you understand that taking that from me was wrong?" He barely refrained from shouting as he jerked Jenny roughly, inadvertently allowing her to collapse against the carpet. He saw his insurance policy crumple into a heap and snatched a handful of Parker's long hair in his fist. Parker angled toward him and clamped her hands over his wrist attempting to lessen the painful tension on her scalp. She fought a wave of fear and refused to let it cloud her ability to defend herself.

"Bryce, please. Just tell me what you want, something I can actually help you get. You're going to get caught in here. Someone will eventually come this way." Parker swept her gaze around the corridor, assessing the possibility of escape. She forced away the same panic she recognized from the last time she stood this close to Bryce.

"No way out for you, you snotty bitch. I know every entry and exit in this whole building. They didn't see me come in and they won't see me leave." His bravado looked more like madness and he kicked a boot into Jenny's side causing her to cry out. "Get up," he growled cruelly at Jenny who managed to stand, holding her side. Jenny reached for Parker's hand.

"What, you sleeping with her, too?" Parker felt his spit reach her ear and she tried not to react.

"Walk that way. Make a sound and I'll shoot you both, understand?" He shoved them into a door marked *IT—Authorized Access Only*. He pushed them between two upright racks and turned to check that the door was secure. Parker shifted Jenny behind her just as Sydney had done during her confrontation with Bryce.

Jenny took a ragged breath and tilted her forehead into Parker's shoulder. Bryce paced the small area lit only by a single fluorescent emergency fixture at the corner of the room. He sweated profusely despite the constant blast of cold air being pumped through the vents. He skimmed his fingers along the bottom of a large server unit and smiled, coming away with a thick envelope. Parker could see stacks of cash as he brushed his fingers over the paper. She scanned the room listening for anyone who might be searching for them.

Bryce paced and dragged a forearm across his sweaty brow, seemingly deep in thought. He folded the large envelope and tucked it into his waistband under his shirt. Jenny raised a hand, guiding Parker to lean against one of the racks. Parker noticed as Jen begin to disconnect the cables plugged into the switches near her hip. Parker chanced a glance behind her and realized what her crafty friend was doing. There was no slack in the cables so they weren't obvious as they dangled among the multitude of the other blue wires.

Slowly she shifted Parker to the other rack, intently watching the gun-wielding fugitive who seemed consumed with wearing a path over the industrial carpet squares instead of monitoring his unintended captives.

❖

Sydney glanced toward the distant hallway and then back to Mack and gestured. They met in the center of the room. Mack looked tense, a fact that made a normally overprotective Sydney feel more justified in the vibrations that gripped her gut.

"Have they been gone a long time or is it just me?" Mack asked Syd who was clenching and unclenching her fists at her sides.

"Twenty-three minutes, but I'm not counting." Syd glanced toward the hall as Mack stepped to scan over the room. Mack led their quiet walk down the hall, flexing her right hand, still in a soft cast as a precaution. Syd walked quickly behind her, waiting outside the restroom door while Mack searched inside.

"Not in there. Where would they go? We're being nuts, right?"

Mack peered down one end of the hall as Syd scanned the other.

"Probably," Syd responded automatically. She watched the alarm panel blink a gold light. She knew the flashing LED indicated a communications failure. Sydney idly thought that the new CSO had her work cut out for her.

Mack pushed open several large doors along the hall, finding only dark cavernous rooms, empty but for the abandoned furniture waiting for Monday morning occupants. Sydney kept a solid pace on the other side until they met again at the end of the hall. Two card readers flashed yellow outside doors, one marked with the CEO's nameplate and the other on the telephone room just past it. Syd grabbed Mack's arm and pointed at the indicator.

She whispered in Mack's ear, "That's Bailey's office. Somehow I think those should be working, don't you? I recognize the model, and this company designs all their systems to be fail-open which means the whole building could be unsecured right now."

Mack nodded and slid her fingers over the gun at her right hip. When a faint alarm tone found Sydney, she reached under her jacket and behind her back, folding her hand over the butt of the small Sig she dropped against her right thigh.

The women crept down the hall skimming shoulders against the canvases hung along the executive wing. A lever handle angled down as light shifted from the IT room. Mack pushed Sydney into a small alcove holding a janitor's room and a water fountain. She jerked her head toward the door as they watched Bryce Downing force Jenny and Parker toward the exit door at the opposite end of the long hall.

Mack caught her partner's eye as she jerked out first. Sydney followed in a quiet run. They had no plan beyond separating Parker and Jenny from the fugitive. The carpet muffled their approach until they were just feet behind Bryce. He wheeled around to see Mack and barely registered the intruder before feeling Mack's elbow drive into his stomach. As he involuntarily bent to catch his breath, Syd twisted the gun from his hand and drove the butt of the weapon into his neck, collapsing him to the floor. Bryce, who still held Parker's arm, forced her into the wall with his folding body.

Mack held Bryce to the carpet and allowed Sydney to once again peel his hand from Parker's skin.

"You all right?" Syd asked them both on an anxious breath feeling the heat rise up her spine when she replayed the last few seconds.

Jenny nodded and looked at Mack, her fear visibly trans-forming into anger. "He came to get a big packet of money from that room. It's in his pants." She snarled at the prone man still groaning from his injury.

Mack jerked him on to his back, kneeling hard on his upper arm, while Syd extracted the envelope. "Well, I guess you couldn't leave town without the rest of your money, huh?"

He spat at Mack before he was shoved roughly back toward the floor. He could see only Sydney's face as she jerked his other arm painfully behind his back. She waited for Mack to muscle his wrists into cuffs.

"You're just pissed I wrecked your precious little car, bitch."
He couldn't stem the flow of drool leaking from the corner of his
mouth as he was pressed into the rough carpet.

Mack laughed as she knelt heavily against his neck while di-
aling 911. "Actually, I think it was the time you hit on her girlfriend. She *hates* that."

Syd pointed the gun she had no intention of firing and pushed
it hard against Bryce's nose, driving him even more roughly into
the floor. "You know, Mack, I *do* hate that. Okay if I put a hole in
his head?" Sydney's words were joking but her voice was toxic
with the fear and the fury and the chaos the greedy murderer had
brought into the lives of so many people she cared about.

"Fine by me," Mack answered happily, "but I thought he
might enjoy *all* his senses while he's making new friends in the
pen."

"Good point"—she spoke in a low snarl as her lips stopped
just shy of his ear—"you try to fuck with what's mine again,
Downing, I won't feel nearly as charitable. And Mack might forget
her manners if you ever touch her wife again."

Syd slid her gun home under her jacket and, using her shirt
tail, unloaded what she knew was the weapon that had killed Sandy
Curran. Mack took the clip and free round, shoving them into her
pocket. She then took the gun from Syd who held it by the trigger
guard.

"It's a Glock 20, Syd." Syd nodded as Mack jerked Bryce up
by his cuffs, awkwardly forcing his arms up and farther behind his
back. They began pushing him toward the lobby.

"You're some kind of idiot coming back here, Downing. And
even bringing the gun and admitting you caused our little accident—I guess an ego that big will trip you up every time."

Mack looked over at her wife. Jenny's fingers slid around her
elbow. "You okay, sweetheart?"

"Better," she sighed, still caressing her side.

❖

Bryce was suddenly mute as he looked down the hall and into the lobby. A semi-circle of remaining guests and CTI employees had formed as three SLPD cars stopped on the apron outside the front doors, unaware that their most famous ex-employee was being led through the crowd from the back. Dawn Turner walked quickly toward them, eyeing the man she knew only from the news.

She acted as crowd control, moving people gently aside as the now swearing, sweating murderer was led to the waiting officers. Darcy followed Taylor as she broke through the crowd to stand near her boss. Syd squeezed Taylor on the arm as they walked past, reassuring her that they were all fine. She'd helped push Bryce Downing through the front doors of CTI for the last time.

❖

Officer Perry switched out the cuffs Downing wore with his own and handed the empty set back to Mack. "Thanks, Sarge."

She slid them back over her belt, chuckling. "It was a total fluke that I even had these. Force of habit I guess."

"The chief called and said to handle the paper in the morning. This guy's not going anywhere." Perry placed a palm over the prisoner's head as he bent him into the caged back seat. "Have a good night."

❖

Mack nodded as she found Jenny and framed her face in her palms and kissed her gently. Mack whispered, "I'm so sorry. Let's go get you checked out."

"No way. I'm fine. I've had quite enough of hospitals. Let's just go home." Jenny inhaled as if the insanity she'd experienced an hour ago had returned.

Mack smiled. "We have to take Syd and Parker home first."

"Actually, no, you don't. I think we're going to walk a bit," Syd looked down at Parker who had closed her eyes, her head pressed against Syd. She simply nodded at Syd's unspoken question. Jenny walked over and kissed Parker soundly on the mouth.

Parker whispered, "I love you, Jen." Jenny replied in kind holding her best friend for an extra moment. Jenny whispered a thank you to Syd before walking to the car with her wife.

Now Sydney gathered Parker against her, unconcerned about the audience that still clustered inside the glass walls. Parker gripped the front of Sydney's jacket as if it were a lifeline to her sanity; perhaps it was. Sydney felt Parker shivering in her arms, and Syd shrugged out of her jacket. Parker allowed herself to be swallowed by the darkness around her before Sydney led them slowly toward the lake where the moon melted into the still water made silver by the light.

CHAPTER TWENTY-TWO

I've never seen so much brass in all my life. It looks like a military funeral." Parker leaned against Sydney, whose heavy platinum watchband rested against Parker's hand as Syd held it nervously.

"It's ridiculous that we've been to three political functions in six months." Syd scanned the crowd.

"How about we swear off anything requiring a tie or an evening gown for the rest of the year?" Parker adjusted the sleeve on her ruched crepe dress and smoothed the skirt under her legs.

"You have a deal." Syd tapped a kiss on her cheek. Parker thought the three-inch scar on Syd's neck looked much better and the mark at her side was almost healed. She had begun her workout regimen too early for the doctors, but Parker accepted that it was just who she was.

A voice from the speakers hushed the crowd. "Welcome, ladies and gentlemen. Every year we're given with the opportunity to recognize some distinguished achievements in the Silver Lake community. First of all, as chair of the Silver Lake City Council, it is my pleasure to welcome, in his first official role as the leader of the Silver Lake Police Department, Chief Mark Cash."

Mack Foster clapped as loudly as she could.

Chief Cash stood in full uniform behind the podium. He looked every inch the distinguished leader, and the SLPD loved him for it.

"Thank you for that very warm welcome. I asked to be here today. I asked for this honor because I wanted to take this moment to recognize a very special member of our police department. Despite the possible personal risk, this officer decided to do what was right. She followed a hunch and we found out too late that she was right." He took a steadying breath before he continued, "This officer cannot accept this today and for that we will always feel a loss. Accepting the Medal of Valor on behalf of Sergeant Sandra Whitney Curran, please welcome her partner Mia Wright."

Waves of coughs and sniffs flowed through the crowd of people who would always feel the loss. Mia stood alone, her hands trembling slightly as she took the blue velvet box and hugged it to her chest. She walked to the podium and cleared her throat, unmistakably trying to swallow her emotions.

"Many of you knew Sandy for much longer than I did. You knew what kind of person she was. All Sandy Curran ever wanted to do is make a difference." Mia glanced up at the sky as she spoke proudly. "You did that, honey. I love you. Sandy would want me to tell all of you thank you." She was one of many crying openly as the crowd stood and a member of the color guard walked her offstage to retake her seat next to Mack. She turned the case in her hand thumbing over the map and accepted Mack's arm around her shoulders.

Richard sat stoically as Allen held a sleeping Olivia. He brushed a hand over Parker's knee. "I can't believe we're at one of these things. Kind of strange, huh?"

"They're really happy you could come, it means a lot." Parker leaned a cheek on her friend's shoulder.

"Next, I would like to introduce a member of our community who went above and beyond the call of duty to make sure justice was served. She continues to serve the justice community in Silver Lake despite *her* significant personal risk and sacrifice. This individual deserves our highest praise and deepest thanks for her contribution. Recipient of the Silver Lake Medal of Honor, please welcome Sydney Hyatt, president of Digital Reconstruction and Independent Forensic Technology."

Sydney straightened from her seat and strode confidently up the stairs to shake the chief's hand. She stood behind the podium and found Parker in the audience, sending her a silent message.

"That was certainly a grand introduction for a small contribution. I know that the minor role I played is something that each one of us would do for a friend. I was lucky enough to be given the opportunity to help find justice for *our* friend, who also turned out to be our hero. I also want to be sure to mention Darcy Dean and Taylor Westin, whose help was invaluable."

"Of course," Sydney continued, "I can't accept any of this without also thanking the person who believes in me no matter what. Parker cheers me on every day and is the most important reason that I get up every morning." Syd paused.

"We have a great community here and the best part is when you get a chance to help. We owe all of this to Sandy Curran for showing us how it's done. Thank you."

Sydney jogged down the steps and toward her seat.

Mia stood to hug Sydney. "Thank you from both of us." Syd planted a sincere kiss on Mia's cheek before reclaiming her chair.

"Finally"—the chief straightened his tie and bent the microphone closer to his mouth—"this is not a customary announcement at one of these events, but as you all know, this has been an unusual year for our community, so here we are." He pushed an index card onto the podium but began to speak without looking at it.

"After taking on an immense investigation with no support, this individual spent every spare moment making sure that a fallen officer would have justice, her department its dignity, and her profession the sense of honor she believes at her core. The department would like to make a special presentation. Along with the much deserved Medal of Honor, please help me announce the latest promotion on the Silver Lake Police Department, Lieutenant Mackenzie Renee Foster."

Jenny leapt to her feet along with the entire assembly. Mack fought the blush she felt rising in her cheeks and strode to the dais with Jenny following close behind. The chief held the medal and firmly gripped Mack's hand as they posed for a photograph. He turned to a beaming Jenny and placed a brass bar in her fingers. At his nod, Jenny stepped to her wife and pinned it to Mack's dress uniform. Jenny put both her hands to the new lieutenant's cheeks and kissed her to the sound of renewed applause. Tears uncharacteristically filled Mack's eyes and she rigidly stood behind the podium.

She adjusted the microphone unnecessarily and stood quietly for a moment, as if sorting through words she could say without being swept under by the emotional tide. She took a deep breath and looked appreciatively at Mark Cash.

"Thank you, Chief. It's an understatement to say we're very lucky to have you. Most of all, thank you to Sandy." She grazed her teeth across her lip, "The irony is that the only reason I'm standing here is because Sandy Curran isn't. I hope, one day, I can be the officer she always was." She gripped Jenny's hand tightly and stepped off the stage.

"I would never believe that I would one day be on vacation with Darcy Dean and some random woman from one of Mack's cases." Sydney Hyatt strolled into the blue waters of Sunset Key. Her aqua blue board shorts and sports top didn't hide the fading scar along her rib cage or behind her ear but Sydney had come to view the battle wounds as a visual aid to a pretty interesting story.

Jenny and Allen sat with Olivia on the sand and Richard took off for a run. Syd watched as Mack lugged bags of sandwiches and a cooler, which she wedged under their umbrella. Darcy lay on a towel near Taylor who was reclining on a folding chair, reading a paperback. Syd marveled that four couples had managed a simultaneous vacation, if only for five days.

"Reality is much more astounding than fiction, my love. I think we can all agree on that." Parker held firmly to Sydney as the water pulsed around them.

Syd said quietly, "Do you still feel like this is enough for you? Us?"

Parker looked at Sydney sideways, managing to stifle a smile at her nervous tone. "What do you mean?"

"I mean, like Mack and Jenny. Do you need that?" Sydney angled to watch them pull a bucket up to reveal a sand castle. Olivia, oblivious to the effort, smashed a pudgy fist delightedly into the wet pile.

"Ah." Parker rested her forehead against the heated skin at Sydney's chest. "You mean do I need to be legally married and have a plethora of your babies?"

"Well, I'm not sure how many is in a plethora, but yes, that's what I mean." Sydney focused with uncertainty on Parker's amused expression.

Parker locked her legs around Sydney as the building surf pounded against them. Parker couldn't hold her tightly enough. She once again felt the terror that had found her the night she thought she lost her, until she'd forced herself back to the present and the spell created from sun block, palm trees, and piña coladas.

"If you remember," Parker continued, "I had the wedding, for a relationship that will never come close to being as right as this one is. I'm more than happy to be part of Olivia's life but I don't feel compelled to have one of my own...of *our* own." She kissed Sydney gently as a wave crashed loudly onto the shore. "To be honest, I want nothing to ever be different or to alter this. I would be too afraid to change anything we have. I was married to you the moment you kissed me and will be your wife, your partner, and whatever else, until I take my last breath. So, no, I don't need that. I only need you."

"Wow. I guess I needed to hear you say that." Sydney stared at Parker, "You are mine always. Everything I have belongs to you. All I care about is your heart." Parker felt Sydney's mouth suddenly on hers and wound her arms securely around her neck. She gasped at the heat that could engulf them in any place, as if they walked in a solitary space constructed solely for the two of them.

"Didn't you say there would be a lot of sex and massages on our vacation?" Parker joked trying to ward off the primal need for her lover that gripped her.

Syd held her tightly against her, pushing her fingertips a little too hard into her flesh. "Well actually, you suggested it and I did agree. I've devised a two-for-one special back at our cabana. You game?" Syd glanced her fingers possessively across Parker's thighs, making her gasp into Sydney's neck.

Parker held on to the life she would never take for granted. "So much."

Syd walked with Parker toward the sand. "Don't let go."

About the Author

Cass Sellars is a certified fraud examiner and criminal justice professional. She has led white-collar criminal, corporate and financial fraud, and theft investigations. Formerly an editor of a small magazine, a creative journalist, and a public speaker, she's always been a writer at heart. The Lightning Series has allowed her to explore the world of romantic-suspense fiction.

After life-changing experiences as a victim of corrupt "justice," she felt compelled to write about powerful lesbian characters that have the opportunity to fight for those who have been victims and seek justice where money and politics are not always the only winning assets.

Sellars grew up in the Midwest and in Great Britain, but spent much of her adult life on the East Coast. She currently lives with her wife near San Francisco. She dabbles in interior design, event planning, singing, travel, and women's music and works at being a vital part of the lesbian and creative communities.

Cass can be reached via her website: www.casssellarsauthor.com.

Books Available from Bold Strokes Books

Beauty and the Boss by Ali Vali. Ellis Renois is at the top of the fashion world, but she never expects her summer assistant Charlotte Hamner to tear her heart and her business apart like sharp scissors through cheap material. (978-1-62639-919-8)

Fury's Choice by Brey Willows. When gods walk amongst humans, can two women find a balance between love and faith? (978-1-62639-869-6)

Lessons in Desire by MJ Williamz. Can a summer love stand a four-month hiatus and still burn hot? (978-1-63555-019-1)

Lightning Chasers by Cass Sellars. For Sydney and Parker, being a couple was never what they had planned. Now they have to fight corruption, murder, and enemies hiding in plain sight just to hold on to each other. Lightning Series, Book Two (978-1-62639-965-5)

Summer Fling by Jean Copeland. Still jaded from a breakup years earlier, Kate struggles to trust falling in love again when a summer fling with sexy young singer Jordan rocks her off her feet. (978-1-62639-981-5)

Take Me There by Julie Cannon. Adrienne and Sloan know it would be career suicide to mix business with pleasure, however tempting it is. But what's the harm? They're both consenting adults. Who would know? (978-1-62639-917-4)

The Girl Who Wasn't Dead by Samantha Boyette. A year ago, someone tried to kill Jenny Lewis. Tonight she's ready to find out who it was. (978-1-62639-950-1)

Unchained Memories by Dena Blake. Can a woman give herself completely when she's left a piece of herself behind? (978-1-62639-993-8)

Walking Through Shadows by Sheri Lewis Wohl. All Molly wanted to do was go backpacking...in her own century. (978-1-62639-968-6)

A Lamentation of Swans by Valerie Bronwen. Ariel Montgomery returns to Sea Oats to try to save her broken marriage but soon finds herself also fighting to save her own life and catch a murderer. (978-1-62639-828-3)

Freedom to Love by Ronica Black. What happens when the woman who spent her lifetime worrying about caring for her family, finally finds the freedom to love without borders? (978-1-63555-001-6)

House of Fate by Barbara Ann Wright. Two women must throw off the lives they've known as a guardian and an assassin and save two rival houses before their secrets tear the galaxy apart. (978-1-62639-780-4)

Planning for Love by Erin Dutton. Could true love be the one thing that wedding coordinator Faith McKenna didn't plan for? (978-1-62639-954-9)

Sidebar by Carsen Taite. Judge Camille Avery and her clerk, attorney West Fallon, agree on little except their mutual attraction, but can their relationship and their careers survive a headline-grabbing case? (978-1-62639-752-1)

Sweet Boy and Wild One by T. L. Hayes. When Rachel Cole meets soulful singer Bobby Layton at an open mic, she is immediately in thrall. What she soon discovers will rock her world in ways she never imagined. (978-1-62639-963-1)

To Be Determined by Mardi Alexander and Laurie Eichler. Charlie Dickerson escapes her life in the US to rescue Australian wildlife with Pip Atkins, but can they save each other? (978-1-62639-946-4)

True Colors by Yolanda Wallace. Blogger Robby Rawlins plans to use First Daughter Taylor Crenshaw to get ahead, but she never planned on falling in love with her in the process. (978-1-62639-927-3)

Unexpected by Jenny Frame. When Dale McGuire falls for Rebecca Harper, the mother of the son she never knew she had, will Rebecca's troubled past stop them from making the family they both truly crave? (978-1-62639-942-6)

Canvas for Love by Charlotte Greene. When ghosts from Amelia's past threaten to undermine their relationship, Chloé must navigate the greatest romance of her life without losing sight of who she is. (978-1-62639-944-0)

Heart Stop by Radclyffe. Two women, one with a damaged body, the other a damaged spirit, challenge each other to dare to live again. (978-1-62639-899-3)

Repercussions by Jessica L. Webb. Someone planted information in Edie Black's brain and now they want it back, but with the protection of shy former soldier Skye Kenny, Edie has a chance at life and love. (978-1-62639-925-9)

Spark by Catherine Friend. Jamie's life is turned upside down when her consciousness travels back to 1560 and lands in the body of one of Queen Elizabeth I's ladies-in-waiting...or has she totally lost her grip on reality? (978-1-62639-930-3)

Taking Sides by Kathleen Knowles. When passion and politics collide, can love survive? (978-1-62639-876-4)

Thorns of the Past by Gun Brooke. Former cop Darcy Flynn's heart broke when her career on the force ended in disgrace, but perhaps saving Sabrina Hawk's life will mend it in more ways than one. (978-1-62639-857-3)

You Make Me Tremble by Karis Walsh. Seismologist Casey Radnor comes to the San Juan Islands to study an earthquake but finds her heart shaken by passion when she meets animal rescuer Iris Mallery. (978-1-62639-901-3)

Complications by MJ Williamz. Two women battle for the heart of one. (978-1-62639-769-9)

Crossing the Wide Forever by Missouri Vaun. As Cody Walsh and Lillie Ellis face the perils of the untamed West, they discover that love's uncharted frontier isn't for the weak in spirit or the faint of heart. (978-1-62639-851-1)

Fake It Till You Make It by M. Ullrich. Lies will lead to trouble, but can they lead to love? (978-1-62639-923-5)

Girls Next Door by Sandy Lowe and Stacia Seaman eds.. Best-selling romance authors tell it from the heart—sexy, romantic stories of falling for the girls next door. (978-1-62639-916-7)

Pursuit by Jackie D. The pursuit of the most dangerous terrorist in America will crack the lines of friendship and love, and not everyone will make it out under the weight of duty and service. (978-1-62639-903-7)

Shameless by Brit Ryder. Confident Emery Pearson knows exactly what she's looking for in a no-strings-attached hookup, but can a spontaneous interlude open her heart to more? (978-1-63555-006-1)

The Practitioner by Ronica Black. Sometimes love comes calling whether you're ready for it or not. (978-1-62639-948-8)

Unlikely Match by Fiona Riley. When an ambitious PR exec and her super-rich coding geek-girl client fall in love, they learn that giving something up may be the only way to have everything. (978-1-62639-891-7)

Where Love Leads by Erin McKenzie. A high school counselor and the mom of her new student bond in support of the troubled girl, never expecting deeper feelings to emerge, testing the boundaries of their relationship. (978-1-62639-991-4)

Forsaken Trust by Meredith Doench. When four women are murdered, Agent Luce Hansen must regain trust in her most valuable investigative tool—herself—to catch the killer. (978-1-62639-737-8)

Her Best Friend's Sister by Meghan O'Brien. For fifteen years, Claire Barker has nursed a massive crush on her best friend's older sister. What happens when all her wildest fantasies come true? (978-1-62639-861-0)

Letter of the Law by Carsen Taite. Will federal prosecutor Bianca Cruz take a chance at love with horse breeder Jade Vargas, whose dark family ties threaten everything Bianca has worked to protect—including her child? (978-1-62639-750-7)

New Life by Jan Gayle. Trigena and Karrie are having a baby, but the stress of becoming a mother and the impact on their relationship might be too much for Trigena. (978-1-62639-878-8)

Royal Rebel by Jenny Frame. Charity director Lennox King sees through the party girl image Princess Roza has cultivated, but will Lennox's past indiscretions and Roza's responsibilities make their love impossible? (978-1-62639-893-1)

Unbroken by Donna K. Ford. When Kayla and Jackie, two women with every reason to reject Happy Ever After, fall in love, will they have the courage to overcome their pasts and rewrite their stories? (978-1-62639-921-1)

Where the Light Glows by Dena Blake. Mel Thomas doesn't realize just how unhappy she is in her marriage until she meets Izzy Calabrese. Will she have the courage to overcome her insecurities and follow her heart? (978-1-62639-958-7)

boldstrokesbooks.com

Bold Strokes Books

Quality and Diversity in LGBTQ Literature

victory EDITIONS

Drama

MATINEE BOOKS

SCI-FI

E-BOOKS

erotica

MYSTERY

SOLILOQUY

EROTICA

YOUNG ADULT

BOLD STROKES BOOKS

LIBERTY

Romance

W·E·B·S·T·O·R·E

PRINT AND EBOOKS